GRAVITYS HAMMER

GRAVITYS HAMMER

Jerry Reynolds

ISBN: 0996326200
ISBN 13: 9780996326209
Library of Congress Control Number: 2015907136
CreateSpace Independent Publishing Platform, North Charleston, South
Carolina

To Vicki
for being my wife, inspiration, and best friend.
You have always stood with me and supported me in all
circumstances that have come our way. Thank you.
It has been an amazing ride so far! Let's keep going!

To Jim Conrad
for inspiring me to revisit this project and get it done, and
for your guidance through the publishing process and an
endless maze of options. Thank you.

CHAPTER 1

Mark Hunter crouched down inside the drop tube, trying to make himself more comfortable and growing more impatient by the moment. Waiting to planet dive was always the hardest part of any mission. The droning of the ship's engines combined with the boredom of simply having to wait always seemed to dull his senses, making it difficult to concentrate on the upcoming mission. Straining against the straps that held him firmly in place, Mark twisted his head around, looking out of the portal in the top of the tube.

The jump compartment was dark; the only illumination was a single combat light suspended from the ceiling. It cast a dull red glow over everything, lending a certain eeriness to the setting.

"Thirty seconds to drop!" the intercom crackled.

Mark had been inside his tube for a little over an hour and was beginning to get anxious as the ship approached the release point. He flexed his muscles, performing exercises in a futile attempt to relieve the tension from being cramped inside the tiny tube for so long. He mulled over what he was about to do, hardly able to believe it.

Getting from a ship to the surface of a planet could hardly be done in a more dangerous way. Mark was part of an elite group of fighting men, similar to military storm troopers of the past, who specialized in attack-and-destroy missions behind the lines. The key to a successful mission was keeping transit time from ship to surface down to a bare minimum. This was where the drop tube came into play. By using this tiny, self-contained ship, the descending storm troopers provided the enemy with many fewer opportunities to fire on them, leading to a much higher survival rate than old-style parachute methods employed by armies in the past. The only problem with the drop tube was that it was somewhat akin to lying in a coffin and being pushed over a cliff. The experience was unnerving, to say the least, and required several years of specialized training to master. Mark had been on many drops in his past as an intelligence operative, utilizing the drop tube system on any mission where a clandestine, rapid approach was crucial to the success of the mission.

The tube itself was roughly eight feet long, and the bottom half was tapered to a point. This helped reduce drag when reentering the atmosphere, but it gave the drop tube the distinct shape of a bullet. The shape, along with a radar-absorbing coating on the outer skin, made it all but impossible to detect on radar. With only small viewing ports at the top and bottom, the occupant had to trust totally in the onboard systems to safely guide the descent. Before the technology was perfected, more than one soldier met his end because of a systems failure before he even had a chance to engage the enemy.

During a drop the ship would swing as close as possible to the dark side of a planet and release its drop tubes into a decaying orbit. If the tracking systems were functioning correctly, the tubes would enter the atmosphere somewhere over the target area. After a brief period of free fall, the onboard systems in the tube would fire a burst from a small rocket mounted on the outer casing. This was intended to slow the tube to a less-than-fatal impact speed, but more often than not, the physical constitution of the passenger determined whether the final landing speed proved to be lethal. Internal compensators and padding softened the blow some, but it still made for a rough ride going down.

"Five seconds to drop!" blared the intercom.

Mark tightened his grip on the brace bars inside the tube and gritted his teeth as he prepared himself mentally for what was about to happen.

"DROP!" the voice boomed as the tube was released from its moorings and fired into an orbital trajectory. Mark's stomach leapt into his mouth and struggled to get free as his tube continued in a rapid downward spiral. He looked up through the overhead portal to see the USS *Hercules*, a Freedom-class battleship, roaring away into the blackness of space. A brief wave of fear washed over him as he realized he was on his own, success or failure resting totally in his hands.

As the tube hit the atmosphere, violent vibrations began beating through the hull so forcefully Mark was sure it would fly apart before he made it down. A deafening screech began as the thick atmosphere whistled around the tube's casing, buffeting the tiny ship back and forth as it rammed its way to the surface. Mark looked up to see a dull red glow obscuring his vision through the portal as friction caused by the atmosphere began to burn the outer skin of the tube. Even though he knew it was impossible because of the shielding built into the tube, he swore he could feel the heat of reentry searing the soles of his feet. The tube shook violently, rattling Mark's teeth in their sockets. After several seconds the glow began to fade, and the screeching subsided and was replaced by an eerie silence as the tube broke into the lower atmosphere.

Watching the surface approaching rapidly through the lower portal, Mark's apprehension built as he began to wonder if the tube's engine would fire in time. As the ground continued to rush toward him, Mark's tension level increased proportionally to his lack of distance from the surface. The engine finally roared to life, rapidly reducing the descent speed of the tube. Mark breathed a heavy sigh of relief. As the engine continued to fire, the pressure on his body increased dramatically, the g-force making it difficult for blood to flow to his brain. Unconsciousness crept up on him, enveloping him, causing him to see bright flashes of light in his peripheral vison. Just before the darkness could overwhelm him, his years of training took over, and he began performing blood-flow exercises to fight off the unrelenting pressure. When Mark was sure he was going to black out, the engine abruptly ceased firing, causing the g-force to subside. Momentarily disoriented at the sudden rush of blood to his brain, Mark shook his head to regain his composure. As he reoriented himself, a synthesized voice announced in a calm, detached manner, "Please brace for impact."

Heeding the advice, Mark crouched down into a fetal position—knees tucked into his chest, eyelids clenched shut—and prepared for the most difficult part of the descent. As the tube impacted the surface of the planet, Mark suddenly remembered why he had retired from special forces. The shock was so severe he was stunned and could do nothing for several seconds, not even breathe. The tube hit the ground violently, bounced, and skidded to a stop at the base of a pile of large boulders. Gravel and dust were thrown into the air, settling over the area and coating everything with a fine layer of gritty sand.

An insistent warning light flashing on the small control panel in front of him brought him back to his senses. As his vision focused, the disembodied voice of the computer chimed a simple warning: "Drop tube will self-destruct in ten seconds. Please vacate immediately."

Instantly alert, Mark knew the tube would detonate whether he was in it or not. He reached beneath his seat and grabbed his backpack. He popped the hatch on the tube, exposing himself to the alien atmosphere. Tossing the pack through the open passageway, he leapt out after it, scooping it up in his arms as he ran away from the tube. He sprinted for several seconds before stopping. Mark turned and looked back in the direction he had come. As he watched, a warm, green glow came from the tube's interior, building in intensity as bright fingers of electricity began to skitter across its hull. He heard a low hum as the self-destruct mechanism built up a charge, filling the air with static electricity. He ducked down as a bright flash emanated from the hull of the tube and the entire ship disintegrated and fell into a small pile of ash. He walked back over and spread the ashes around to remove the evidence of his arrival.

As he surveyed the area, Mark noted with satisfaction that it was still dark; the only light was a dull glow coming from a cluster of distant buildings. He opened his backpack, removed a small transceiver, and keyed it up.

"Home Base, descent complete. Moving to primary objective," Mark said softly into the communicator.

"Acknowledged," came the almost-instantaneous reply.

Stowing his communicator in his backpack, he pulled out a geolocation device that contained a map of the area and tried to get his bearings. The data on this planet were minimal—as it had only recently been identified as an alien outpost. Glancing around, Mark could see that he had come down almost precisely as planned. He was only four hundred yards from the enemy compound. As far as he could tell, his presence had, as yet, gone undetected, thanks in part to the special electromagnetic absorption properties of the tube's coating. It would not reflect any kind of radiation, making it impossible to detect with conventional radar equipment. The only danger would be from a direct visual sighting, and it appeared that he had been lucky in that respect.

The sky was as black as ink, allowing Mark to approach the enemy compound without being spotted. Unable to detect any security devices, Mark was worried. It meant that these people either were stupid or had capabilities of which he was not aware. He would have to be even more careful.

He knelt next to the outer wall of the largest building as he removed a rope and grappling hook from his backpack. Fastening the rope onto the hook, he stood and swung the hook in a wide arc over his head, releasing it as it reached the top of its arc. The hook sailed toward the roof and lodged firmly into place with a muffled clank. Mark tugged on the rope to make sure it was secure and began scaling the wall, pulling himself up the rope toward the top of the building. His muscles cried out in pain as he hoisted himself up the rope. He was using parts of his body that had not been exercised this way since he had retired. He felt vulnerable and visible as he ascended. If someone saw him, his mission would be over before it started. Finally reaching the roof, Mark pulled the rope up after him and hid it in the shadows. He surveyed the area, noticing what appeared to be an air shaft that would suit his needs perfectly, providing access into the building and getting himself out of the open. Making sure all was clear, Mark pried open the shaft cover and climbed in, putting it back in place as he carefully descended the shaft.

Peering out of a vent into what appeared to be a large warehouse, Mark saw that the entire space was deserted. Pushing the vent cover out, he dropped to the floor, careful to make no sound. He moved quickly across an open area into a darkened hallway. As he made his way, Mark couldn't help but sense an electric feeling of tension in the air. It had been over five years since he had done any fieldwork, and the adrenaline was pumping through his body just like it had on his first combat mission behind enemy lines so many years ago. He had not had much time to prepare for this mission, but he was glad to see that his old skills had not left him yet. Once in the hallway, he glanced to his left, noticing a glow coming from an adjoining room. He approached cautiously, not wanting to alert anyone to his presence. He pushed the door open slowly and peered inside.

The room was occupied by a blue-skinned humanoid behind a computer station with many monitors and flashing lights. The alien was facedown, oblivious to his surroundings. At least Mark thought it was oblivious. He really did not know for sure—intelligence had little to no information on this alien race. Mark silently drew his weapon from its holster, taking comfort from the balanced weight of it in his hand. He crept into the office slowly, his nerves stretched to the breaking point.

Silently approaching from behind, Mark confirmed that the alien was unconscious, breathing shallowly, face-down on the desk. He observed one hand holding an empty glass and the other a half-full bottle of a foul amber liquid. Bending over slightly to smell the contents of the glass, Mark was disgusted by what he smelled. Mark assumed from the scene that this alien had stayed late and tied one on, drinking whatever passed for alcohol on this planet—whether out of celebration or depression Mark had no idea, nor did he care. Wanting to raise no alarms and having no desire for a confrontation at this point, he quietly left the room, closing the door. Glancing toward the end of the hallway, Mark saw a large, secure-looking door protecting a room that was a likely candidate for the source of the information he had come for.

Proceeding down the hall with as much stealth as he could muster, Mark came within inches of the door. Expecting elaborate security precautions, he paused to examine the door as closely as he could in the dim light of the hallway. It appeared to have no hidden security devices, instead relying on simple strength for deterrence against an intruder. While not as large, the door reminded him of the main entry doors he had seen at the North American Aerospace Defense Command headquarters—ridiculously thick to withstand a direct blast of almost any magnitude.

Removing a small sounding device from his pack, Mark positioned it against the door, causing it to activate itself and attach to the surface with a gentle click. He pressed a small button, and the sounder sent out a out a pulse of sonic energy that passed through the door and reflected off everything on the other side. The sounder received these signals and built a three-dimensional map of the room that was behind the door, including thickness and density data for walls and the surrounding area, and presented it to Mark on a small display. Mark could hardly believe the information being displayed. The door was over three feet thick, made of a substance that he had never seen before. Its molecular structure was so dense it would be impervious to explosives. Knowing that it would be impossible to breach the door by brute force, Mark decided his only chance for entry was to attempt to breach the security access panel on the wall.

Examining the panel closely, Mark could not tell exactly how it worked. There were instructions, but they were printed in an alien language. As he pondered his next move, his ears perked up at the sound of a low conversation reverberating from the opposite end of the hallway. Mark stowed the sounder device and retreated into the shadows, pressing his body flat against the wall as he waited.

Two aliens, dressed in what appeared to be military uniforms, were coming directly toward Mark's position.

They were conversing casually, the tone of their conversation assuring Mark that no alarm had been raised and that they were unaware of his presence. Retreating further into the shadows, Mark held his breath as he waited to see what would happen next.

The older of the two aliens stood before the massive door and placed his hand firmly on the security panel, which promptly began to glow. Mark flinched as a loud clang sounded from within the door. It began to slide back on its guide rails, a low rumble echoing down the hallway as it moved. Both aliens entered the room as soon as the door was open. Mark stared in after them. He made an instant decision as the door began to roll shut, leaping into action. Looking up and down the hallway to ensure that no one else was coming, he covered the space between himself and the door in a single bound. With almost no room to spare as he slipped in, the door closed behind him with a dull thud that reverberated off the ceiling. He was grateful for the noise; it covered any sound he had made while entering.

The aliens were standing with their backs to him, still unaware of his presence. He crouched, slipped his knife from its sheath, and readied himself for the attack. His blade was thirsty for blood, and he was intent on satisfying that thirst. The room was still dark, so he had to allow time for his eyes to adjust. He could see his targets standing close together, silhouetted against the glow from several banks of equipment on the far wall. Mark leapt into action. Seizing the older one by the throat, he placed his blade against the blue flesh and slid it across in a firm, powerful stroke. The alien stiffened in surprise, then immediately went limp, and Mark could feel a warm, sticky substance flowing over his hands as he let the body drop to the floor. He knew the alien was dead. Stepping over the body, he heard a gasp from the other alien as it reacted to what it saw playing out. Eyes widening in fear, the alien started to cry out. Mark swung around and brought his knife handle down hard on its skull. He heard the satisfying crunch of bone as the second alien fell to the floor next to its companion. He looked around the room to make sure no one else had been alerted by the action and bent over to get a closer look at the aliens he had just terminated. Their skin was blue, fleshy to the touch, their bodies were basically humanoid in appearance. A small ridge of bone ran from the tip of the nose all the way around the crest of the skull, giving them the appearance of a Roman centurion of old. Their bodies were lean and very muscular, and their legs were somewhat larger than those of an average human. Mark guessed that the gravity on their planet was somewhat higher than on Earth, which would account for the heavier musculature of their bodies.

Wiping his blade on the uniform of one of the dead aliens, he sheathed it and stood up, taking in his surroundings. The room was still too dim for him to see clearly, even after allowing several minutes for his eyes to adjust. He retrieved a flashlight from his backpack and turned it on, causing a bright beam of light to split the darkness. Quickly surveying the room, he noticed a large bank of equipment covering the far wall and several large strategy-planning tables in the middle of the room. Playing the flashlight over the surface of these tables, Mark was staggered by the information that was displayed there..

The tables contained images of the surrounding areas in space, with each planet clearly marked as to its position. Earth was dead center on the table, the obvious target. The table contained markers to indicate alien fleet placement. There were massive squadrons of alien ships, and there were many of them, positioned in such a way as to surround Earth and leave no avenue of escape. Mark took in what he was seeing, a feeling of dread slowly overcoming him as he also saw Earth's entire fleet clearly marked on the display, tiny in comparison to the alien fleet. The actual location of the fleet was a closely guarded secret, yet here it was on display for anyone to see.

The planning for an invasion of Earth had been in progress earlier in this very room. Fleet dispersion and positioning were all laid out in graphic detail right in front of him. Removing a small camera from his backpack, Mark began snapping photographs of every table. The strategic information in front of him would be invaluable in the coming war. Mark continued to take pictures of everything he thought might be of use until his camera beeped softly. He glanced down and realized that its memory was full. He stowed the camera and began to scrutinize the room again, looking for any other valuable information he could glean. The glowing monitors along the back wall of the room caught his eye. He approached them in order to get a closer look.

Mark examined the control consoles closely. The system was controlled by the same type of biometric security panel that had controlled access to this room. As he inspected the panel, an idea occurred to him. Mark returned to the body of the alien who had originally opened the door with his hand. He lifted the body onto his shoulders and carried it over to the system access panel. Supporting the alien's body against his own, he placed its hand on the access panel. The panel glowed briefly, scanning the alien's hand, and then went out. Mark held his breath and hoped his ruse would work. It was just possible that it would raise an alarm and jeopardize the entire mission, but he had to try. This might be his only chance to break into the system.

Within seconds he was rewarded when a faint whirring sound began to emanate from the equipment banks. Mark dropped the body in a heap as the systems sprang to life. A screen next to the security panel glowed with some type of prompt that he did not understand. Having no way of comprehending the data before him, Mark had all but given up on getting any useful information from the system when he noticed two small slots on the front of one of the workstations with a stack of metallic disks next to them. Taking a chance on this being a default action that would not set off any alarms, Mark inserted the disks into the slots, causing the system to respond by dumping information onto them. He continued to swap out disks as each disk was filled with data. Once the last one was full, he placed them into his backpack and slung it onto his back. Turning around, he saw the aliens he had dispatched earlier. Not wanting to raise any alarms if someone came into the room, he dragged the alien bodies across the floor to hide them in a small anteroom. He cleaned up the area, removing all traces of his incursion.

Sure he had everything he could use that was within his ability to get, he approached the door cautiously, unsure of how he was going to get out. When he got within three feet of the massive door, he was startled by a low rumble as the door again began to slide to one side. Mark jumped back out of view, fully expecting someone to enter. When no one did, he carefully peered out of the doorway. Relieved at seeing no immediate danger, he hurriedly exited the room and made his way down the hallway. He heard the door close behind him.

Making his way down the passage, he once again peered into the first room he had entered just to make sure the inebriated alien was not a threat. The alien was no longer there. From behind, Mark heard the whine of a weapon building up a charge and a growled statement in a language he could not understand. Not knowing the capabilities of the alien's weapon, he decided not to try anything and froze in his tracks, quietly laying his hand on the butt of his own weapon.

The alien barked again in such a way that Mark thought it best to turn around. He did so, slipping his weapon out of its holster and holding it behind his back. Mark eyed the alien, waiting for the right moment to act. An automatic door slid shut in the back of the room, distracting the alien briefly.

Knowing he might not have another chance, Mark seized the opportunity to level his weapon and fire a single shot at point-blank range into the alien's chest. The impact of the slug flattened the alien against the far wall, where, with a stunned look on its face, it slid into a crumpled heap on the floor, leaving a streak of blue blood on the wall. Mark held his breath for a few moments, sure that the weapon's discharge had alerted someone else. After holding his position for a few seconds, Mark decided that his luck was still holding as no alarms sounded.

The alien's body had fallen in a rear corner of the room, so Mark didn't have to worry about someone discovering it before he could get away. Holstering his weapon, he turned off the lights in the room and crept out into the hallway. Mark looked up and down the length of the corridor; the coast was clear. He made his way to the closest window, opened it, and climbed out onto the ledge.

The air was hot and muggy. He carefully checked the area as he wiped the sweat from his brow. Quietly closing the window, he adjusted his pack, making sure the disks were still tucked inside. He found the rope he had used earlier and slid silently to the ground, rolling to absorb the impact. Landing with a grunt, he brushed the dirt from his face and activated a control that released the grappling hook. The rope and hook fell into a pile in front of him. He coiled the rope, stowed it and the hook in his pack, and then waited in a hidden spot for the way to clear.

Seeing no alien activity, Mark ran away from the compound, making his way back to the drop point without further incident. He fished out his communicator and keyed in his retrieval code. Within minutes a transport came around a bend in the clearing and hovered to a stop about fifty yards from his position. He used his communicator to key in a security code that only his contact would be able to answer. An acknowledgment came back immediately, so he came out from the underbrush and made his way toward the transport. He opened the door and climbed into the vehicle, quickly buckling himself in. The pilot gently eased the nose of the transport skyward, increasing their thrust as they climbed. The ship quickly disappeared from sight, fading into the darkened sky.

CHAPTER 2

As the transport left the surface far behind, the muscles in Mark's neck began to relax. He adjusted himself in his seat, trying to get more comfortable.

"Quit wigglin' 'round back there, boy!" said the pilot.

Mark could hardly believe his ears. Only one person he knew talked like that.

"Jo? Is that you?"

"An' who else would risk their butt just to save a peasant captain like you? Hmm?"

Mark grinned from ear to ear. The man in the pilot's seat was none other than Johann Switzer, one of his closest friends from his academy days. Johann was a native Jamaican, dreadlocks and all. Even though his accent was not real, he insisted on using it at times to spice up what he called his "mystery." Mark had not spent time with Johann since they had graduated and embarked on different careers.

"It's really good to see you, man. I just wish it were under different circumstances."

"Likewise," said Johann as he brought the ship's speed up to maximum.

"And how, may I ask, did you get involved in this project?" asked Mark.

Johann chuckled. "Not much sense in working on anything else, is there?"

"Yeah, right," said Mark, settling himself into his seat, closing his eyes in a vain attempt to shut out the whirlwind of events that had swept up everyone's lives and turned them upside down. For perhaps the millionth time, his mind replayed the last several days.

A little over two weeks earlier, a large radio telescope in the Arizona desert had intercepted what appeared to be some type of coded military transmission. The personnel on duty that day were not unduly alarmed because even though their telescope was currently being used to examine a remote star in a newly discovered planetary cluster, it was not unheard of for stray electromagnetic radiation to become jumbled in with the signals they were receiving from the stars. However, standard procedure was to report all unusual occurrences to the director of the telescope station. Unable to determine exactly where the message had originated, the director had sent a printout of the message to Pentagon intelligence as a precautionary measure for evaluation and recommendations.

When the printout was received, all hell broke loose. What should have been a simple decryption job baffled even the most powerful supercomputers at the intelligence section's disposal. The top cryptologists in the world were brought in to analyze the message. They all marveled at the level of sophistication and degree of encryption. As hard as they tried, they could discern no patterns at all that would aid in their efforts to decrypt the message. Laboring over the data for several days and getting nowhere, intelligence made an urgent call to the station that had intercepted the message, requesting as much detail as possible about its origins. The personnel on duty that day had thought the message originated on Earth, so they had not paid that much attention to it, believing it was simply chatter that had bled into the frequencies they were monitoring. At the latest request from the Pentagon, they realized they had stumbled onto perhaps the first intelligent message that was definitely extraterrestrial in origin. Digging into their records and recordings of the transmission, the telescope station team was able to pinpoint the location of the signal and forwarded this information to the Pentagon.

With the additional information, the Pentagon's cryptography team determined that a mathematical pattern did exist in the message based on the location and orbit of the planets in the system of origin. Using this new information, the team was able to decipher the message. It was a code based on a coordinate system. The message contained sets of coordinates that directly triangulated with the new planetary system the telescope had been studying and Earth's own star, Sol. Once the coordinates had been mapped out, much to the chagrin of the Pentagon, each and every one lined up precisely with every military installation on Earth. This news threw the entire world into a double shock: first, there was indeed extraterrestrial life in the galaxy, and second, the extraterrestrials knew the exact location of Earth's planetary defense systems.

Further intercepted communications seemed to indicate that the civilization in that area was indeed planning a full-scale invasion of Earth. The fact that the astronomers had been fortunate enough to intercept the message was the sole reason Earth forces had been able to mount a credible defense. Once the invasion plans had been confirmed, the military had gone into an immediate and massive buildup of weapons, both conventional and nuclear, in an attempt to prepare for the coming attack. Along with the weapons buildup, a corresponding increase in manpower had been achieved through a hastily passed law that required every able-bodied male on the planet to immediately report to the nearest military installation for duty. The entire planet had been a hive of activity ever since.

While all this was going on, Mark's old unit commander had come looking for him to enlist his services. His previous job had been in military intelligence as a field operative. It had been his assignment to infiltrate enemy lines and perform intelligence reconnaissance. He had been quite good at his job and had kept up his skills during his retirement. He supposed that was why he had been chosen to go on this mission.

In his mission brief, the details of the overall situation and his assignment were laid out before him. The alien military had successfully established a forward base that initially appeared to be an outpost built for support operations for a large invasion force.

The alien base was located on an asteroid that had been transformed to make it habitable and give it an atmosphere very similar to Earth's. The technology involved in this feat was incredible and beyond anything available on Earth.

Because the asteroid was in a stable geosynchronous orbit out of a direct line of sight, the alien forces had been able to build the base without being discovered by any of the observation stations located on Earth. It had only been discovered during a NASA space shuttle mission while the shuttle had been practicing emergency recovery maneuvers. Cameras onboard the shuttle had inadvertently captured an image of the unusual asteroid. When these images were analyzed back on Earth, scientists realized this was not a naturally occurring phenomenon and it warranted further investigation. Once the location of the enemy base had been spotted, the eye of the Hubble telescope had been trained on the coordinates provided, and what was discovered there made even the most jaded skeptics believe.

An alien installation, large enough to provide support for a full-scale invasion, had been built and embedded into the asteroid—a massive war machine. The intercepted messages mentioned the exact coordinates for the alien installation, confirming once and for all that this base was indeed part of the coming invasion. The facility had been under constant observation ever since, and on more than one occasion, brief glimpses had been caught of the aliens themselves.

Basically humanoid in appearance, they were generally a bit taller than the average human male, and their skin was a very pale blue. When this information was made public, the nickname Blue Devils was quickly adopted. However, the official name given to the alien's star was Jerrol-1, after the man who had first discovered it. The aliens came to be known as Jerrollites.

Weaponry was a whole different matter. Single-occupant spaceships had been spotted engaging in mock combat maneuvers over the asteroid. Their firepower was staggering. Most of the technology and tactics witnessed were so alien they defied understanding. The military leaders on Earth could only guess and prepare the best that they could.

Military forces on Earth had been able to monitor the alien base's activity without being discovered, which gave them a tactical advantage that they did not intend to waste.

Mark's mission was simple but dangerous. He was to go on a recon mission to that base and gather intelligence information on the pending invasion. Because the base was totally alien, he would be going in blind. It was with this sketchy information in hand that Mark had shipped out on the first high-speed vessel to leave the planet, ready to do his part in the defense of his home.

"Coming up on the *Hercules*," Johann said.

Shaking himself out of his memories, Mark straightened in his seat, leaning forward to get a better view of the ship they were approaching. They flew beneath it in a gentle arc that passed within meters of its outer hull. Its skin was stark white in the reflected starlight, causing the ship to stand out against the blackness of space. Bristling with armament, the *Hercules* was all business, all the time. This craft was the best that human engineering had produced, the very pinnacle of technology upon which rested the defense of Earth. Mark felt the stirrings of an immense pride as they approached the docking bay.

Johann swung the transport into a wide arc that encompassed the breadth of the ship. Both men stood in awe of the battleship just outside their cockpit window, thrilled by the strength and power represented but at the same time nervous about the future of humanity being placed in the hands of the military machine. Humanity had never before undertaken a mission of this magnitude.

Johann spotted the docking collar off in the distance and engaged his automatic docking system. The flight computer chimed in acknowledgment and began the docking sequence. The system began bringing the rear docking collar in line with its mate on the ship, making minute adjustments to their speed and flight path until it looked like both ships were standing still. Once both ships were stationary to each other, the transport began moving slowly toward the battleship. The transport's docking collar eased into perfect alignment with the one on the ship, and the two collars met and mated. A clang resounded through the hull as magnetic grappling hooks locked into place.

"Seal is secure," said the docking system as a green indicator light on Johann's panel lit up. Hissing could be heard as the ship's air pressure began to equalize with that of the battleship. A soft whine emanated from several panels on the transport as various flight systems began to power down. Turning in his seat, Johann addressed Mark.

"I hope you got what you went in for, Mark. Matheson has been on pins and needles ever since you left."

"I think he'll be happy with the presents I brought," Mark said. The men shared a laugh. "Are you here for the duration?"

Johann's eyes sparkled with excitement. "Oh yeah, boy! I done been assigned to dis ship till de fighting is over!"

"Good. Let's get together later. I'm buying!" Mark said.

"Okay, boy. You got a deal!" Johann waved him off as he returned to his control panel. Mark grabbed his backpack and climbed out of the transport through the rear airlock into the docking bay of the *Hercules*.

The bay was a bustle of activity. Mark looked over the gigantic room and took in all the activity that was going on. Technicians and flight crews swarmed over the entire bay, checking and rechecking equipment, working together in an ordered frenzy that reminded Mark of a beehive. Mark's observations were cut short by a loud whine followed by a shout.

"Watch out, sir! Coming through." He turned around to see a munitions cart stacked with seven large missiles coming directly at him. The sergeant driving the cart had a very annoyed look on his face. Mark quickly stepped aside to let the cart pass, returning the salute of the driver as he whizzed by, barely missing Mark's feet.

Mark continued looking around, and his eyes came to rest on rows of one- and two-man tactical, single-wing fighters lining the walls of the bay. Nicknamed TAC-WINGs by the crew, these ships were agile and vicious fighter spacecraft built specifically for close quarters combat. Each had a particle beam cannon mounted in the nose, along with wing mounts for dozens of different kinds of missiles and armament that could be quickly changed depending on the mission. Each TAC-WING was sitting next to a set of rails that faced an iris-shaped port. When the ships were ready to be launched, they would be hoisted onto the rail system. Exhaust diverters were mounted on the rails behind each ship to channel hot exhaust gas down and away from the bay. This configuration would allow flight crews to scramble and launch in the minimum amount of time possible.

The two-man version of the fighter was also capable of near-light speed interstellar flight in a pinch, thanks to the newly developed particle drive engine. Originally developed to send microscopic nanoprobes into the far reaches of the universe, these engines would only have been useful for that purpose. The technology had taken an unexpected colossal leap forward when researchers at a university back on Earth had stumbled onto a unifying principle that allowed them to force billions of the nanoengines to work together in a synchronized fashion, effectively creating a single engine that could be scaled up to propel any size spacecraft. This revelation had allowed them to adapt the new technology for use in manned spacecraft that would give those ships the ability to approach light speed for the first time in human history. The engines functioned like small particle accelerators, shooting a conductive stream of nanoparticles from their exhaust ports, driving the ships forward to incredible velocities. The technology was experimental and had just been released to the military for field-testing. However, the current state of affairs had forced the military to push the engine through the normal testing process quickly in order to get it into production as fast as possible. There were still potential issues with its use, and Mark was in no hurry to be one of the first to use the technology in a live mission, although it was comforting to know it was available if required.

Each TAC-WING fighter was being swarmed over and serviced by a team of technicians and mechanics who were fueling it and loading as many munitions as the bird could carry. Final checks were being performed on each craft, making sure each one was flight ready.

Mark oriented himself and began to make his way toward the main briefing room where General Matheson was waiting to receive Mark's information. He was amazed at the buzz of activity and the focus and determination on every face. Everywhere he glanced, he observed crew members running back and forth, intent expressions on their faces and a definite purpose in their strides. He understood their determination and felt the same way. Mark was tempted to lend a hand in the activity he saw going on around him but realized he didn't have time; his destination was just around the next corner.

Approaching the briefing room, Mark noticed that the security panels were active and that the room was locked down. This most certainly meant that something bad had happened to require such tight security. Smoothing his uniform, Mark pressed the access button.

"Come," a deep voice said from inside.

The retina scanner on the wall began to glow, waiting to confirm his identity. Mark placed his eye in the scanner; the brief flash of light caused it to water. When the scan was complete, a synthesized voice said, "Mark Hunter, Agent ID 3761-1." A green light came on, accompanied by a loud click. Mark placed his hand on the door and pushed. The door swung open to reveal a smoke-filled room containing arguably the most powerful men on Earth. Every military commander of any consequence was present and seated around the conference table. Mark digested the scene without comment, still wondering what was going on. General Roy Matheson sat at the head, a commanding presence, obviously in charge.

The general was an imposing figure, hair cropped close to his head in a style reminiscent of the US Marines in the late twentieth century. His trademark chewed cigar was in his mouth at all times. This and his usual demeanor had earned him the nickname Bulldog. It was a name not only descriptive of his personality but also a fairly accurate description of his looks. No one ever used this nickname to his face, as to do so might have been the last thing the offender remembered before waking up in the brig. Even though he was feared, he was respected and loved by his men. They always knew that Matheson would have their backs, and his men would fight for him to the death if necessary. General Matheson had been Mark's commanding officer many times throughout his active duty career, and Mark had grown very fond of the general, viewing him as a second father.

Usually in a foul mood even at the best of times, Matheson was angrier than Mark had ever seen him, his face flushed as he chewed nervously on an unlit stogie.

"Get in here and shut the door!" said the general.

Mark shut the door and secured it.

"What did you bring us?" the general asked without preamble.

Mark reached into his backpack and pulled out the camera, passing it to the ensign on duty.

"Project these on the main wall, please."

"Yes, sir," the ensign said. He took a position next to the projection screen as he waited.

As the pictures appeared, Mark heard gasps of surprise from his audience.

"How did you get this much detail?" asked a commander.

"Honestly, I was a bit lucky. I was able to get into the alien command staff briefing room without being detected. The fleet positions were laid out in detail on planning tables, so I photographed them."

Several nods of approval and whispered remarks came from around the table.

"Also," Mark said, as the buzz of conversation in the room abruptly ceased, "I was able to gain access to their central computer network, and I downloaded as much information as possible. I don't know if intelligence can get anything useful out of these," he removed the silver disks from his backpack, holding them up for everyone to see, "but there could be something of value on them." He tossed the disks onto the table, directly in front of Matheson. The general fingered the disks, raising his eyes to Mark.

"Outstanding job, son. I'll send these disks to the lab to be analyzed immediately." The general scooped the disks off the table and put them in his pocket. He stood and approached Mark, talking in a voice only he could hear. "You are dismissed. Take some time and relax. I'll contact you soon about your next assignment."

"Uh, yes, sir," Mark said, confused at the abrupt dismissal. He left the briefing room and headed toward his cabin. Once in the hallway, Mark considered what had just occurred. It made him very uneasy to be quickly dismissed and shoved aside like that. The magnitude of the information he had brought in seemed to be lost on Matheson and the others.

Mark had a reputation as one of the most relentless people in the world when searching for information, and he wasn't about to let this strange behavior pass unnoticed. He wasn't sure what was going on, but he had a gut feeling that something was wrong.

CHAPTER 3

Mark entered his cabin, causing the lights to come on at full intensity. The harsh glare made him squint, so he turned the lighting down to a more tolerable level. He removed his backpack and tossed it across the room, where it landed with a thud in the far corner. He stretched his sore muscles, trying to restore some semblance of flexibility. His back always seemed to be in knots after a mission. Rubbing his hand over a nagging pain at the base of his neck, Mark made his way toward the shower, discarding his uniform as he went. He stepped into the water and let its heat take away the pain he was carrying. As the tension began to ebb, Mark relaxed, glad that the reconnaissance mission was over. Ever since his old commander had found him, Mark had wondered if he could still perform his duties like he had in the old days. He had retired from the military five years ago but had stayed abreast of developments in his field, trying to keep up his skills as an intelligence officer. Even though retired, he felt he had done pretty well for an old-timer. He shut off the water and toweled himself dry. Getting a cup of coffee from the dispenser in his room, he sat down on his bunk, sipping slowly. As the hot liquid made its way down his throat, a wave of fatigue washed over him, forcing him to lie down. The adrenaline rush of the mission was finally beginning to fade. While his mind was still busy processing the events in the briefing room, his subconscious was telling him there was a reason to worry. General Matheson simply did not act like that except when something was wrong. As he began to fade into sleep, Mark resolved to find out what was going on when he awoke. Finally he allowed sleep to win the fight, drifting off into a deep, dreamless slumber.

Mark awoke with a start, blinking his eyes rapidly to clear his vision. He got up from his bunk and walked over to the sink, yawning. He glanced at his watch and was startled to see that nine hours had passed since the briefing.

"Man, guess I was more beat than I thought," he said. Mark washed his face and put on a new uniform. He figured Johann was probably just about ready for that drink he had promised. Looking himself over again in the mirror, satisfied with what he saw, he made his way toward the door. He was startled when the entry chime sounded.

"Come."

The door slid aside to reveal General Matheson, a look of severe agitation on his face.

"You need a light for that thing?" Mark asked, gesturing to his ever-present cigar.

"Hell, no. You think I want to get cancer or something?" Matheson said.

"Come on in, sir," Mark said, stepping aside.

The general entered the room without further preamble. Walking over to the desk, he sat his large frame down and methodically began chewing the end of his cigar. Mark could tell by his expression that he had unwelcome news.

"What's wrong, General?" Mark asked, all business.

"Mark, I'm sorry for the way I sent you out of the briefing this morning, but we had just received a dispatch from Command Central that contained some very distressing news." Matheson adjusted his position in his chair, leaning forward to bring his face closer to Mark's.

Mark could feel the hair on the back of his neck begin to rise. The general looked at Mark, trying to ascertain his reaction before going on.

"We've known each other for a long time, Mark, so I'm not going to pull any punches with you," he said.

"I appreciate that, sir. What's going on?" Mark asked.

Matheson removed the cigar from his mouth and set it on the desk. Without further delay he removed a folded paper from his pocket and passed it across the desk to Mark. He gingerly picked up the paper, unfolded it, and began to read. The first thing that caught his eye was the designation stamped in bold red letters across the top of the page. *Top Secret—Commander's Eyes Only*. The message had come from the Central Earth Military Command on Earth. Mark cleared his throat as he began to read aloud.

Message Dispatch	*Origin*: Marcell Brighton, Commander
Urgent	Central Earth Military Command

Time: 0900 CST

At 0830 CST, the Jerrollite fleet attacked Earth without warning. All major command posts were destroyed within minutes. The disposition of the enemy fleet was such that every military installation on the planet was attacked simultaneously. Within hours the entire planet was under Jerrollite control. All Earth governments were ordered to surrender control or risk annihilation. Resistance proved to be futile, as was demonstrated when the Russian government refused to cooperate and launched all its nuclear missiles against the Jerrollite fleet. Every missile was destroyed before it could get anywhere near even the smallest of the enemy ships.

In response to this attack, a small portion of the Jerrollite fleet opened fire on every major population center in Russia. The barrage continued until nothing was left but piles of rubble. No reprieve was given.

It is currently believed that the entire government of Russia has been wiped out, along with approximately 85 percent of its population. No communications have been possible to verify this estimation.

Every other Earth government has capitulated to Jerrollite control. This command post is the last operational communications facility left untouched by the attack. Its location will undoubtedly be detected when this message is transmitted. Do not attempt to respond to this message. You are now our only hope. You carry the only remaining torch of freedom and as such serve as our only hope against our oppressors.

No further communications will be possible. All evidence of your existence is being destroyed to preserve whatever element of surprise you may have.

May God deliver us all.

Gen. Marcell Brighton, Commander
Central Earth Military Command

End Transmission

Mark sat down heavily on the edge of his bunk, his mind swirling with the implications of the message. He folded the paper and dropped it on the desk. He sat in silence, stunned, unable to believe what he had just read.

"Have you confirmed any of this?" Mark asked quietly.

"Long-range scans have confirmed the destruction in Russia. We've also been receiving sporadic reports from different places, but I'm afraid they all paint the same picture as what you just read."

A flurry of emotions threatened to overwhelm Mark as he contemplated the degree of death and destruction that had just swept over Earth. His family and friends were either dead already or in grave danger. No help would be coming from Earth.

Mark turned his emotions inward, refusing to show his true feelings. General Matheson must have seen the look on his face. "I feel the same way, son. Just make sure you control your anger so it can be channeled into something useful. We have some serious planning to do if we want to liberate Earth from the control of the Jerrollites," he said, placing his hand firmly on Mark's shoulder. "We're all in this together."

"Yes, sir," Mark said simply, knowing nothing else to say.

The general picked up the message, placing it in his pocket. "I'll be announcing this to the entire ship in a few moments, so there is no need to keep it a secret. I think the crew has a right to know exactly what we're fighting for," he said. He turned and left without saying another word.

Mark decided that dwelling on the subject would accomplish nothing except drive him insane. After a few moments, he decided to go to the officers' club anyway. He really didn't feel like being alone.

CHAPTER 4

The door to Mark's cabin slipped shut as he made his way to the officers' club. The announcement of what had happened on Earth began coming over the ship's intercom system. Mark continued walking as the grave news was shared with the entire crew. The looks of shock and fear on the faces he passed served only to strengthen his resolve.

The events had grave implications for the human race. Central Earth Military Command's fleet had been in space dock undergoing refits to prepare for the coming war. Because the attack was unexpected, the devastation had been complete; only the *Hercules* was spared.

Since the attack, the *Hercules* had been unable to establish contact with any other ships. If any had escaped, they were unable to respond. Mark assumed that they were pretty much alone.

Deep in thought, he almost didn't realize what happened as a thunderous crash reverberated through the corridor. The ship rocked violently to one side, slamming Mark's body against the bulkhead. Muffled explosions

were coming from below deck, setting off sirens and klax-
ons all over the ship. Sprinting down the corridor to the
access way that led to the bridge, Mark passed several crew
members who had been hurt by the sudden violent shift.
He made his way to the nearest intercom and called for
emergency medical assistance before going on. Reaching
the access way, Mark shimmied up the ladder and hurried
onto the bridge. He stumbled as another explosion rocked
the ship. Fighting to maintain his footing, Mark shouted,
"What's going on?"

Matheson, who was standing in the middle of the
bridge, turned to face him. "We're under attack by a
Jerrollite patrol ship! If he reports back to his command,
we're going to be in big trouble," he replied.

"Understood, General." Mark was all business. "Are
any of the TAC-WING fighters available yet?"

"One wing is available and ready for launch. The
crews are at their ships." Turning to the tactical officer,
Matheson barked a command. "Hold launch clearance
until Hunter gets there." To Mark, he said, "They're waiting for you, so *go!*"

"I'm on my way!" Mark said as he sprinted from the
bridge.

He made his way to the launch area quickly and scrambled into the cockpit of a single-man TAC-WING the

flight crew had mounted on its launch rails and prepped for launch. Dropping firmly into the pilot's seat, Mark reached back and removed the BWI helmet from its storage area in the rear of the cockpit. The helmet was the one feature that really set this fighter apart from earlier models. Using sensors mounted in the shell, human brain waves could control every aspect of flight or combat. If the pilot thought it, the ship did it. That was where the name of the helmet came from: BWI stood for brain wave inference.

Mark slid the helmet over his head and activated its Heads-up display. The helmet performed a retinal scan and recognized him as an authorized user. The onboard computer acknowledged him. "Welcome, Captain Hunter. You are now in command." Mark ordered the computer to bring the ship to flight-ready status. As the ship's systems began to come online, each one reported its status directly to the display. Mark began running down the preflight checklist, verifying that all systems on the fighter were ready and all armament was responding to the ship's computer. Mark was relieved that, operationally, not much had changed since his retirement, the ships systems still working the same way they did when he was on active duty. Inside the cockpit, he felt secure and comfortable.

He gave a thumbs-up to the crew chief and called over his communications system, "Clear for launch!" The flight crew immediately disconnected everything from the craft as the hatch directly in front of his ship irised open. The fighter was moved smoothly into the launch tube by small induction motors in the rails. The hatch slid silently shut behind him, the only light coming from indicators on his dashboard and helmet. At the far end of the launch tube, another portal opened to reveal the blackness of space and the distant light of the stars.

As the engines of the fighter ignited, they began to thrum with power, making Mark feel as if the fighter had become a part of his own body. His senses were its senses, and his brain received direct input from the fighter's vast array of sensing capability through his helmet. As power levels began to increase, Mark felt as if he could barely restrain the spacecraft, almost as if it wanted to burst free of its bonds and take flight.

Performing a final communications check, Mark radioed the other nine fighters in his wing.

"This is Wing Commander, prepare to launch!"

"We're ready, sir!" came the eager response.

The radio crackled in his ear. "Wing Commander, this is Flight Control. You are cleared to launch. Good luck."

Mark felt the ship throbbing with unbridled power, waiting for a simple thought to streak toward the fight.

"Roger, Control. All fighters...LAUNCH!"

Ten simultaneous fountains of fire leapt from the rears of the TAC-WING spacecraft, filling the launch tubes with flame and hot exhaust gases. Each pilot was pressed against his seat with a force equivalent to eight times Earth's gravity, gritting their teeth against the pressure. Each ship rocketed down the launch rails, picking up more and more speed until finally reaching launch velocity. Passing through the outer shield, the fighters vaulted from the launch rails into cold, dark space.

Once clear of the launch area, the wing took up formation on Mark's ship. Curving high in a graceful arc over the top of the *Hercules*, Mark saw that no real damage had been done by the Jerrollite attack—yet. Activating his proximity scanner, he began to search the surrounding area for the enemy ship.

"All units, stand by. Target is approaching from twelve o'clock. TAC Two through Five, with me. TAC Six through Ten, fall back and maintain a defensive posture around the *Hercules*. If they get past us, you will exercise all means possible to prevent them from reaching the *Hercules*. Remember, there is no try on this mission! You must succeed! If you don't, we all die," he said.

Each ship peeled off the formation, headed toward its assigned post. Mark's group swung around, each pilot performing a tight spiral roll to bring the ships directly into an attack formation.

"Bring weapon systems online," Mark ordered.

"Yes, sir. All systems are online and ready," was the response.

Sweeping in a wide arc to his left, Mark engaged his gravitational compensator, a device that allowed the TAC-WING to execute maneuvers that were normally beyond the physical capabilities of human pilots by generating a field that served as a cushion against the increased g-force experienced during violent combat.

Bringing his forward sensors to bear, Mark instructed the computer to triangulate on the enemy ship and lock the coordinates into its memory. Selecting a Shrike antispacecraft missile, he removed the firing safety and prepared to launch. The targeting system had locked on to the Jerrollite ship, displaying crosshairs in his HUD as it tracked the enemy ship.

"Begin jamming all communication channels!" Mark said.

"Roger, leader. Jamming is in progress."

Knowing the Jerrollite would not be able to contact his ship removed some of the pressure and allowed Mark to concentrate on making the shot. He engaged his aft rockets, roaring after the enemy fighter and rapidly closing the gap between them. The Jerrollite pilot began swinging his ship violently from side to side in a vain attempt to shake the TAC-WING from his tail.

"TAC Three and Four, swing around in front of me and cut him off!" Mark said.

"Roger, TAC One!"

Mark watched intently as the two fighters leapt from their positions, nosediving into a path that directly intersected that of the fleeing Jerrollite ship. Realizing that its only options were a kamikaze death by colliding with the oncoming TAC fighters or a fight with Mark, the Jerrollite pilot chose the latter. As the alien ship came about in a razor-sharp 180-degree turn, it kicked in its own boosters and began a high-speed attack run directly toward Mark. Dual energy beams leapt from the nose of the Jerrollite ship in an attempt to blast the TAC-WING from the sky.

Anticipating the Jerrollite's tactics, Mark had already begun to move his ship out of harm's way. The beams lanced across the bow of Mark's ship, harmlessly fading into the distance. As the enemy vessel passed directly in front, onboard tracking systems sounded a shrill alarm, indicating that the Shrike missile had locked on to the alien ship and was ready to fire. Enabling the missile's shields, Mark mentally ordered the computer to launch. The TAC-WING shuddered as the missile blasted free of its mounting under the nose of the ship, racing after the target.

The Jerrollite began firing frantically from its rear-facing weapons in the direction of the missile to detonate the warhead but was unable to obtain a lock on it quickly enough. Once the missile had obtained a positive lock, the Jerrollite could only sit, watch, and die.

The missile impacted the alien ship just below the cockpit area, shattering glass and spraying fragments of metal in several directions. Mark could see the pilot's pale-blue face contort in terror as the missile penetrated the hull of its spacecraft, venting the internal atmosphere. The Jerrollite locked eyes with Mark, impending death evident in its expression, surprised that it had been beaten.

The spacecraft was vaporized, followed by a blinding flash. Automatic systems on the TAC-WING darkened the canopy to lessen the impact of the flash on its human occupant. Outboard sensors indicated that the hull temperature increased momentarily to over seven thousand degrees. The flash faded, leaving nothing except a faintly glowing cloud of ionized gas to tell passersby what had occurred. As the cloud began to dissipate, Mark swung his ship around, ordering the wing to fall in on his position.

"Nice shootin', Tex!" one of his pilots commented.

"Thanks," Mark said.

As they headed back to the *Hercules*, Mark continued scanning the area for additional enemy ships just to make sure that the single alien fighter had not been able to get off a message. He instructed the other pilots to do likewise.

Finally satisfied that they were at least momentarily safe from enemy attack, Mark radioed the ship.

"*Hercules*, this is Wing Commander. The area is secure."

The response came almost instantly. "We were watching. Great shot, sir! You are clear for landing in Bay Two. Bring 'em home, boys!"

Mark smiled in response to the exuberance in the controller's voice. Looking over his left shoulder, he was impressed by the precision of the formation off his wing. The pilot in the nearest ship was looking at him, grinning like a kid with a new toy on Christmas morning. Mark smiled back but wondered what this kid would feel like when this mess was over.

The *Hercules* came into view, starkly visible against the black backdrop of a large asteroid. It sure didn't seem like much, all alone, to be humanity's last hope. Starting braking maneuvers, the wing began its descent into the landing bay.

As their ships touched down, the pilots were greeted by cheers from every hand on deck. Mark knew how they felt. Any victory, no matter how small, was a morale booster. As he taxied his fighter into its holding area, Mark opened his canopy and raised his hand in a thumbs-up to let them know he was unhurt. This action was promptly greeted by another chorus of yells and shouts. He removed his BWI helmet and climbed down onto the deck of the battleship. As each member of the wing emerged from his ship, Mark saluted him.

The deck chief walked up to Mark as he was removing his gloves and emergency air supply. The chief was dressed in a standard-issue, white flight deck coverall, covered head to toe with grease.

"The general wants you to report to the bridge as soon as you hit the deck," he said, jerking his thumb over his shoulder in the direction of the bridge.

Mark acknowledged his message with a curt nod, placing his gloves and backpack into the chief's hands. "Take care of this for me, will you?" he asked.

"No problem, sir. Good shootin' today!"

Mark smiled and nodded, walking off to find the general.

Stepping onto the bridge, he was greeted again by a cheering crew. Mark acknowledged their praise with a small smile and made his way to the center platform where General Matheson was standing. Mark could see the twinkle in his eye as he approached.

"You really blew that son of a bitch right out of the sky!" he exclaimed.

"Yeah, piece of cake," Mark replied shakily.

The general grinned and let out a genuine laugh. The entire bridge crew joined in, allowing the mood of the moment to carry them away. Regaining his professional demeanor, the general pulled Mark to one side, speaking in a subdued voice so none could overhear.

"Mark, you did a good job, but now we have to decide what to do next. Meet me in the briefing room."

Mark nodded curtly and left the bridge.

"Helm, plot a course to take us out of the system. Keep that asteroid between us and the Jerrollite base at all times. I don't want this ship detected while we try to get the hell out of here."

"Aye aye, sir," acknowledged the ensign at the helm console.

After confirming that his orders were being carried out, Matheson turned over control of the ship to his first officer.

"You have the bridge, Lieutenant."

"Aye, sir! I have the bridge," he replied.

Mark was sitting alone in the briefing room thinking about the events of the last few hours when General Matheson entered. Before Mark could come to attention, the general waved him off.

"At ease, at ease," said Matheson, smiling. Removing a cigar from his pocket, he began to chew on it while eyeing Mark. In a move that belied his stress, Matheson withdrew a small lighter and allowed the flame to dance over the tobacco, causing it to glow as he pulled on the cigar. Mark watched in silence, knowing that the general actually lighting up was a prime indicator of the amount of stress he was under. Mark waited for the general to continue. Finally coming to a decision, he lowered the cigar, took a deep breath, and began.

"Mark, desperate times call for desperate measures. As far as we know, we represent the only military forces left from Earth. And since we are currently in a state of war, I am implementing two priorities. The first will be to guarantee our survival. We can accomplish that by moving the *Hercules* into a safer position. I have already implemented this phase. The second, and perhaps the more difficult, will be to begin planning and implementing a counterattack, the ultimate goal of which is the liberation of Earth from Jerrollite control." He paused, taking a long drag from his cigar and slowly exhaling a large cloud of smoke before continuing.

"The first phase of the counterattack will be up to you, along with a team of specialists I will assign to you. Your primary objective will be to retrieve several experimental weapons that have been under development for the past few years, along with any scientific personnel you may find along the way, specifically those who developed the weapons, and return them here, to the ship." Matheson looked carefully into Mark's eyes, searching for any hint of fear or self-doubt. Finding none, he continued.

"I am granting you a field promotion to the rank of colonel. You will be second in command only to me," he said, tossing a set of silver eagles onto the table. "Any questions?"

Mark swallowed convulsively, picking up the eagles and looking at them in the palm of his hand. "Just one, sir. When do I meet my team?"

"Right now," Matheson said, stepping around the table and opening the door. The bright light from the hallway kept Mark from seeing the face of the individual who walked in the door, but the hairdo could only belong to one person.

"Johann! It's good to have you on this mission!" Mark said, standing and pounding him on the back.

"Easy, boy, easy! You're gonna kill me before we get there."

Embarrassed, Mark stopped his exuberant display. Johann gestured to the insignia in Mark's hand. "Say, those be some beautiful birds you got there, mon. Put 'em on!"

Glancing at the eagles, Mark looked back to General Matheson.

"I would be honored, sir, if you would do this for me." The general smiled, taking the eagles from Mark's hand and pinning them on his uniform. When he was finished, he stepped back and saluted. Mark returned the salute and shook his hand.

"Thank you, sir."

"My pleasure, Colonel Hunter. Let's go meet the rest of your team," he said. The three men left the briefing room together, heading for the men's quarters below decks.

CHAPTER 5

Back on Earth

Stepping out of the shower, Bill Johnson decided he had better get a move on or he was going to be late for the morning briefing at the Pentagon. Ever since the Jerrollite presence had been detected in the asteroid belt, the military had been in the highest state of alert possible without actually going to war. Part of that readiness was morning briefings, which had grown to be such a necessary, if somewhat inconvenient, part of Bill's life. Grabbing his suit from the closet, he dressed quickly and made his way downstairs.

Miscalculating the last step, Bill went sprawling into the kitchen. He slid across the tile floor and stubbed his toe on the far wall, causing a reaction that made him lose his balance and fall toward onto the table. With a loud crash, he ended up facedown in his two-year-old daughter's bowl of cereal. As he raised his head and wiped the milk from his eyes, he saw his daughter staring at him with her spoon held above her head in what appeared to be a defensive posture, a wild look of disbelief on her face. His wife, Marilyn, was almost in tears from hysterical laughter.

"Way to go, graceful!" she said, chuckling, as she picked up his breakfast from the stove and brought it to the table. "Here you go—try not to fall in it!" she said as her fit of laughter started again. By this time, his daughter had picked up on her mother's cue and had begun laughing and squealing in delight. Bill couldn't help but smile at her as he wiped his face with a napkin.

"Agent Smart, reporting for duty," he said, making a face at his daughter. This brought a renewed burst of laughter. Born to amuse the masses, I guess, he thought as he sipped his coffee. He had never been the most graceful person on the planet, but fortunately in his chosen career, grace was not a requirement for success.

Bill was a physicist who had recently developed a new theory that described a process for the creation of a singularity, more commonly referred to as a black hole, in a laboratory environment. As there was currently no reliable technology available that would ensure the containment of one of nature's most dangerous objects, originally his work was mostly theoretical. However, his team had taken his theory, pushing it to the limits, and had come up with an actual working generator. They had successfully created black holes for a billionth of a second in the lab, but there was no way to really test it safely on a larger scale. The prototype generator had become the object of discussion by weapons designers as a possible superweapon that could be used against the Jerrollites. If they could get everything working, it would be a most fearsome weapon. Because planners were not leaving any option on the table, Bill was required to attend design sessions with the weapons team and to participate in the daily morning briefings at the Pentagon for military personnel to keep them appraised of his team's progress.

"Thanks for breakfast, sweetheart," he said to his wife, Marilyn. Standing up and taking one last sip of coffee, he wiped his mouth and walked toward the door. Marilyn was waiting for him.

"Bye, honey. Be careful not to attack any more walls with your big toe!" she chided. He smiled as he took her into his arms for a passionate kiss. As the moment ended, he held her at arm's length, looking at her intently. She and their daughter were Bill's entire reason for living. He shuddered to think of life without his family. Giving her a last embrace, he headed out the door toward his car. It was a beautiful day outside, and the sun felt warm on his skin. As he fumbled to retrieve his keys from his pocket, Bill heard an ominous, low rumble coming out of the east, growing louder and louder as he listened. The intensity of the noise increased until it was almost deafening. The ground began to tremble underneath his feet, vibrating with the roar in the air. He clapped his hands over his ears, grimacing in pain as he searched the sky for the source of the sound.

At that moment the world as he knew it came to an end. The street was rocked by a loud explosion, and he fell to the ground. The peaceful scene of only moments before was now pandemonium and chaos. Bill looked up at the horizon to see a scene straight from *Dante's Inferno*. The skyline was on fire. Sirens began wailing somewhere close by. Standing in confusion, still looking skyward, Bill saw a large group of airborne vehicles making sweeps across the city, raking the streets with concentrated beams of energy. Every place the beams touched burst into flames, rapidly followed by secondary explosions. While he watched, horrified, several people fell into the line of fire and were vaporized instantly. Only a black smudge was left behind where once a living, breathing human being had stood. Heavy antiaircraft fire was coming from the military bases around the city, but it was bouncing harmlessly off the shields of the attacking craft.

With a sudden realization of horror, Bill recognized the shape of the attacking ships. Jerrollites! He couldn't believe what he was seeing. The military had just assured the president yesterday that this could not possibly happen anytime soon. A cold fear swept over him as he realized that if they had so badly underestimated the timelines, it was quite possible that they had also underestimated everything else. His heart broke as he watched building after building go up in flames. Watching the futile attempts of the military to counter the attack, Bill realized that Earth didn't stand a chance.

As he watched, a single fighter broke off from the main group, flying low and fast directly toward him. As the ship began to strafe the ground, the air itself began to churn as the heat and fire sent huge clouds of black smoke roiling into the sky. Bill realized too late that the beams from the fighter were advancing directly toward him.

Dropping his briefcase, he turned and ran back toward his house to protect his family. He got as far as placing his hand on the doorknob before the beams hit his house. Bill heard the air crackle as the extreme heat caused the air inside the house to expand violently, ripping it apart from the inside out. The gas feed ruptured as the house came down, igniting a massive fireball. The force of the explosion hurled Bill high into the air and slammed him against a parked car across the street. As he lay on his back, stunned, he looked up to see his home and family gone, an inferno in their place.

The Jerrollite ship completed its strafing run and rose high into the air to rejoin the other ships that were attacking different parts of the city. Bill watched through the smoke and haze of what was once his neighborhood. The attack ended as fast as it had begun. The sounds of war echoed in the distance. He struggled to his feet, holding his aching ribcage.

He could not fathom what he saw. Every house, as far as he could see, had either been destroyed or was burning. There was nothing left of his house but a burning pile of smashed lumber. The emotion welling up in him was too much to bear. He fell to his knees, sobs wracking his entire body. His beautiful wife and child were gone, killed by a faceless enemy he couldn't get his hands on. An anguished moan escaped his lips as he withdrew into his own mind, squeezing his eyes closed, recoiling from the terror that lay all around him. Mercifully he lost consciousness.

Pounding. Pain. Life? Bill's blinding headache reminded him that he was indeed still alive. Pushing his grief momentarily aside, he opened his eyes slowly, embracing an insane hope that it had all been a bad dream. Putting his hand to his head in a vain attempt to ease the throbbing pain, he stood up and looked around. The sky was no longer blue but a dingy gray, filled with the smoke of hundreds of burning buildings. The attack had left the streets filled with rubble and debris, making passage by motor vehicle impossible. Gathering up his briefcase, Bill stumbled toward the remains of his house. Not really expecting to find anything, he began to search the charred hulk.

Lifting burnt studs and kicking still smoldering furniture out of the way, he found no evidence of his family. Bill began to cry quietly, mourning his loss and venting his frustration at having been unable to do anything to save them. He was startled to hear a voice from behind him.

"They are in a better place, you know," a frail old woman said.

Wiping tears from his face, Bill turned to face her. It was a neighbor he had never really met.

"The only way for you to honor them is to survive," she said.

The woman's words got past his anguish, causing a glimmer of rational thought. He glanced down at the briefcase in his hand as realization dawned. Looking up and down his street again only confirmed his suspicion. The Jerrollite line of fire had been aimed specifically at his house. They had been attempting to kill him! His family had not been the victims of a random attack by a faceless soldier but were casualties in a premeditated act of murder.

"Oh my God!" he said.

He was considered a military target because of his research into the singularity generator. All of his notes on the project were still in his briefcase, which meant he was still a target. Bill was not a large or physical man, but the resolve that formed in his mind at that moment would have put many mighty warriors to shame. He would indeed survive, and his weapon would be used to exact vengeance for his family.

Bolting down the street, Bill yelled back at the old woman, "Find shelter and get off the streets! Those bastards may be back!" He decided it would be best to make his way to the Pentagon, to retrieve the experimental versions of his weapon. Only preliminary models, they could still be used as a guide to construct the most fearsome weapon man had ever seen.

Picking his way along the street, dodging in and out of the shadows, he left his neighborhood and his old life behind. His resolve continued to build as he saw more and more death and destruction. It gave him new strength to go on. The old woman was right, he thought. I must survive.

CHAPTER 6

Rounding a corner, Bill drew up short and jumped back out of sight into the shadowy crevice of a building. A Jerrollite patrol ship had landed in front of the Pentagon, and ground troops were rapidly deploying in an attempt to encircle the building and prevent anyone from escaping. On the verge of panic, Bill tried to calm down and think of what to do next as his heart pounded in his chest. If the Jerrollites were able to gain control of his weapon, Earth would be doomed forever. He had no choice; he had to act.

"Think, man, THINK!" he said to himself, wiping sweat from his brow and breathing hard. He suddenly remembered a secret entrance to the Pentagon building. If he could only get to it without being discovered, he could retrieve everything possible and destroy the rest.

Circling around the huge building, he made himself invisible to passing enemy troops by staying in the shadows. The entrance he was searching for was used to evacuate personnel in the event of an accident or attack. It was connected to an underground tunnel that ran directly to the research lab. Bill could only hope that the security system had not been breached yet.

Reaching a wooded area directly behind the Pentagon, he found the entrance to the tunnel without being discovered by Jerrollite troops. The security panel on the door glowed green, which meant that until now no one had been this way. He removed the access card from his wallet and ran it through the slot. A soft chime prompted him to enter his access code. His fingers trembled slightly as he did. Bill heard a soft click as the door swung open. He entered quickly and closed the door.

The tunnel was pitch-black. Bill looked around, trying to get his bearings. He felt his way along the wall until he found a large button. Hoping it was a lighting control, he pushed it and was relieved when dim overhead lighting came on. As he continued forward, Bill's footsteps echoed hollowly down the length of the tunnel. Dimly lit and dusty from lack of use, the passage had an eerie feel to it, oddly quiet amid the chaos going on outside. Finally reaching the end, he approached the main security barrier and entered his access code again. After what seemed like an eternity, the panel glowed green, and Bill heard a light rumble as the lock mechanism rolled back. Gingerly pushing the door open and peering inside, he faced the business end of an M-16 automatic rifle not more than three inches from his forehead.

"Freeze, you alien son of a bitch!" the guard said in a trembling voice. A loud click suggested that the bolt on his weapon had slammed home and was ready to fire. Not wanting to be killed by one of his own people after surviving the initial Jerrollite attack, Bill spoke cautiously.

"I am cleared for this area, Sergeant."

The guard took Bill's badge and examined it closely, turning it over in the dim light to make sure it wasn't a forgery.

"Sorry, Mr. Johnson, but things are pretty hairy around here right now. When we saw the access light for this tunnel go green, we were afraid that the Jerrollites had found a way in," said the sergeant as he handed Bill's access badge back to him.

"Thanks, uh…" Bill read the man's name from his badge. "Carson. No problem."

Bill retrieved his badge and returned it to his wallet. Not wanting to waste time in idle chatter, he gave Carson instructions to lock down access to the tunnel and allow no one but himself to exit. Pushing open the door to his laboratory, he was relieved to see everything just as he had left it the day before. He opened his locker and removed a duffel bag large enough to contain the models of his weapon.

Startled by a series of muffled thumps from outside, Bill guessed that the Jerrollites had begun attacking the building, attempting to breach it through brute force. He quickly gathered the models and notes he had come for, knocking several pieces of equipment to the floor in his haste. After carefully placing them inside the bag, Bill zipped it shut and headed for the lab's safe. In it were schematics and diagrams for larger versions of his weapon, as well as alternative recovery area instructions. These would tell him where to meet up with his colleagues in the event of an emergency. He couldn't think of anything that more thoroughly qualified as an emergency than what was going on now. He opened the safe, grabbed the documentation and directions as well as a minimal survival kit, and stuffed them into his bag.

Before leaving, Bill entered the computer room. If the Jerrollites got their hands on the plans for his weapon, it would all be over. He entered his access code into a control panel to initiate the irreversible self-destruct sequence that would destroy the laboratory and everything else in this area of the building. The computer responded by sounding a klaxon to warn all personnel to evacuate and initiating emergency lighting. A secondary panel sprung open, and a synthesized voice prompted Bill through the remainder of the procedure.

"Enter secondary access code."

Wiping the sweat from his eyes, Bill entered the second code.

"Engage primary detonation cylinder."

Grasping the blood-red handle, Bill turned it clockwise until he heard it lock into place.

"Primary cylinder engaged. Self-destruct will occur in T minus forty-five seconds. Please vacate the area immediately," the computer said.

A large red light began flashing in the center of the room as the computer switched to the main PA system for its announcements.

"Thirty seconds to self-destruct," the computer said.

A white mist began hissing out of nozzles located in various parts of the room. The noise level was deafening. Bill gathered up his bag and briefcase and bolted from the room.

In the tunnel the voice echoed down the walls. "Ten… nine…eight…seven…" As he ran, his heart racing, he began screaming at the guard as he approached.

"RUN! This whole place is going to self-destruct!"

The guard's eyes grew large, and, realizing what Bill had done, he frantically began punching the open code into the security panel. His fingers trembled as he fought to keep them steady. At last the door hissed open just in time to allow Bill to run through. Carson was right behind him as they headed for the exit. The self-destruct system automatically slammed the door shut behind them. Somewhere in the back of his mind, Bill realized that door might be the only thing that saved their lives—it would prevent the explosion from entering the tunnel, if it held. Approaching the exit door, Bill saw that it was closed, and the access light was glowing red, indicating that it was locked. Hoping the door was not as heavy as it looked, Bill and Carson hurled their bodies against it. Yielding to their combined weight, the door sprang open as they tumbled out of the tunnel and onto the ground.

A low rumble began emanating from the tunnel, followed by a series of loud, percussive explosions. Looking back down the tunnel, Bill could see a fireball swiftly making its way toward them. Grabbing Carson by the collar of his uniform, Bill heaved him to one side and jumped to the other just before a column of fire erupted from the opening with a loud *whoosh!* The flame shot fifty feet, igniting several trees and bushes.

"Holy shit! I ain't never seen anything like that!" Carson said.

"Me neither." Bill replied, groaning. But that's nothing compared to what the Jerrollites are going to get when I get this baby working, he thought as he patted the duffel bag.

"We have to get out of here. The Jerrollites had to have seen that explosion!" he said to Carson.

As if to prove his point, a patrol pulled up on the main road about seventy-five yards from where they were sitting and began to unload troops. Their commander was screaming orders and pointing in the direction of the tunnel, which was now on fire.

"Follow me, Sergeant," Bill said as he ran deeper into the trees. Dodging undergrowth as he ran, he heard a Jerrollite soldier begin to yell. Carson had been spotted. The air began sizzling and crackling with the energy being released by the beam weapons the aliens were firing at them. Bill continued to sprint toward cover. He turned around to motion to the sergeant to follow him, just in time to see Carson's body explode as he took the full brunt of a particle beam in his back. Bill had never seen a man killed by a beam of light before, and it was not a pleasant sight. The beam superheated the moisture contained in each cell, causing them to burst. It was a messy, ugly, painful way to die. The sergeant's body, a pile of burnt flesh, fell slowly forward to land at Bill's feet and splatter across the plant growth, still sizzling as the heat from the Jerrollite weapon slowly dissipated.

Bill retched as he jumped back under cover. His heart was pounding so hard he thought it would leap from his chest. He dug into the underbrush to create an effective cover for himself as the Jerrollites searched the area. Several of them were looking at remnants of the sergeant's body, repeatedly firing bursts into it to make sure he was dead.

Bill couldn't understand their language, but when they all started heading back toward their transport, he breathed a sigh of relief. His entire body shook violently from the adrenaline pumping through it. Apparently the Jerrollites were convinced that the sergeant had been the only person in the area, and they had dealt with the situation. Carson's death had given Bill the opportunity he needed to escape. His life had purchased Earth's chance to fight back. Bill swore that his sacrifice would not be in vain, but now it was up to him to get his plans into the right hands.

Bill unfolded the map to the recovery area and examined it closely. It was a topographical map covering a hundred miles in all directions. His assigned area was a cave located in the countryside approximately thirty miles due east. Bill could see hills in the general direction he needed to go. He would use these as a landmark.

Deciding it would be best to wait for nightfall before attempting the journey, he placed the map back into his bag and dug in a little deeper, covering himself with dead leaves and twigs. He might as well get some rest while he had the chance.

Closing his eyes brought visions of his family to his mind. He saw his daughter playing that morning. He remembered Marilyn's laughter at his clumsiness. He saw the Jerrollite fighter sweep his house with weapons fire and saw it explode again and again and again.

"No!" Bill screamed as he woke with a start. Sweat was pouring down his face. He looked around, coming to his senses, and realized it was not just a bad dream. His family was gone. His life was gone. The only thing he had left was his burning desire for revenge on those who had destroyed them. Bill pushed that rage deep into his heart, where it smoldered and seethed, waiting for a chance to erupt in fury.

Night had fallen while he slept, so Bill gathered his belongings, removing evidence of his presence, and fled under the cover of darkness.

CHAPTER 7

Mark examined the men who stood at attention before him as he paced back and forth across the room. He wondered if they were capable of withstanding the pressures and dangers of the upcoming mission to Earth to retrieve experimental weapons and, hopefully, some of the scientists who had been working on their development. Each man stepped forward as Matheson called his name. When the last one had stepped up, the general moved from behind the podium.

"At ease, men." They all took seats in the briefing area. "All right, gentlemen. I'll cut directly to the chase. You've all been selected to participate in a mission that is as vital as it is dangerous. Colonel Hunter is in command of this little excursion, so I'll allow him to brief you on your mission. Good luck," said Matheson as he turned and left the room.

"Auhhhtenshun!" one of the soldiers growled. Everyone in the room snapped to attention until the general was gone. Mark moved to the front of the room and laid his notes on the podium.

"At ease," he said. "We might as well get to know one another and dispense with the formalities. We'll be working closely together in a very difficult situation, and the succ—"

"How difficult, sir?" one of the men interrupted. Looking at the notes he had prepared, Mark sighed and came to a decision. He lifted the notes and tore them in half. This action was greeted by several nods of approval and a surprised chuckle from around the room.

"Look, guys. I'm not going to feed you a line of official crap. You're all aware of the situation on Earth. What some of you may not know is that top secret weapons research was being done in underground labs at the Pentagon. Several of those weapons were close to being complete, and if we can retrieve them, they just might give us the edge we need to beat the Jerrollites at their own game." Quiet filled the room, the only sound coming from the faint rumble of the ship's engines. The men were sitting on the edges of their seats, anxiously awaiting Mark's next words. He understood the feeling.

"This mission is vital to the continued survival of the *Hercules* as well as that of Earth. Without those weapons, we don't stand a rat's ass of a chance against the Jerrollites."

The statement hung heavily in the air. Mark looked at his men as he continued. "Our only chance is to retrieve those weapons and the scientists who were working on them. All I ask of you is that you obey my orders without question, holding the goal of the mission above all other considerations. Even your own life."

The mood was somber as he continued. "Johann here will be my second in command." He turned and pointed toward the large Jamaican standing behind him. "If anything happens to me, he is in charge." The fierce-looking black man stood stiffly behind the colonel, his arms crossed, gazing fiercely at the men. He exuded an air of ferocious confidence. Several of them swallowed nervously as they met his eyes and quickly looked down.

"Any questions?" Mark glanced at each man in turn, giving him the opportunity to speak. "Good. Gather up your belongings and follow Johann to the special quarters we've set up for you. Get a good rest period in because you're going to need it! Good day, gents." Mark caught Johann's eye and grinned.

"Atten...hut!" Johann roared as he returned Mark's grin.

Each man bolted to attention, startled by the ferocity of Johann's voice. As Mark left the room, Johann was shouting about one thing or another, and each man was trying to stand as stiffly as possible, terrified of drawing attention to himself. It was good to be on top of the military food chain for once, Mark thought. He chuckled to himself as he continued down the corridor. Coming around a bend, Mark spotted General Matheson and hailed him.

"General, I need to talk to you. We need to go over some equipment requirements and timelines for the mission," Mark said, falling into step beside him.

Matheson stopped and turned to Mark, removing his cigar from his mouth so that he could speak. "I'm giving you carte blanche on your requests. Take what you need. You can see the quartermaster down on Deck Twenty-Seven for your supplies." Stuffing his cigar back into his mouth, he continued, "Report to me when your team is ready to depart." He spun on his heel and left Mark standing alone.

After Mark finished his procurement duties, he decided to look up Johann and buy him that drink he had promised. He stopped at the nearest intercom panel and punched in the code for Johann's cabin.

"Johann, you up for a drink?"

"Sure, mon. Always time for a cool one."

"I'll see you in the officers' club in five, okay?"

"I'll be there."

Mark clicked off the intercom and made his way to the club. On a battleship with such a large crew, it was important for people to have a place to let off a little steam every now and then. The officers' club was pretty Spartan in comparison with some of the better planet-side establishments, but the drinks were free, and the company was good. Mark entered the lounge and seated himself at a table away from the main concentration of people. He did not really feel like being sociable, his mind occupied with the details of the upcoming mission.

Johann entered the club with his usual flamboyance, dressed in some of the wildest clothes Mark had ever seen. He made his way over to Mark's table.

"Those clothes aren't exactly regulation, are they?"

"Not really, but I figured what the hell? I might not ever get to wear 'em again, right?"

Mark grinned, unable to come up with a valid argument. Johann slid into the seat opposite Mark.

"How do the troops look?" asked Mark.

"Oh, they'll be okay. Some of 'em are kinda green around the gills, but as a whole, I think they'll be able to get the job done."

Mark was relieved to hear that. He trusted Johann's assessment of men more than anyone else's, even his own. He stared aimlessly into the amber liquid of his drink.

"You know, Matheson gave us whatever I asked for. Didn't even question me when I requested one of the new

TAC transports. Just signed a blank order and told me to get whatever I wanted."

"The old man is goin' all out, eh?" Johann said.

"Yeah. Means he must be serious about our success."

"That or he's giving us a grand send-off for our funeral."

The men eyed each other. Matheson was usually conservative, holding as much as possible in reserve. If he was willing to throw everything into a first effort, it could only mean that this was going to be their only chance. Shrugging it off, Johann tossed down the rest of his drink. Mark quickly followed suit.

"Let's hit it, brother. I think we got a long day ahead of us tomorrow."

"Good idea. I'll see you in the morning."

They exited the club and headed for their quarters to try to get some rest before launch time. Both knew it was probably going to be a wasted effort but felt they should at least try.

CHAPTER 8

As the team was assembling in the cargo bay, General Matheson approached Mark to brief him on the plan for his team's mission. As Matheson drew near, Mark could tell he was tense by the set of his shoulders and the grim look on his face. Matheson knew the continued existence of the human race as free beings depended on the outcome of the mission.

"Attention on deck!" came the cry. The entire squad quickly fell into formation and faced forward, standing at attention. The general stopped directly in front of the squad and stood with his hands clasped behind his back, ready to address the men.

"We will reach our drop point in approximately thirty minutes. The *Hercules* has been moved to a position on the far side of the moon to avoid Jerrollite detection. Your job is to recover the weapons and the weapons designers at all costs! Do you understand?" he asked. Several affirmative responses emanated from the group.

"Good luck, men. Our future is in your hands." Turning to Mark, he said, "Drop will be on my command. Get your men into the transport."

"Yes, sir," Mark said. After saluting the general, he turned to his team.

"All right, you mama's boys, load 'em up!" Mark said, his voice reverberating through the bay.

With a shout, each soldier gathered up his gear and began to climb into the TAC transport, a craft generally used for transporting men and critical goods into high-risk situations. Mark looked at its squat, round shape and chuckled; it reminded him more of a fishbowl than a spacecraft. After the last man had boarded, Mark climbed into the cockpit and secured the ship's main hatch. A hissing sound emanated from nozzles in the wall as the cabin began to pressurize in preparation for departure. Mark took his place in the pilot's seat, buckling himself in. Toggling the intercom switch, he addressed the men in the back.

"Make ready for planetfall, gentlemen. We're gonna make a power dive straight into the atmosphere to avoid detection, so I can't promise that the ride is going to be very smooth."

Each man took the hint to double-check his safety harness and cinch it up even tighter. Mark's reputation as a pilot had preceded him with several members of the team; he could tell by the look of dread on several faces. He overheard two men in the back of the cabin.

"You know, Jim, you better hang on to your shorts. The old man is flying this bucket, and he don't pull no punches."

Jim's gulp was audible, even in the cockpit.

Smiling, with just a hint of a mischievous glint in his eye, Mark prepared for a takeoff that these guys would never forget. To his right the comm unit crackled to life.

"Transport One, you are cleared for launch." Grinning devilishly, Mark slammed the throttle lever forward to maximum thrust. The transport screamed down the launch rails, gaining speed with every second.

"Oh my God, we're gonna die!" Mark heard Jim moan under his breath. Checking the passenger video monitor, he could see the soldier turning a little green around the edges. The transport leapt free from the launch tube, bursting through the atmosphere containment field. Switching the view screen to an aft view, Mark saw the *Hercules* receding rapidly from view. Satisfied, he switched the view forward in time to see the crescent of Earth appear just over the horizon of the moon.

As Mark guided the transport toward their destiny, he tried to relax a little while he had the chance. Johann stuck his head through the cockpit access hatch.

"Are you having fun up here?" he asked, a cross expression on his face. "I got guys pukin' their guts up back here."

"Sorry, Jo. Just trying to get 'em ready for the hellfire."

"Oh, man! You're gonna use the hellfire maneuver?"

Mark's eyes lit up in anticipation.

"Yeah. Go back and get 'em ready. We're coming up on atmospheric insertion in…" Mark checked the chronometer, "three minutes."

Johann shook his head, retreating to the cargo bay where his men were. He stood in front, addressing the entire squad.

"Suck your seats and grab ahold, boys—we're goin' in!" Johann laughed, amused by the obvious displeasure on the faces surrounding him. Several moans came from the rear of the cabin.

Executing a violent swing around, Mark flipped the transport 180 degrees on its axis, placing the heat-resistant rear shield toward the atmosphere. He heard the familiar tortured shriek as the thick air buffeted the transport, causing the heat shield to glow a fiery red. The air pounded at the hull of the transport, sending horrendous sounds reverberating through the ship. Glancing at the monitor, Mark could see the anxiety in the men's faces. Having compassion for his squad, Mark toggled the intercom.

"No sweat, guys. Everything is completely normal so far. All systems are nominal." Mark finished his announcement as the screeching abruptly ceased, causing a momentary silence to fall inside the transport. Pirouetting the craft so its nose was facing down toward the surface, Mark deployed his atmospheric maneuvering engines. With a loud clank, the engines fired up and began to whine loudly as they sucked thin atmosphere into their intakes, combined it with fuel, and blew it out the back, thrusting the transport forward. The renewed thrust pushed everyone back into their seats as the engines fully engaged with the atmosphere. Mark saw mixed signs of relief on the faces of the men as they realized the reentry had been successful but were unsure of what was coming next. Johann simply sat in front and displayed a wide, toothy grin.

As the ship descended, Mark brought up a topographical coordinate map on his screen, pinpointing their location. The ship was approximately thirty-five miles north of the emergency relocation area where the scientists should be hiding, assuming they had been able to escape from the Pentagon.

"Brace for hellfire…"

Mark kept the nose of the craft straight down, giving the engines maximum throttle. If the men in back had had Mark's view, he would have had an instant mutiny on his hands. The hellfire maneuver provided a planned, controlled way of reaching the surface of a planet as rapidly as possible. The only problem was, to the uninitiated, it looked more like a serious attempt at suicide.

As the ship broke through the upper cloud cover, Mark throttled back, forcing the ship into a last-minute braking maneuver, whipping up a cushion of air that slowed their descent. He fired the landing thrusters to complete their descent to the surface. Stirring up a small cloud of dust, the transport settled into a grove of large, bushy trees that looked like they would give adequate aerial cover. As the touchdown light came on, automatic systems on the ship kicked in and scanned the area for alien life-forms. Mark checked the readings, relieved that they were all negative. He gave the all clear signal to open the hatch. Unbuckling his seat harness, he made his way back into the crew compartment.

"Okay, men, gather your gear and get outside. The area is clear, but we want to use standard camouflage to hide the transport," Mark said.

Everyone stood up, somewhat shaky in the knees but otherwise none the worse for wear. Each man began to make his way out of the hatch and down the access ladder. Returning to the cockpit, Mark entered a security code that would disable the ship until the code was reentered. As an additional precaution, he enabled the automatic self-destruct if the wrong code was entered. Satisfied, he disembarked and sealed the hatch.

"Sergeant! Break out the maps of this area, and let's find out where we are," Mark said.

A gruff-looking man roughly fifty years old came out from behind the crowd of soldiers. He unrolled a map and placed it on the ground in front of him, squatting down to examine it. The alternative recovery area was a cave located in a mountain range to the south. Mark could see the mountains in question, but to his dismay the city lay between them and their goal.

"Do you think we have time to go around the city?" asked Mark.

The sergeant considered his options for a moment, standing to look at the distance between their location and the mountain range.

"I figure if we go around, it'll take at least a week to reach the cave. That cave is supposed to have four days' worth of survival equipment and supplies, so to my thinkin', we really don't have a choice. If we go through the city, we can get there in two days, maybe faster if we can appropriate some kind of transport from the Jerrollites," he said.

Mark exhaled heavily. "I think you're right, Sergeant. The only problem is I'm afraid we might be leading the Christians to the arena to be fed to the lions."

The sergeant looked at Mark carefully. "I don't think so, sir. Every man on this squad had family on Earth when the Jerrollites attacked. They want nothing more than a chance to scrap with the blue devils and give 'em some of their own!"

Mark looked at the men as they went about their duties. He could tell by the grim sets of their faces and the intensity with which they did everything that they only had one thing on their minds—revenge.

He could see the hurt and pain in their expressions. He also saw a dark cloud of hatred. If these feelings went unchecked, they would cloud their judgment in battle, which could cost them their lives. Standing on one of the engine pods, Mark called his men to his side. They gathered around, waiting to hear what he had to say.

"I know what each and every one of you want, and I understand how you all feel. My feelings are the same." He paused a moment and then continued. "Those feelings must be laid aside." A rebellious grumble came from the assembled men. "Ultimate victory over the Jerrollites can only be achieved if our mission is successful. If you have any personal feelings or vendettas that are going to interfere with this mission, put them aside now. The best way we can protect our families and honor our dead is to serve here and now, without question. A time for revenge will come later." He edged the intensity of his voice up a notch. "NOT NOW!"

Dead silence fell over the squad as they looked first at one another and then at Mark. Their faces had hardened into stone; no one moved as the sergeant came forward to speak.

"We're behind you, Colonel," he said. All the men nodded in agreement. Mark felt a wave of relief wash over him.

"That's good to know, Sergeant. All right, men, get your gear together. We move out in ten minutes!"

The squad burst into a flurry of activity. Mark surveyed his group, wondering if any of them were up to the task set before them. Never before in human history had anyone had a mission of such importance. His men had a righteous flame burning in their hearts and the desire to avenge the wrong that had been done to each and every one of them.

God help any Jerrollite that got in their way.

CHAPTER 9

Climbing down from the engine pod, Mark signaled his squad. "All right! Let's move out!"

The squad began moving around with a crisp military orderliness, gathering the materials they were going to need. Motioning for the sergeant to join him, Mark instructed him to pick a man to stay with the ship, someone who could bring it to the recovery area if they needed to blast their way out. The sergeant looked over the men milling around and picked a tall, broad-shouldered young man named Reeves. He called him over.

"Front and center, Reeves!" the sergeant said. Reeves responded quickly, bounding forward and standing stiffly at attention in front of the sergeant.

"At ease, mister," Mark said. Reeves relaxed into parade rest. "I need you to stay with the ship while we go in," Mark said. Reeves started to object but was silenced by a look from the sergeant. "Here is the access code for the computer system." Mark handed him a small scrap of paper. "Memorize it and destroy that paper." Reeves looked at it for a moment, committing the number to memory, and shredded the paper into small bits.

"Make damn sure you remember the code. You will only get one chance to enter it. Make a mistake, and the ship explodes."

Reeves swallowed hard. "I wish I was going with you, sir," he said.

"Your time will come soon enough. Just make sure you're ready when we call. When you come, come in on the deck, flat out, guns blazing. Got it?" Mark asked.

"Yes, sir!" he said, evidently pleased at the prospect of action against the Jerrollites.

Satisfied that Reeves could handle the assignment, Mark walked to the front of the formation and signaled for everyone to move out. The ship had landed in a secluded area that provided excellent cover all the way to the edge of the city. The column of men made good time toward the city limits. After about an hour of steady, double-time walking, the squad came upon a clearing roughly two hundred yards wide. Not wanting to risk crossing during daylight, Mark ordered the men to sit down, rest, and wait for dark.

"We have a long march tonight so take the opportunity to get some rest while you have the chance. You may not have time later. We move out at dark."

Everyone dispersed into the wooded area at the edge of the clearing and sat down, all the while keeping an eye on their surroundings for Jerrollite patrols. Mark made his way back to Johann and the sergeant, dropped his pack, and sat down heavily.

"It's been a long time since I did this type of thing," Mark said, removing his boots and massaging his sore feet.

The sergeant chuckled quietly, but Johann couldn't resist the opportunity for some ribbing. "What's the matter, boy? Been sittin' behind a desk too long?" They shared a laugh.

Mark responded by making his voice sound as stern as possible. "I trust that if for some reason I'm unable to continue, you will carry on in my stead?"

They erupted into laughter. Mark shook his head in disgust, ignoring both of them. He adjusted his pack in a vain attempt to make a comfortable place to lie down. After finally getting into a somewhat restful position, Mark sat back and looked out over the city, noting the mass destruction that had occurred everywhere. It looked more like a bombed-out wreck from WWII than a modern, clean city. The industrial and business sections had been hit the hardest; the destruction was almost complete in those areas. A dark, smoky haze had settled over what was left of the city, covering an area as far as the eye could see with a shroud of death and destruction. As Mark looked out over the nightmarish scene, he couldn't help imagining the anguished screams of the people who had been murdered by the Jerrollites.

He closed his eyes in a useless attempt to block out the scene, but it had already been burned into his memory forever. Mark forced himself to think of more pleasant things. His family, his experiences from the past, his friends. The thoughts filled him, allowing his body to relax and drift off into a world where everything was okay, where Jerrollites didn't exist.

Mark was suddenly jolted out of his reverie. He opened his eyes to feel Johann shaking his shoulder.

"Wake up, Mark," he said. "It's time to move out." Dragging himself back to reality, Mark glanced around groggily at the rest of the squad gathering together, ready to move out.

Mark picked up his pack and weapon and made his way to the front of the squad. The sergeant was at his side as they looked across the field to survey the safest place to cross. The closest building was directly across the field from where they were standing. Mark thought it would be the best place to cross.

"Sergeant, take the men across in groups of two. Johann, you bring up the rear with the last group." Both men nodded in agreement and began to break up the squad into pairs. When each man had been paired with another, Mark decided it was time to cross.

"Fan out! Keep your butts low! First group, on my lead. Let's go!" Mark sprinted across the clearing, followed closely by the sergeant and the first two soldiers.

On the far side of the clearing were several office buildings that would provide excellent cover. Mark and the sergeant made their way to the largest of the buildings, surveying the area for any enemy presence. With their backs flat against the wall, they began to inch their way around the building. As the group came around the first corner, Mark found himself looking directly into the blue face of a Jerrollite soldier. As recognition dawned on the alien's face, its eyes widened, and it began to raise its weapon to fire.

Boosted by a tremendous rush of adrenaline, Mark leapt toward the guard, grabbing its weapon hand and shoving it out of the way. The alien's rifle clattered onto the concrete as they struggled. Mark's muscles were screaming as he exerted every ounce of pressure he could muster to overcome the alien soldier. With a violent move, the Jerrollite managed to twist Mark around and get him into a stranglehold. It began choking the life from Mark's body. The sinewy blue fingers crushed his throat. As Mark's world began to fade into blackness, the thin whistle of a knife sailing through the air reached his ears. Struggling to open his eyes, Mark heard the dull thud of the blade impacting flesh and bone. The Jerrollite released its grip on Mark and spun around, jerking up straight. A knife was embedded in its throat, blood pouring out of the wound. Mark seized the opportunity, kicking the alien hard in the back and scampering out of the way. The alien's lifeless body staggered and fell, a pool of blood rapidly spreading outward.

Mark rolled into a sitting position, coughing and gasping for air, leaning on the wall for support. Turning, he saw the sergeant remove his knife from the throat of the Jerrollite, wiping blood off the blade before sheathing it. He looked at Mark and smiled.

"Damned if you ain't the brave one. I ain't never seen an officer willing to get blood on his uniform." He chuckled as he came to give Mark a hand. "You okay?" he asked.

"Yeah. Thanks for the assist," Mark said. The sergeant grinned at Mark and clapped him on the back.

"No problem. Next time try using your gun instead of your hands." Mark glanced down at his sidearm where it remained in his holster. It had never even occurred to him to pull it out and use it. The sergeant turned, shaking his head and smiling, and signaled for all the other men to join them. As they came up, several were startled by the dead Jerrollite lying on the sidewalk.

"What happened here, Sarge?"

"One of the bastards surprised us. The colonel here decided to make like a kamikaze and jump the sucker before he could fire at us."

Several of the soldiers in the squad looked at Mark, at the dead Jerrollite, and then back at Mark again. He could see a bit more respect in their eyes than had been there before. Mark gathered himself up, signaled the rest of the squad to follow, and proceeded to make his way around to the back entrance of the building.

As the squad approached the rear of the building, they heard the low murmur of people talking. Signaling the squad to come to a halt and be absolutely silent, Mark flattened himself against the wall and peered around the corner. What he saw caused his heart to sink inside his chest.

Across from the building were at least five hundred Jerrollite troops that had set up a camp in the parking lot. Mark saw several guards actively patrolling the area. Withdrawing around the corner, he realized the Jerrollite they had just killed probably had been on guard duty for this camp, which meant that if it didn't report in soon, their commander would become suspicious and start a search. Pausing a moment to think clearly, Mark motioned the sergeant over to take a look.

"Well…hell. I guess we had better come up with an alternative route through the city," he said venomously.

Mark nodded in agreement, looking around the area as he tried to come up with a plan. His eyes settled on a large manhole cover right across from where they were standing. Tugging on the sergeant's sleeve, Mark pointed out his discovery.

"Sewer, huh? I guess that's appropriate. Let's go check it out," said the sergeant.

The men trotted over to the cover and quietly lifted it out of the hole. Removing a flashlight from his pack, Mark cast its beam down into the inky blackness. Discovering nothing more unpleasant than a couple of rats, he motioned for one of the men to pick up the Jerrollite's body and bring it over. The soldier dragged it to the edge of the hole and laid it down. The sergeant searched the corpse and found a map of the surrounding area with Jerrollite facilities marked on it. Counting that as a stroke of great luck, Mark took the map and stowed it in his backpack. The sergeant removed the alien's weapons and placed them in his own pack. After the search was complete, Mark gave the body a shove with his foot, causing it to roll over into the hole. After a brief delay, it hit with a dull thud and splash. Looking into the young soldier's face, Mark saw the grim set of his jaw.

"Casualty of war. Don't worry about it."

"I know, sir; it's just that I've never seen a dead body before," he said, shaking with revulsion.

Nodding, Mark turned and signaled the squad to enter the sewer drain. They sprinted across the street and one by one dropped into the hole. The first man down moved the dead alien out of the way so the others would not have to deal with it. After all the other men were in, Mark lowered himself into the darkness, pulling the heavy cover after him. It slid into place unexpectedly, landing with a muffled thud on his finger.

Stifling a cry of pain, he jerked his finger free, and the lid clanged into place. Grimacing, Mark made his way down the ladder, gingerly feeling his way with his feet. Finally reaching the bottom, he stepped off the ladder and promptly sank ankle deep in sludge.

"Give us some light, Sergeant," Mark said, squelching his revulsion.

Mark heard a slight rustling sound and then a muffled snap as the tunnel filled with an eerie green glow from a bioluminescent tube the sergeant had activated and placed in a holder on his shoulder. Glancing up and down the sewer as far as the glow could encroach on the darkness, they could see nothing. Taking a quick compass reading, Mark decided on the most appropriate direction to proceed.

"Okay, men. Keep it quiet. Every other man activate a glow rod and follow me." Mark led the way quietly. He could hear the sloshing footsteps of the men as they followed. If they could stay in the sewage tunnel long enough to get past the Jerrollite camp, making their way out of the city would be that much easier. Mark could only hope that the dead Jerrollite guard would not be discovered until they had had long enough to get a decent distance away from the area.

CHAPTER 10

As the squad made its way along the tunnel, the smell became overpowering. Several men began to retch as they continued through the slime and sludge.

"Man, what a funky smell!" a voice said, echoing off the walls.

"You said it. This ain't exactly what I had in mind when I signed up," another voice said. Several low chuckles came from the group.

"Cut the chatter!" Mark said through clenched teeth. The noise immediately died down. After walking through the stench of the sewer for more than a mile, they could dimly make out another manhole cover up ahead that might provide a possible exit. Mark reckoned they were well past the alien encampment and all should be safe. Signaling for the squad to halt, Johann and Mark made their way to the ladder.

"I'll go up and take a look around," Mark said. Johann stepped aside, making an after you gesture.

Mark placed his hand on the damp metal ladder and hauled himself up out of the muck. Cautiously he crept up the ladder, choosing his footing with care until he reached the top. He placed his ear as close as possible to the air vents in the cover, listening intently for any sound that would betray the presence of enemy troops in the area. For several minutes Mark heard nothing except the occasional drip of condensation hitting the water below and reverberating off the walls. Satisfied that they were in no immediate danger, Mark braced himself against the heavy cover, lifting it just enough to see.

The surrounding streets were dark, the power long ago shut down. Damage to the buildings was heavy. All that was left of most of them were burned-out shells. Peering through the darkness, Mark could see nothing moving, not a single living thing in the entire area. There was no sound, only an oppressive stillness that suffocated the area.

Lifting the cover and placing it off to one side, Mark bent down and motioned for Johann to come up the ladder. He climbed quickly, bringing himself up to the same level.

"This looks like a good spot to get out," Mark said.

Johann grunted his agreement.

"I'll go first and scout the surrounding area, so when I give you the signal, come out fast and meet by that building over there," Mark said, pointing.

"Let's do it," said Johann.

Mark climbed out of the tunnel quickly and sprinted across the street. Looking around the area, he could still detect nothing in the dark stillness. With a small hand signal, Mark motioned for Johann to proceed.

"Douse your glow rods and follow me," Johann said. He leapt from the manhole, crouching low, and sprinted toward the place Mark had pointed out. The other soldiers came out of the tunnel like ants erupting from an anthill that had been disturbed. The last man out replaced the cover and joined the rest of the squad crouched in the shadows.

Johann fell to the rear as they began to make their way around the building. The lack of lighting made it extremely difficult to see, but flashlights or glow rods would alert the enemy. The building appeared to be some sort of warehouse, and Mark felt it would be a good place to stop and regroup. They approached a large opening in the wall that looked like some kind of vehicle access. Mark came around the corner quickly, crouched low, his weapon raised and ready to fire. Establishing that no danger was within, he gave an all clear signal. The sergeant came in first, followed closely by the squad. Johann was the last to enter. When everyone was safe inside, Mark rolled down an overhead door, closing off the opening to any outside view.

"Give me some light," Mark ordered. Several flashlights snapped on at the same time. Standing in the middle of his men, Mark looked around the room they were in and was staggered by what he saw.

The building was a munitions factory that had been damaged only slightly in the initial attack. The interior was cavernous and stacked floor to ceiling with portable ground-to-air missiles stored in shipping crates, ready for delivery to various sites around the world. Mark wondered at the arrogance of the Jerrollite forces to have left something like this unguarded.

Motioning for two men to join him, Mark slipped his knife out of his boot and began prying open one of the crates. As he was unable to get the cover to budge at first, the other men added their efforts, and the lid gave way fairly quickly. Inside were three brand-new missiles wrapped in grease paper, ready to go. Mark looked over to the sergeant and smiled.

"Are you thinking what I'm thinking, Sarge?" Mark asked.

"I think if we stuck these in just the right place, we sure would give those Jerrollites a really severe case of heartburn," he said, chuckling.

"Exactly. Send a man up to the roof to spot that camp we ran into on the way in."

"Yes, sir!" he said, turning and barking orders to one of his men. Mark examined the missiles again. This particular model was equipped with trail-suppressant exhaust ports, which would allow no flame or smoke to exit the rocket engine, making the missile's point of origin virtually untraceable by visual means. They were also equipped with terrain-following radar, so they could be fired below the level of enemy sensors.

Yes, indeed, Mark thought, these will do nicely.

The young soldier that the sergeant had sent to the roof came running back into the warehouse. Breathing heavily, he could hardly speak.

"Sir, the enemy camp is approximately one and a half miles to the south of our current position," he said.

Allowing himself a small smile, Mark quickly made the calculations in his head. The distance was well within range of this missile. He nodded toward the young soldier, who saluted and returned to the main group.

"Okay, Sarge, here's what I want," said Mark, pulling the sergeant close. "We need to locate a means of transport that is faster than travelling on foot. The only problem is that if we try to use anything other than a Jerrollite transport, of which we have none, we will be attacked immediately. So it seems to me that we need a diversion." The fierce glint in Mark's eye was impossible to miss. "Here is what we are going to do…"

The planning continued for several minutes, punctuated by occasional nods from the sergeant. When they were done, the sergeant sent two men out into the area to attempt to find a Jerrollite transport of some kind. The rest of the squad began to unpack forty of the missiles and set them up on launch racks on the roof of the building. Each missile was wired so it could be fired remotely. Other members of the squad scoured the plant, looking for any high-powered weapons they could take with them.

Watching over the entire operation, Mark looked around the colossal room, noting the thousands of missiles stacked to the ceiling. He motioned Johann to join him.

"You know, it would really be a shame to leave all these nice popguns just lying around for some Jerrollite to find and use against us."

A wide grin split Johann's face. "Hey, boy, leave it to me!" He grabbed one of the explosives men from the squad and pulled him off to one side.

"I want to be able to detonate it remotely, just like the missiles. Got it?" Mark yelled after the departing men.

Johann raised his hand in acknowledgment and continued off into the shadows.

The team that had been sent out to find a vehicle reentered the building. "What did you find?" asked Mark.

"On the roof of the building next to us, a cargo transport that looks like it was abandoned when the Jerrollites attacked is just sitting there, ready for us to use."

"Great—did you make sure it was operational?"

"Yes, sir, we did. Its internal battery was dead, but we were able to scavenge one from the burned-out hulk of another transport. We put it in and checked it out, and everything came up and online. It's completely fueled and ready to go. The access hatch is unlocked and ready to be loaded," the soldier said.

Mark flagged the sergeant down, and the soldier restated his findings. The gleam in Mark's eye indicated how pleased he was with this development. Use of the transport would allow the squad to reach the alternative recovery area and the scientists in a matter of minutes instead of days.

The teams rapidly finished wiring the building for demolition, wasting no time. Forty missiles had been mounted on the roof and were ready to be launched. Johann approached Mark and extended a small black box. Taking the device from his hand, Mark examined it carefully. It was simple, consisting of only two switches and a small antenna on top.

"You can trigger launch within a two-mile radius, so be careful with it. When you flip the first switch, the missiles will launch, and when you flip the second, this building is gonna go up like an incendiary grenade in a fireworks factory," said Johann.

"Great, this ought to do the trick." Pocketing the detonator, Mark turned to the sergeant and said, "Gather up all the men and get them over to the other building and loaded on the transport. We'll be right behind you."

"Yes, sir." After a moment of hesitation, he said, "Don't do anything stupid, sir."

"Have no fear. Now get going!" said Mark.

The squad moved off into the darkness toward the other building. Mark and Johann made a last check of all the connections on the explosives they had set up. Mark armed the rig by attaching a battery to the receiver tied to the transmitter in his hand. Johann and Mark then followed the squad across the street to the other building. The squad had already made their way to the roof, leaving Mark and Johann to find their own way. After a brief search of their surroundings, they found it.

The transport was there, gleaming like a silver falcon in the moonlight. The squad had already begun entering the ship through the passenger hatch. Mark gave the alien ship a thorough once-over to verify operation and check for any battle damage. Satisfied, he climbed up into the cockpit and sat in the pilot's seat. Johann climbed up after him, taking the copilot's seat. This particular ship wasn't much different than the transport they had flown in on, so familiarizing himself with its workings was a fairly easy task and quickly accomplished. Mark heard a noise behind him. He turned and saw the sergeant climbing into the navigator's seat behind Johann.

"Ready to go, boys?" Mark asked.

Both men looked at him with manic grins on their faces and simply said, "Go for it."

Mark switched on the startup sequencer and was relieved to hear the whine of the twin repulsor engines building up an operating charge. Everyone on the ship was tense. If the transport was spotted by Jerrollite ships they would check the security credentials of the transport. Since they had no way for the humans to respond properly, they would be sitting ducks. As the engines came up to full power, the hull of the ship resonated with the harmonics generated by each power plant. When the cockpit indicators all showed green, Mark lifted the transport from the roof, hovering only inches from the ground. He removed the black box from his pocket and fingered the detonator switch. He looked over at Johann and grinned.

"Here we go!" Mark said, slamming the first switch home.

At first, nothing happened. Looking down at the detonator, Mark actuated the switch again. Still, nothing happened. Damn cheap-ass government batteries, he thought.

"Shit! The missiles didn't fire!" Mark said as he hit the switch again.

Just as he was about to land the ship and go back to check on the wiring, a loud *whoosh* filled the air, accompanied by a blinding light as all forty missiles launched simultaneously.

Breathing a sigh of relief, Mark watched the night sky blossom into a fiery spectacle as all the missiles reached their destination within seconds, impacting targets all over the enemy camp. The transport shuddered violently as it was blasted with the shock wave. Mark and Johann watched as it became quickly evident that the destruction wrought by the missile attack was devastating. No enemy response would be coming from that direction.

Mark slammed the throttle to maximum, causing the ship to lurch forward over the edge of the building and swoop down to street level. A jubilant cry erupted from the men in the back of the ship. Feeling his spirits soar, Mark kept the ship in a low trajectory, following a zigzag path across the city to avoid detection. If they were spotted, no one would be able to tell in which direction they were truly headed.

"Your turn, amigo!" Mark grinned, tossing the detonator across to Johann.   Johann laughed and pressed the second switch, which was followed almost instantaneously by a deafening explosion. Mark looked over his shoulder to see a giant fireball rising from the munitions plant. The heat from the explosion scorched the already blackened walls of the surrounding buildings. Secondary explosions continued for several seconds until nothing of the plant was left standing. Looking in the opposite direction, Mark could see scores of Jerrollite bodies strewn about the streets around the camp. One of the missiles had hit an ammunition dump right in the heart of their camp. The resultant fireball and shock wave had succeeded in killing any living thing in a two-hundred-yard radius. The destruction of their camp was almost total, with only a single, heavily damaged ship remaining and a few injured personnel wandering around aimlessly.

Mark piloted the alien ship toward the mountain ranges in the distance. Johann checked the rear scanners for any enemy pursuit. A couple of alien ships approached from the front but did not challenge them. Because of the distractions caused by the exploding munitions building and the missile attack, the Jerrollites were too busy to challenge one of their own. The fates were with them, Mark realized, as he saw dozens of enemy ships swarming over the destroyed campsite and the munitions plant.

"Man, that worked better than I thought it would," said Johann.

"Any pursuit, sir?" asked the sergeant. Mark looked to Johann for an answer.

"None at all. They're so confused right now they don't have any idea what hit 'em," the Jamaican said.

"Good. Let's see if we can get the hell out of here without getting killed, shall we?" said Mark.

Running with normal lights in standard power mode, Mark piloted the ship in the same fashion he had seen many Jerrollite pilots do as they had attacked human cities, blending in to the chaos surrounding the city because of their attack. They stood a good chance of making it to the recovery area without any Jerrollite complications.

CHAPTER 11

As the transport approached the city limits, all that could be seen of the destruction that had been wrought was a dull, flickering, orange glow reflecting off the bottom of the overhanging clouds. Looking forward, Mark noted they were about to leave the city and enter the darkness that lay beyond.

"Enter the coordinates of the Alternate Assembly Area into the flight computer, Sergeant," he said.

The sergeant pulled his map out of his pocket, unfolding it and spreading it out in front of him. After looking at it for a few seconds, he leaned forward and began entering the coordinates into the alien computer, occasionally glancing at the map to confirm his input. He paused, hoping that he was doing it correctly. It was an alien system, after all. He leaned back and looked over at Mark.

"You know, sir, the Jerrollites will probably figure out what just happened and then come after us."

True enough, thought Mark. "We'll be long gone before anything like that happens," he said aloud, with more confidence than he actually felt.

"Hmm. Sure," grunted the sergeant as he shrugged his shoulders and returned to the task of entering the coordinates into the system. Snapping the keypad cover back into place, he sighed heavily and leaned back in his seat. He folded the map neatly and placed it into the map pocket on his uniform. Mark found what he thought was the automatic flight control in the instrument cluster and activated it. The computer would now fly the ship automatically to the coordinates entered by the sergeant, keeping low to the ground and out of enemy sights.

As the ship passed the perimeter of the city, it plunged into an inky blackness, punctuated only by the occasional visible star. Looking up at the night sky, Mark thought how foreign the world had become in just a few short weeks since the war had begun. He no longer felt as if he was on Earth at all, but instead on some alien planet far, far from home.

A gentle beeping sound from the console stirred Mark from his thoughts, advising that the ship was rapidly closing on its final destination. Mark dimmed the lights in the cockpit so they could see out the windows. On the horizon the massive black outline of a mountain could only be distinguished as a deeper shade of black than its surroundings. The ship automatically began braking maneuvers, easing into a slow descent toward the valley floor. Mark toggled the intercom.

"Brace for landing, men—T minus thirty seconds."

He snapped off the intercom as the engines fought to slow down the mass of the transport. The ship stopped its descent only ten feet above the surface, hovering momentarily as its computers calculated the thrust needed for a soft landing. Slowly settling down to the surface, the transport's engines kicked up a large cloud of dust and debris as its landing skids made contact with the ground. Mark quickly ran through his shutdown procedures, bringing the engines to a slow idle.

"Why are we stopping?" the sergeant asked.

"We need to make contact with the ARA to let them know we're coming. That cave is equipped with some mighty fearsome defense weaponry, and I have no desire to be on the business end of it," Mark said.

"Makes sense to me," the sergeant said.

Mark reached across the sergeant to power up the radio, tuning it to a special frequency set aside for emergency use by the military in crisis situations.

"If the ARA is following procedure, they should be monitoring this frequency for messages. Hand me my pack over there," Mark asked, motioning toward his gear stowed in the corner.

The sergeant handed the pack to Mark, who opened it and removed a small security container. He entered the access code, causing the lock to pop open. Inside were several documents labeled *Top Secret*. He rifled through the pages until he found the one he was looking for and removed it from the container. It listed the secret codes required to pass messages over an unsecured channel. Mark took a moment to compose a brief message that would identify him to the base and then began to transmit the information. After several minutes of sending, a brief burst of static, followed by a curt "acknowledged," issued from the radio's speaker. Satisfied, Mark replaced the materials in his pack and stowed it again.

"What did you tell them?" the sergeant asked.

"I told them we would arrive in three minutes and to have everyone ready to evacuate when we got there."

The sergeant nodded as the engines powered up once again, the whine increasing in pitch until it was just out of audible range. The flight computer caused a minor increase in output power, lifting the transport into a low hover. Mark nudged the throttle forward, and the transport shuddered slightly as they once again got under way. Mark scanned the readouts in an attempt to discover whether they had been followed. He was relieved to see that so far no pursuit had come from the city. Mark killed all exterior illumination on the ship and proceeded in total darkness.

Rocketing through the black night, the transport approached the mountain very quickly. When Mark felt they were close enough, he once again settled the ship to the ground and placed its systems on standby. Unbuckling his harness, he motioned for the sergeant to do the same. Johann shut down his console and followed the other men out of the cockpit.

They exited the cockpit on the underside of the transport and stood together, looking up at the dark, silhouetted shape of the mountain before them. Far up on the hillside, Johann saw a brief flash of light, indicating where they were supposed to go.

"Look, up there!" Johann said, pointing out the signal.

"Okay, that's our signal. Let's get the men unloaded. Sergeant, prepare a plan for getting to that point as quickly as possible," Mark said.

"Yes, sir," he replied, already trotting toward the back of the ship where their equipment was stored.

Mark activated the access ladder leading to the crew compartment. He climbed in, followed immediately by Johann. He was pleased to see the men were already gathering up their gear, preparing for the trek up the hillside.

"All right, gents, let's go. Follow Johann," Mark said.

"Okay, all you pretty boys, it's time to earn your pay! Get your gear and assemble outside in one minute! MOVE IT!" Johann bellowed. The cabin erupted into a flurry of activity as each man grabbed his pack and scrambled for the hatch. Johann refused to let up.

"MOVE IT! MOVE IT, MOVE IT, MOVE IT!" he yelled at each man as he went down the access ladder. The cabin rapidly emptied out, the bustle of activity replaced by an eerie silence.

"Man, Jo, try not to kill 'em before we even see combat," said Mark.

"No problem, mon. It only takes their mind off of how scared they are," Johann said.

Questionable as his tactics were, Johann had a point. Mark could ill afford to have a man go nuts on him at the wrong moment. He just smiled and clapped Johann on the back.

"Let's do it," he said.

Climbing back down the ladder, Johann went to the front of the assembled men, going over their plans, making sure they were all ready. The sergeant joined him. While the squad was occupied, Mark decided to take the opportunity to prepare a little surprise for their Jerrollite hosts. He climbed back up into the cockpit, knelt in front of the flight computer keyboard, and proceeded to program in a course that would fly the transport back to the city and crash-land it in the middle of the Jerrollite camp. That would take care of the last remnants of the camp. Mark had a self-satisfied smile on his lips as he snapped the cover back on to the keyboard. Not only would sending the ship back to the city throw the Jerrollites off their trail, but crashing it into their camp would provide another great diversion.

Mark climbed down the cockpit ladder quickly and secured the hatch. He walked to where the sergeant and Johann were standing.

"You better tell everyone to get away from the ship," he said matter-of-factly.

"What's the hurry?" the sergeant asked.

"The ship is going back to the city," Mark said.

"WHAT!"

"You heard me. I don't want any Jerrollite patrol ships to spot this thing out here in the middle of nowhere. It sticks out like a sore thumb. Besides, Reeves will be picking us up in our own transport when I call him. Got it?" said Mark.

"Yes, sir, Colonel," Johann replied. The corners of his mouth twitched slightly, wanting to form a smile. "Present for the Jerrollites, huh?" he whispered under his breath. Mark met his level stare head on.

"You got it, my friend," he said, a roguish glint in his eye. "Should keep 'em busy for a while, don't you think?" Johann broke into a hearty belly laugh, thinking of the Jerrollites scrambling for cover when they realized what was about to happen.

"That it should, Mark, that it should."

As the automatic takeoff sequence started, the faint whine of the engines built in pitch as the now-unmanned ship began to rise on a cloud of dust. Executing a sharp turnaround, the transport flew off into the night in the direction they had come, the noise of the engines fading into the distance. That Jerrollite camp was in for a nasty surprise in just a little over twenty-five minutes.

With Johann taking the lead, the squad began to make their way up the hillside. Although it was fairly steep, they were able to make good time, reaching the perimeter of the ARA in a little over an hour. Johann motioned for the squad to halt while Mark stepped forward to identify them to the security system. Finding the entrance to the cave was proving to be no easy task; it was extremely dark, and the entrance was very well camouflaged. To the naked eye, it appeared to be a solid stone wall. Feeling his way gingerly, Mark finally located the security panel. Wiping the sweat from his eyes, he keyed in one of the secret access codes he had been given earlier by General Matheson.

The code was accepted, and the main entrance to the cave slid aside with a silent *whoosh* as air rushed in to fill the void left by the door. Signaling the men to join him, Mark entered the cave. Light was almost nonexistent, allowing them to see only vague shapes in the darkness. As the last man crossed the threshold of the door, it rumbled shut automatically, sealing the entrance to the cave and leaving them in total darkness.

The hackles on the back of Mark's neck began to rise as he realized how vulnerable they were in the dark. He could not even tell where Johann or the sergeant were standing. He called out, "Is anyone here?"

He was answered only by the sound of his own voice echoing off the walls. He was reaching toward his pack to pull out a glow rod when the chamber filled with an intense white light, momentarily blinding everyone. Mark's eyes began to tear as he rubbed them to regain a clear field of vision. He could hear weapons being cocked and readied all around him. A single man stepped away from the wall toward their position.

Mark crouched low, his rifle leveled at the approaching man. The man cringed as he realized he was on the business end of several very nasty weapons.

"Wh-who are you?" the man asked timidly.

Mark lowered his weapon, motioning his men to do the same. "Colonel Mark Hunter, United Military Forces. This is my team," he said, indicating the men standing behind him. "And just who might you be?"

"My name is Bill Johnson. I was a research scientist at the Pentagon."

Mark extended his hand. Bill shook it firmly. "Good to meet you. We're here to take you and the rest of your people back to the USS *Hercules*." Looking around the room, Mark asked, "By the way, where is everybody else?"

"I would appear to be the only person who made it. The Pentagon was under attack when I left. The only reason I got out was because of a hidden entrance the Jerrollites had not spotted. As it was, I barely escaped with my life."

"I see," Mark said. This did not bode well for their mission. They could not spare the time to wait for anyone else who might or might not show up. "Are you ready to go?"

"Yeah. I've got nothing left here. My family was killed in the first wave of the attack. All I really care about now is a chance to even the score." As timid as he appeared to be, Mark saw that his eyes burned with the same fierce determination he had seen in his men's faces.

"We'll leave tomorrow night, at dusk."

Bill nodded. "I'll be ready. Your men can follow me. I can show you where the sleeping quarters are," he said. He turned on his heel and began walking away.

Mark motioned for the sergeant and Johann to follow and began walking in the direction Bill had gone.

CHAPTER 12

Mark rubbed the knotted muscles in his neck as they made their way down the passageway toward the sleeping quarters. It seemed like forever since he had been able to simply relax under a hot shower. He looked around at his men and could see the same fatigue on their faces; giving them time to rest while they had the chance was a good idea. He personally was looking forward to dropping like a stone into a bed. Mark was startled by a slap on the back and a voice in his ear. He turned to see Johann standing next to him.

"How you doin', ol' boy?" he asked in quiet tones.

Mark grinned. "Fine, I guess. At least for an old dog who's been out of commission for a while." Johann chuckled under his breath, clapping Mark on the back once again as he made his way to the front of the squad. Mark was amazed at Johann's stamina. He never seemed to show any signs of weakness. He decided after watching him for a few minutes that Johann could simply hide it better than most men.

Their brief chance to rest suddenly ended. The ground bucked violently beneath Mark's feet as a colossal explosion ripped through the cave. The massive doors covering the entrance collapsed inward like a waterfall of stone and mortar. A geyser of flame shot through the main entrance, coming toward the squad like a blazing demon released from the pits of hell. Bodies scattered and fell as the fireball passed, scorching everything in its path. Mark could hear several muffled gasps as his men tried to breathe the oxygen that had just been consumed by the jet of flame. As Mark was sure his own burning lungs were going to explode, a fresh wash of outside air passed over him. Automatic systems had kicked in and begun pumping in large amounts of air from external vents.

Whoomp! Mark gasped as the ground once again leapt up to meet him. He could hear Johann shouting at the men, trying to get them to scatter so they would be less vulnerable. Mark heard several muffled thumps coming from outside the cave as energy beams hit the side of the mountain, vaporizing huge chunks of earth. He got into a crouching position, leaning on the wall for support. As he was gathering his gear, he looked up, and amid the swirling smoke he caught a clear glimpse of the attackers. Jerrollites!

The alien force had been able to track the transport all along and had only been waiting for it to arrive at its destination before attacking. Mark cursed under his breath as he realized that their entire mission was in jeopardy because of his carelessness. Scooping up his pack, Mark signaled Johann to follow him with the men and ran in a low crouch toward the gaping hole in the far wall of the cave. From behind a large piece of fallen rubble, Mark peered at the pandemonium going on outside. On the ground below, almost in the same spot where they had landed, a Jerrollite troop transport was disgorging its contents onto the valley floor. Jerrollite soldiers were swarming out of the ship, sprinting toward the cave entrance. Mark quickly ducked back inside. While his heart pounded in his chest, his mind played out possible scenarios of defense. Searching for and quickly finding the sergeant, Mark picked his way through the debris to get to him. Both men stayed low behind a large piece of fallen machinery.

"Sergeant! Gather the men around the rear of the cave and wait for my signal. I'm going to call Reeves to come and get us out!" Mark yelled over the uproar. Several Jerrollite energy beams lanced through the smoke, vaporizing everything in their path.

Mark ducked his head as a Jerrollite soldier appeared in the doorway, rapidly firing its weapon in random directions. A beam missed Mark's head by inches, singeing the hairs on the side of his skull.

"Watch out!" the sergeant said as he knocked Mark off his feet, shoving him down into an undignified heap.

His hand covering the side of his head, Mark turned to the sergeant. "Damn! That was close. Thanks." The sergeant's only answer was in his actions. He rolled to his right, leveled his rifle at the alien soldier, and fired a sustained burst. The slugs struck the soldier in its midsection, almost cutting it in half. Mark felt his stomach turn as the Jerrollite wilted into a quivering pile of flesh, a large pool of blue blood spreading out from what was left of the body.

"Well, well, I guess they do bleed after all," the sergeant said sarcastically. He trotted up to the opening in the cave wall, took a position behind several large boulders, and began rifling off shots into the smoke and haze. The occasional scream from below bore witness that his aim was true. Mark removed his communicator from his pack and keyed in the access code that would contact Reeves back at the ship. He could only hope that Reeves would remember the code to activate the ship. At first the sole response from the radio was a loud squawk of static, but finally Reeves's voice came through, loud and clear.

"Colonel Hunter, is that you?" the tinny speaker said. Mark recognized Reeves and was relieved that he was still okay.

"Yeah, it's me. Are you ready to fly?" Mark asked.

"Yes, sir. Just tell me where and when!"

"We're under attack by Jerrollite forces. No enemy air cover has been detected, but it's dark, so make sure you're careful. We're located at the ARA, in grid seven at coordinates a-one slash g-nine. We need your firepower to get us out. We're pinned down but can hold till you get here."

"Message received, sir. I'll be there as quickly as I can."

"Godspeed, Reeves. Out." Mark closed the communicator and placed it in his pack. He drew his sidearm and took up a position next to the sergeant, who had already been very successful, as indicated by the many bodies lying facedown in the dirt. Mark motioned for the rest of the squad to take up positions along the wall. If they were to last until Reeves arrived, they would have to make every shot count.

Across the room, Mark saw Bill Johnson crouched down behind several large pieces of equipment. He motioned for three men to converge on Bill's position and defend him. All they needed now was to lose the only surviving weapons scientist they had to make this entire trip a colossal waste of time.

Shouting at the senior soldier of the three guarding Johnson, Mark made sure that he truly understood the importance of his task. "You make sure that man gets out of here unharmed! Understand?" A curt nod relieved Mark of that worry momentarily. As he turned to rejoin the battle, Mark heard a scream from the other side of the cave, directly across from where he was crouched. Through the haze Mark saw a young man, not more than twenty, staring down at a gaping hole in his chest, a look of disbelief on his face. An energy beam had struck him in the chest, leaving a hole the size of a man's fist all the way through his body. Where his heart once had been, now there was only empty space. As Mark and several other soldiers watched, the young man attempted to say something and then collapsed into a heap on the floor. Mark glanced around into the faces of his men. The looks in their eyes hardened as they returned fire even more fiercely than before.

The battle would not last long at the rate they were consuming their supplies. The squad was running low on ammunition, and it was getting harder and harder to see targets below. Firing continued for several minutes as both sides succeeded in decimating the forces on the other side. Mark was sickened at the sight of several of his best soldiers sprawled in heaps on the floor of the cave, their lifeless eyes staring out at nothing. He pulled out his communicator and again contacted Reeves.

"Reeves! This is Colonel Hunter—where the hell are you?"

"Approaching your position now, sir; ETA is fifteen seconds!"

Mark looked up beyond the confusion of battle and could just make out the running lights on the transport. The sight immediately lifted his spirits. He signaled Johann and the sergeant, pointing. Both men understood immediately. Johann ordered the squad to drop back from the cave entrance so they would not be hit by any stray fire from the transport. Mark's communicator burst into life as Reeves announced his arrival.

"Yee-HAH! The cavalry is here!" Reeves shouted. Mark did not want to distract him, so he made no reply, instead only waiting and watching.

Mark could just hear the high-pitched whine of repulsor engines running at full throttle. The whine continued to grow in intensity until it was almost deafening, eliciting confused looks skyward from the Jerrollite ground forces. Mark concluded that the Jerrollite commander had figured out what was about to happen, because it was standing up, frantically waving its arms to get the soldiers loaded onto their transport before all hell broke loose. Mark smiled grimly to himself, realizing that the commander was only succeeding in making a much more attractive target. If Reeves followed procedure, the first thing he would hit would be the alien ship. Almost as if on cue, Reeves and the transport burst into view, coming out of a low-lying cloud with the nose of his ship pointed straight down, the front cannon spitting jets of flaming death toward the enemy ship.

The Jerrollites were caught completely by surprise. The initial volley ripped through the outer skin of their ship like it was paper before it finally exploded, sending dead Jerrollites spinning through the air to land in broken piles all over the battleground. As the fireball rose into the air, chased by an oily black tail, a shout of victory tore itself from the lips of the men under Mark's command. Every dead alien body added fuel to the fire that was burning in the hearts of his men. Reeves brought the transport around in a wide arc, raking the enemy camp multiple times with thirty-millimeter cannon fire. The depleted uranium slugs destroyed everything in their path, passing through metal, flesh, and stone with little or no delay. Several enemy soldiers attempted to bring their weapons to bear on the transport but dropped them and collapsed before they could fire a single shot. Mark looked down the line and saw Johann and the sergeant, rifles at their shoulders, picking off single Jerrollite soldiers as they attempted to fire on the transport. He returned his attention to the scene playing out on the ground below. After the transport made two more passes, the area was transformed into a scene of carnage and death accompanied only by the eerie whine of the transport's engines.

"All clear, sir!" Reeves said over the radio.

As Reeves brought the transport in for a landing, Mark stood up with a triumphant yell and called to the other men. They answered his yell with an even louder one of their own. Holding their weapons high over their heads, they ran out of the cave toward Reeves, who was just coming out of the cockpit access hatch. Grabbing him and hoisting him onto their shoulders, they began to whoop and yell, rejoicing in their victory.

"Great job, mister!" Mark said from his perch, waving his hand in Reeves's direction.

"Thank you, sir! My pleasure!" Reeves said enthusiastically.

As he turned around, Mark saw Bill Johnson trying to bundle something into a bag and walked over to help him load his gear. "Let's go home, Bill," said Mark. Bill looked at him somberly for a moment and then nodded rapidly.

"I'm ready," he said, gathering his equipment. Both men walked outside and joined the squad standing around the transport. Ordering the sergeant to get the men loaded, Mark took his place in the cockpit, showing Bill to the jump seat located in the rear.

"All hands, prepare for liftoff," Mark said over the intercom.

A jubilant cry went up from the rear of the ship. Mark smiled to himself as he started the launch sequence. The whine of the engines built up rapidly as the ship pushed itself skyward, breaking free of the gravitational bonds that tried to hold it down. Turning the nose of the craft skyward, Mark pushed the throttle forward to maximum, reveling in the feel of the thrust against his body as they blasted their way toward space—and home.

CHAPTER 13

As the transport broke free from Earth's atmosphere, Mark entered a course into the ship's computer that would take them to a prearranged rendezvous point with the *Hercules*. Engaging the autopilot, he unbuckled his harness and made his way to the rear cabin. Several of the men were already resting, their eyes closed and their arms cradling their rifles like mothers holding children.

Making his way quietly through the ship, Mark checked on each man, offering comfort and thanks for their efforts. When he got to the back of the cabin, his foot bumped against something solid on the floor. His eyes came to rest on a dull-green body bag, a grim reminder of what they were fighting for and how much they were willing to give up to win.

Mark composed himself and made his way back into the cockpit. Squeezing into the cramped pilot's seat, he secured his safety harness and sat back, reflecting on the mission.

"I'm sorry you lost some of your men, Colonel," Bill Johnson said from the rear of the cockpit. Turning his head slightly, Mark could see a look of genuine concern on Bill's face.

"There's a price that must be paid for freedom. They gave their lives so you would have a chance to help us. Don't mourn their loss—just make sure their sacrifice wasn't in vain."

"I will, Colonel. I will," he said as he clamped his hand on Mark's shoulder. The resolve in his eyes was evident. "Thanks for coming to get me." The moment was interrupted by a flashing light on the panel.

"What's that?" Bill asked.

"Automatic guidance system. We're coming up on the *Hercules*." Turning his attention to the controls, Mark said, "Make sure you're strapped in good. This is going to be a rough landing." Bill scrambled to get himself situated in his seat, going over his harness once again to make sure everything was buckled properly.

Glancing over his panel, Mark began to make the necessary preparations for landing the transport on the flight deck of the *Hercules*. Because of the clandestine nature of their mission, along with the need for speed, the transport was going to attempt a special high-speed landing procedure. To remain undetected, the *Hercules* could not reduce speed even for a fraction of a second. Mark had never had to actually perform a high-speed landing except in flight simulators but felt reasonably confident. The procedure would maintain the highest degree of protection both for the ship and the transport. The maneuver consisted of accelerating the transport to twice the cruising speed of the *Hercules* and then, with the precise timing only a computer could achieve, the shields would be lowered and the transport allowed to enter the landing bay. Shields would be raised immediately, and automatic systems in the bay would prevent the transport from crashing into the far wall.

Toggling the radio to a secure channel, Mark called in his recognition code for landing permission. The terse reply came quickly. "Permission granted. Speed is point three seven six." The *Hercules* was giving them as much leeway as possible—that fraction of light speed was as slow as the ship could cruise and still maintain invisibility to enemy sensors. Programming the flight computer for twice that speed, Mark made the final preparation for landing by initiating an inertial damper field around the transport. Without the field, the contents of the transport would be smeared on the inside walls like grape jelly on toast. Flipping the intercom switch, Mark made a brief announcement.

"All right, gentlemen, prepare for high-speed landing." Several groans came from the rear cabin.

Placing his hand on the activate switch, Mark took a deep breath and engaged the computer. The star field blurred to the edges of vision as the transport leapt forward to its destination. A distant point of light appeared to be hurtling toward the transport at breakneck speed. The blur of light rapidly resolved into the landing bay. Mark closed his eyes and braced himself.

As the transport blazed toward the *Hercules*, the ship's computers began working in tandem with the transport's onboard system to calculate speed and distance millions of times per second. Just before the transport impacted the *Hercules*'s shields, the computer lowered them for the fraction of a second necessary for the transport to gain entrance. As the transport streaked into the bay, the computer engaged a magnetic grappling field to seize the ship as it passed. Everyone inside was thrown violently forward against their safety harnesses. Even with the inertial damper field field in place, the rapid deceleration produced a crushing force that made it impossible to breathe. Mark's vision faded, dark blotches beginning to dance across his field of view. A horrendous ripping noise filled the cabin as sparks erupted from the console, filling the cabin with smoke. The pressure on Mark's body increased to the point where he was sure he was going to burst a vital blood vessel somewhere or become violently ill.

As abruptly as it started, the pressure stopped. Only the quiet licking of flames on the console reminded Mark that he was still alive. Slowly opening his eyes, he winced at the throbbing pain in his head from the massive influx of blood. He looked around the cabin and realized they had made it! Grabbing a fire extinguisher from the side of his seat, Mark pulled its pin and doused the console. He released his harness and activated the emergency ventilation system to remove the smoke from the transport's atmosphere. Coughing hoarsely, Bill Johnson sat back in his seat and moaned in pain.

"Man, you weren't kidding when you said get ready, were you?" he said, shaking his head and rubbing his eyes, attempting to orient himself.

"As they say, 'Any landing you can walk away from is a good one,'" Mark said. Bill laughed gingerly, still holding his head as he unbuckled his harness and picked up his gear. Mark opened the cockpit hatch and descended the ladder to the deck below. General Matheson was already coming toward the transport, the gleam in his eyes giving away his feelings. As he approached, Mark came to full attention.

"Colonel Hunter reporting in, sir," he said, saluting smartly and snapping back to attention. Matheson eyed him for a moment and then clapped him on the back so hard Mark almost lost his balance.

"At ease, boy, at ease!" Matheson laughed heartily. "Thank God you boys made it back. We've been dodging

Jerrollite patrols ever since you left. It's a bloody miracle we haven't been discovered yet!" he said, pausing to catch his breath. "Were you able to recover any of the weapons or scientists?" he asked, apprehension in his eyes.

Unable to keep the disappointment from his voice, Mark said, "When we reached the ARA, only one person had been able to make it in safely." The general's spirits quickly came crashing down.

"Damn. Who was it?" he asked.

"Bill Johnson, sir. He was working on some sort of black hole generator that the Pentagon thought could be used as a weapon."

"I see," he said, mulling over the situation as he chewed his cigar.

Bill had climbed down from the cockpit and walked up to where both men were standing. He introduced himself to the general, and soon they began discussing in earnest the facilities that would be needed to complete the research and development of the generator. As Bill educated the general on the potential uses of his singularity generator, Matheson grew more and more intrigued.

Mark excused himself from their discussion and made his way over to the sergeant, who was supervising the disembarkation of his troops. Glancing up at the ship, Mark examined the abuse that the transport had taken. The exterior hull was a mess. It was stretched out of shape in several places where the magnetic grappling hooks had locked on to it. Black scorch marks ran up and down the entire length of the ship where Reeves had been raked by enemy ground fire.

"Looks pretty bad, doesn't it?" asked Mark.

"Yes, sir, but at least it's in one piece," the sergeant said.

"True enough. Debrief the men, and then give them twenty-four hours of R & R. Also, take a day off yourself. You all deserve it," Mark said, smiling.

"My pleasure, sir!" Grinning, he saluted Mark and returned even more vigorously to his task of getting the transport unloaded. Mark watched as several body bags were stacked on carts to be taken down to the ship's morgue for processing. His heart was heavy as he thought of the sacrifice that these men had made. Johann's voice didn't even startle him.

"You did a good job, Mark." Mark turned and saw the compassion in his eyes.

"I've never had anybody die under my command before. It really gets you, right here," he said, gesturing toward his heart.

"You won't ever get used to it. When you do, that's a pretty good indicator that you've been at it too long."

"Yeah, I suppose you're right," Mark said with more conviction than he felt. Johann lingered a moment longer and then went off to help the sergeant get things in order.

Mark could hear them bellowing good-naturedly at the men all the way to his cabin. Opening his door, he threw his gear into his locker and collapsed onto the bed. All the tension and stress of the last few days finally caught up with him. His body was telling him to shut down, to withdraw into himself, and get some much-needed rest. After fighting the impulse for several seconds, Mark finally surrendered, drifting off into a deep and dreamless sleep.

CHAPTER 14

Bill had been working continuously since his arrival on the *Hercules*. His head ached, and his back hurt from stooping over his experiments for so long. He had never really intended his invention to be used as a weapon, so he had not incorporated any type of targeting or fire control into his original design. He had been laboring to design a housing that could not only withstand the tremendous energy that would be generated when the weapon was fired but also be capable of transport by a small TAC-WING fighter.

The task was a daunting one. He had already come up with several radical new devices that were required to make the black hole generator a reality instead of merely a theory. Each new device had required an entire development and testing process of its own. All of this took time, which they were quickly running out of. The general had assigned a team of engineers and technicians to assist him in any way they could, but because he was the only person who could understand the theory behind the generator, he had to personally oversee every single aspect of its development.

All the pressure was rapidly becoming more than any normal man could handle. Bill pushed himself away from the bench that held the latest incarnation of the generator and rubbed his eyes. He was tired and wanted to take time off to sleep for a month. Walking over to a dispenser, he poured himself a large, steaming cup of the synthetic garbage that passed itself off as genuine coffee. At least it had the same kick as a good cup of Colombian like his wife used to make.

Sudden and unexpected thoughts of his wife and daughter made his heart sick as his mind replayed for the millionth time their violent and fiery deaths. Again the rage built inside him as he screamed silently at the injustice that had been done. He was trembling with rage and mourning as tears began to flow from his tightly closed eyes.

"Bill, are you okay?" a gentle voice said. He turned and saw Mark Hunter standing behind him with a genuine expression of concern on his face. Wiping the tears from his eyes and sniffing, he smiled at Mark and accepted the offered handkerchief.

"I'll be fine. I was just thinking of my family," he said.

"All of us feel the same way. You sure look like you could use some rest. When was the last time you slept?" Mark asked.

"I don't remember. I try to catch a few winks here and there while we're working. I have a cot in the back," he said, indicating a storeroom at the back of the lab with a wave of his hand. "I'll be okay, Mark. Really."

"Okay. If you need anything, just let me know."

"I will. Thanks," Bill said.

Mark left the lab. Bill returned to his work at the bench and began tinkering with the device that was mounted in a brace. His hand slipped, and he dropped the tool he was holding. His thoughts again turned to his family and their lives together. Despair began to grow in his mind as he thought of facing life without them. On the verge of giving up and succumbing to the desire to retreat from the world of the living, he looked up at a sound in front of him. An older technician had entered the lab and was checking several experiments running on the far side of the room. The sight of the woman reminded him of his neighbor back on Earth, the old woman who had survived the attack and snapped Bill to his senses in the aftermath of the destruction.

What was it she had said? Bill struggled to remember through the haze of time. Suddenly her words came ringing through the cloud that surrounded his brain. "The only way to honor them is to survive." Bill pondered the wisdom of that statement. He had survived, all right. He had been through a living hell ever since the first attack, but he had come through unscathed. Now he had a chance to honor not only his family but the millions of others who had been slaughtered during the war. By God, he decided, he would survive. The old woman's words once again gave him strength to carry on. Silently he whispered a prayer for her safety as he bent to his work with renewed fervor.

Several days later, a working prototype lay on the bench. Although it could not be tested safely inside the ship, Bill was confident that it would work. He had been over the circuits and reworked the algorithms at least a hundred times. He had pored over the charts with his assistants, looking for any flaw in the design, any defect that might prove dangerous when the weapon was tested. Finally satisfied that everything had been thoroughly checked, the team had begun assembly on the prototype that lay before him. Every circuit had been tested and every component verified individually. If everything went according to his design, this device would make it possible to generate a black hole of any size at any coordinate position relative to the generator. Because black holes were extremely dangerous, the generator could not be tested anywhere close to an inhabited system.

Gathering up his notes and a small model of the prototype, he left the lab and made his way to the briefing room where General Matheson, Colonel Hunter, and all the other military commanders were waiting for him. He entered the room and was met by a chorus of greetings from those assembled. They all knew the deadlines he had been working under and did not want to pressure him, even though they were anxious to hear the results of all the work that had been proceeding in the lab. The *Hercules* had been cruising just outside the Sol system during development of the generator, and most of the commanders were getting restless sitting around doing nothing.

Bill fumbled with his notes as he prepared to present his findings to the group. Organizing his thoughts, he began.

"As you all know, several weeks ago we began attempting to apply a theory I had developed to the construction of a working weapon that could be used against the Jerrollites. After many long, hard hours, I am pleased to report that we now have a working prototype, ready to be tested." Several of the men around the table smiled at the prospect of a return to action. "Because you have not really had the opportunity to understand our work, I'll give you a chance now to ask any questions you may have concerning the generator."

Several of the commanders began speaking at once, creating pandemonium in the room. General Matheson stood to his full and impressive height and rapped on the table for attention. One by one the other officers turned in his direction. When he had the full attention of the room, he said, "One question at a time, gentlemen." They all nodded their agreement, so the general returned control of the meeting to Bill. The nearest man at the table asked the first question.

"Exactly what will this generator do?"

"The purpose of the generator is to create a singularity, or black hole, in any location we desire," Bill said.

"What's a black hole?" said an anonymous voice from the back. Several subdued chuckles came from around the room.

"Well, stated simply, a black hole is an object with such an intense gravitational pull that not even light can escape its surface. It's not really a true hole in the sense you might be thinking of, but if you were to see a black hole up close, that is what it would appear to be."

"How can that be put to use as a weapon?" another officer asked.

"By being able to precisely control the location and appearance of a black hole, we can conceivably destroy any physical object in the universe. For instance, to understand the incredible power we're talking about, suppose that we materialized a black hole the size of a pinhead in the middle of an enemy ship. To us, the ship would seem to disappear instantaneously. In fact what really would happen is that the entire ship and its contents would be violently attracted to the surface of the black hole and crushed. Theoretically this could even be done to an entire planet," Bill said as several astonished gasps came from around the room.

"Drawbacks?" General Matheson asked.

"Well, right now this weapon is still in an experimental stage. We don't have enough material on board to construct another prototype, so we are limited to only one generator. Also, if we attempt to generate a black hole larger than a pinhead, stability problems may result, and we could lose control of the hole. If that happens, the results will be catastrophic and definitely not something we want to happen."

Matheson's eyebrows went up. "Catastrophic?"

"Yes, sir. If we lose control of the process, the hole could continue to expand until it achieves enough mass to start a fusion process. In effect it will become an unstable star. Most likely it will go supernova and destroy everything around it."

General Matheson stared at him for several seconds before responding. "Hmm. Sounds like we had better be careful."

"Yes, sir. Right now we need to come up with a way to test the generator without alerting the Jerrollites," Bill said.

"What would you suggest?" asked the general.

"I would like to see it used on a small body, such as an asteroid, as an initial test," Bill said.

The general seemed lost in thought for a moment, and then he continued. "Major Smith, plot a course for the nearest charted asteroid outside of the Sol system. Make sure that it is at least ten parsecs from the nearest known Jerrollite installation. Bill, get your generator ready for testing. Mount it in the front cargo bay and rig it so it can be controlled remotely from the bridge. All right, men, you have your assignments. Testing will commence within two hours after we arrive at the asteroid. Good luck." With that statement, the general turned and left the room.

Bill gathered up his materials and followed the rest of the officers out, readying himself for the monumental task at hand.

CHAPTER 15

Bill returned to the development lab to gather the things he would need to install the generator in the cargo bay. The general had selected the bay because it faced forward and was located on the front of the main command module. It would provide an excellent platform from which to run the generator.

He entered the lab and motioned for his assistants to gather around. "All right, everybody. Our objective is to get the generator installed in such a way that it can be controlled from the bridge. Everything needs to be set up so the generator becomes an integral part of the weapons systems of this ship. Put on your best engineering hats, and let's get this thing installed!"

The lab exploded into a frenzy of activity. Bill's assistants collected the tools and materials necessary to mount the generator and wire it into the ship's weapons systems. A virtual army of technicians made their way toward the front cargo bay with Bill in the lead. The strange entourage was the focus of many curious stares in the ship's narrow corridors. When they arrived at the cargo bay, the team began to install the equipment to accomplish the task at hand.

Not only did the generator have to be installed, but the test would have to be monitored closely, which necessitated the installation of several sophisticated pieces of monitoring equipment. Bill examined the bay to decide on the best way to mount the generator. This cargo area was one of the smallest, used mostly for storing nonperishable food. Currently it was almost empty, which was fortunate because the support and test equipment for the generator would fill most of it. There was a single large opening in the far wall that let equipment be loaded in and out. The most logical way to mount the generator was to suspend it from a brace that would center it on the opening in the far wall. Techs began to fabricate the brace with the help of the ship's maintenance engineers. Welding torches crackled and popped as the framework went up. The ship's ventilators and air-recycling system could barely keep up with all the smoke and debris. After about an hour, the framework was complete. Bill motioned for the generator to be brought in. Carefully wheeling it in on a special cart that had been assembled back at the lab, the technician slowly made his way over to where a small hoist was waiting next to the brace. Bill walked over to supervise the operation.

"Make sure that line is secure," Bill said.

"Yes, sir," the young man said.

All the lines were checked and double-checked before Bill gave the okay to raise the generator from its cradle on the cart. As it went up, Bill and several other technicians kept their hands on it to steady and guide it into its receptacle in the brace. The generator was lowered slowly into the freshly constructed arms of the brace. When it was resting securely in its cradle, Bill and the others began to clamp it securely into place. Once it was accomplished, Bill stepped back to admire his handiwork.

It sure doesn't look like much, Bill thought. What it looked like was a scene right out of Frankenstein's lab. The generator was mounted in a complex lattice of supports and braces that all but obscured the large cargo entrance. A mass of wiring ran from the generator to several computer outlets along the wall and into many pieces of test and support gear scattered throughout the room. Bill walked over to one of the programming consoles.

"How's it goin', Mike?" he asked.

"Fine, Bill. I'm just finishing up tying in fire control to the generator. We can monitor it from the science console on the bridge, but it will have to be fired by the weapons officer from the weapons console."

"Great. How much longer will you need?" Bill asked.

"I'm finished now. All the preliminary checks are complete, and system communications with the bridge have been tested and verified," Mike said as he shut down his console and stood, arching his back and stretching to relieve some of the pent-up tension.

"All right. Let's get this area clear, and I'll inform the general," Bill said.

Mike trotted off to supervise the final cleanup, double-checking all the connections as he went. Bill located the nearest intercom and paged General Matheson on the bridge.

"Sir, this is Bill Johnson. Installation of the generator is complete. All control has been routed to the bridge. We are ready to commence the test whenever you are."

"Excellent. We will be arriving at the asteroid in about fifteen minutes. Be on the bridge by then. Out." The intercom clicked off with finality.

Bill raised his voice to address the entire room. "Make sure any loose articles are removed when you leave. Secure your stations and evacuate the room."

After the last person left the bay, Bill shut the access door and locked it with his personal code. When he reached the bridge, the door opened with a quiet swish, and a puff of cool air hit his face. He made his way to the science console and opened the program that would monitor and control the generator. After he was satisfied that everything was in order, he turned to the general.

"Everything's ready, sir. All systems are showing green on my board. The weapons officer has control."

"Very well, gentlemen. Helm, reduce speed."

As the *Hercules* approached the asteroid, its speed reduced slowly until it came to a halt three hundred kilometers from the slowly spinning body.

"Helm, bring the ship around and line up Cargo Bay Charlie with that asteroid," said Matheson.

The *Hercules* swung around gracefully, stopping its spin just as the cargo bay containing the generator lined up perfectly with the asteroid. As the ship was being maneuvered into position, Bill began the initial warm-up sequences to bring the generator into a state of readiness. He also brought all the monitoring equipment online and started the recorders. Once the ship was in position, General Matheson stood up in the center of the bridge and began calling commands to different stations.

"All hands, prepare for test sequence to begin."

"Aye, sir."

"Open cargo bay door."

The ensign at the ops console complied with his order. On the monitors around the bridge, the massive door of the cargo bay could be seen sliding silently to one side until it locked in place at the end of its track. The generator sat in the center of the opening, glistening in the starlight like a slender needle of death.

"Power up to nominal levels," the general said.

Technicians all over the bridge began bringing up the power levels to the generator. A low-frequency hum could be felt throughout the ship as each circuit came online. The building charge could be seen on the monitors as a bright blue corona dancing around the tip of the generator, sizzling and crackling with barely restrained energy.

"Generator has charged and is ready to target, sir," Bill said from his station.

"Excellent. Bring targeting system online," Matheson said.

"System is online and ready, sir," a young officer at the fire control station said. Clasping his hands behind his back, the general took a deep breath.

"Target asteroid body."

"Done."

"Set generator to minimum power, duration of one nanosecond." The general glanced at Bill to ensure that the requested levels had been set. Bill wiped a bead of sweat from his face as he nodded.

"Everything's ready."

"Very well. You may fire on my mark," said Matheson.

Watching the chronometer mounted over the main viewing panel, the general raised his arm. Breathing stopped on the bridge as a tense hush fell over everyone present. The officer at fire control struggled to suppress the tremble in his hands as he waited for the signal. All eyes were on the asteroid as the general's hand dropped.

"Fire."

What happened next was almost as impossible to believe as it was anticlimactic. When the generator was triggered, a brilliant blue beam shot across the intervening space between the ship and the asteroid. It danced on the surface for the briefest of moments. The massive asteroid then simply ceased to exist. It was as if it had disappeared into the vacuum of space, nothing left to even hint at its existence. The entire bridge crew sat in stunned silence. The general was the first to break the spell.

"Oh my God. That was minimum power?" he asked hoarsely. Momentarily flustered, he struggled to regain his composure.

"Y-y-yes, sir, minimum pulse duration, minimum power level," Bill said.

"Oh my God," the general said again, standing. "I want a complete scan of the area. The mass of that rock had to go somewhere. I want to know where!" His order sent the bridge into a flurry of action. Readings were taken, recorded, and then passed along to the general. He glanced over them for a moment and then handed the printout to Bill for his analysis. Bill's face was ashen as he finished reading the reports.

"What is it, Bill?" the general asked worriedly.

"Well, instead of only causing the breakup of the asteroid, as we predicted, its entire mass has been compressed into a ball roughly one centimeter in diameter. It has also caused the core of the asteroid to become superheated, almost to the point of thermonuclear fusion!" Bill said excitedly.

"What the hell does that mean?" the general asked, his foul mood evident by the way he was chewing on the end of his unlit cigar.

"What it means is that if that asteroid had contained any more mass than it did, it would have just given birth to a new star," Bill said with awe in his voice. The general's jaw dropped, and his cigar hit the floor with a thud. Finishing the general's train of thought for him, Bill said, "And if that had happened, this ship, along with everyone on board, would have been incinerated."

"Oh my God," the general said yet again as he sat down. "You mean to tell me that we can't use this thing without destroying ourselves in the process?"

Bill considered carefully before replying. "As long as the appropriate calculations are made, we should be able to use it to destroy enemy cruisers. Anything larger than that, and I'm afraid it would be terminal for us as well."

The general considered Bill's comments. He quietly came to a decision. "I want a safety governor installed on the system so that the generator cannot be fired in a situation that would be dangerous to us as well as the enemy. I also want an override capability tied into the bridge, keyed on my voice. Any questions?" He paused, looking at Bill. "Good. Do it."

Bill left the bridge elated that the weapon had worked but at the same time very apprehensive about the destructive power he had unleashed. He remembered the words of Robert Oppenheimer, the father of the atomic bomb. "Now I am become death, the destroyer of worlds." Bill understood those words now in a way that very few human beings ever would.

Perhaps in a time of peace, the generator could be put to good use helping to create habitable systems where once there was only dead rock in space. Perhaps. But right now his invention would be the savior of humankind, an instrument of judgment to be used against their oppressor, bringing peace and hope where now there was only war and hopelessness.

His thoughts turned to his family. He imagined the liberation of Earth from the hands of the Jerrollites. Bill's mind continued to turn these thoughts over and over as he made his way to his lab.

CHAPTER 16

Modifications were being made at a dizzying pace. A new mood pervaded the ship as crew members finally saw a spark of hope on the horizon. Small as it was, it was enough to ignite the hearts and minds of everyone on board. Even Bill had a hard time resisting the excitement. At last he would be able to justify the sacrifices that had been made to get him to the *Hercules*.

Once the generator had been fully integrated into the ship's systems, General Matheson called a planning meeting for all his top staff. Planning for the counterattack was finally under way. As Mark made his way to the briefing room, he could not help but feel a surge of adrenaline. He stopped by the lab on the way to the planning session to see how Bill was making out. The door whispered aside as he entered. Looking around, Mark saw a familiar white-coated figure hunched over some contraption in the far corner. He chuckled to himself as he was reminded once again that Bill could be relentless in the search for perfection. Walking over to where Bill was standing, Mark tapped him on the shoulder. Bill responded by jumping like a scared cat, dropping the tool he was holding.

"Man! Don't do that!" Bill said.

"Sorry, Bill, just wanted to stop by and see how things are going," Mark said, chuckling.

"No problem. Other than a little fatigue, everything is fine."

"Great. Why don't you take some time to relax and let us handle things for a while?" Mark said. Bill removed his glasses and rubbed the bridge of his nose with his thumb and forefinger, his face looking like a sunken, hollow facsimile of itself.

"You may be right. I am kind of tired, now that I stop to think about it," Bill said.

"Go to your cabin and get some rest. You're not going to do us any good if you kill yourself before we engage the Jerrollites. I'm on my way to the planning session now, and I'll stop by and let you know how it went when we get through. Fair enough?" Mark asked.

Bill nodded his head in agreement, giving a few last orders before leaving the lab. Mark left with him and headed in the opposite direction.

When Mark arrived, the session was already under way. The room was congested with a thick haze of smoke and filled with arm-waving, finger-pointing men all trying to make a point at once. It resembled an experiment in chaos more than an orderly battle planning session. Mark wondered at the ability of these men to produce anything useful from these meetings. He took a seat next to General Matheson at the head of the table. A large, muscular soldier with the rank of captain, whom Mark recognized as the commander of the ground forces, was currently standing in the center of the room, pointing at a map of the solar system on the wall.

"We must provide a diversion from the rear, General. If you can get enough of my troops on the ground, we will be able to mount a campaign against their main communications facility, which they have established in the Pentagon. Without that, they won't be able to send for help from their home world. They won't be able to 'phone home,' as it were." The reference elicited several muffled chuckles from around the room. Feeling that he had made his point, the captain took his seat.

"Very well, Captain," the general said. Turning to Mark, he asked, "How are preparations going?"

"We've fitted the *Hercules* with all the control systems you asked for. I also took the liberty of outfitting one of the TAC-WING fighters with a harness to hold the generator if necessary."

"Why?" the general asked.

"If the *Hercules* becomes crippled, we will be able to preserve the generator by launching it on a fighter."

"Good idea. Okay, here's what we're going to do." The general continued for several hours, hammering out every possible detail and contingency. Many times the discussion threatened to get out of hand—some wanting to go in full tilt and simply blow the Jerrollites out of the sky, others wanting to maintain secrecy for as long as necessary. Mark watched as General Matheson skillfully manipulated the meeting, gently guiding it in the direction he thought was best. Finally a plan was worked out and agreed to that incorporated the best elements from the ideas that had been thrown on the table. After generating all the necessary papers and orders required to implement the plan, the general dismissed the session. As the other men trudged out of the room, exhausted by the meeting, General Matheson leaned over to where Mark was sitting and rubbing his eyes with the back of his hand.

"You think it's going to work?" Mark asked.

"I figure the odds are against us right now," he replied, scratching the stubble on his chin thoughtfully. "But with God's help and a dash of luck, I think we can pull it off!" He grinned as he stood up to leave the room.

"Godspeed, sir," Mark said, standing with him. A strange emotion filled him as he watched the general leave the briefing room. He had an unspoken son-to-father attachment to the old man for sure, but there was something more, something deeper that he couldn't quite put his finger on. When the general reached the doorway, he turned back to look at Mark, his figure silhouetted against the bright lights in the hallway. Seeing that image jarred Mark's mind. Struggling hard to remember his Greek mythology, he was struck suddenly by the story of the phoenix, the bird that was destroyed but rose up from the ashes of destruction to a new and even greater glory. This ship and all the humans on board were the phoenix, rising up from destruction to reclaim what was rightfully theirs. Mark choked up as he thought about his metaphor.

"Sir," Mark said.

"What is it, son?" the general asked.

"I propose that this operation be code-named 'Phoenix,'" Mark said, staring at the general as the words left his lips. Realization dawned in the general's eyes, unspoken comprehension passing between the men.

"Very well. Operation Phoenix it is," he said as he turned and left the room.

CHAPTER 17

High in orbit above Earth, five Jerrollite command ships were stationed in geosynchronous, equidistant positions. No spot on the surface could avoid surveillance. The flagship was positioned over North America, immediately over the Jerrollite communications facility in the Pentagon building. Floating in space, the flagship's conical shape gave it a benign appearance belying its true nature. Jerrollite battleships were perfect examples of efficiency in design—design for a specific purpose. Their gleaming white surfaces were interrupted only by the occasional extrusion of sophisticated sensor arrays and bays full of equipment. The ships bristled with hidden armament, which could be deployed within seconds. They were machines of war, not exploration. The body of each ship flared toward the rear where the main propulsion units were housed. The great engines emitted an eerie, greenish glow as they exerted a gentle thrust to offset the pull of Earth's gravity and maintain a geosynchronous orbit.

Since the initial invasion, the fleet had dispersed across the surface of the planet. Every landmass had been assigned a squadron of ships to serve as an occupying force under the direct control of a local commander. Each squadron operated symbiotically with the others, intermingling and supporting one another when necessary. Each squadron was tied into one of the orbiting battleships via a communications link and through that to the supreme commander in the flagship, who in turn could control every aspect of the Jerrollite presence on the planet. The entire invasion had been coordinated from above by the supreme commander through direct communications and control links to the flagship, a supremely efficient arrangement that allowed for complete control and coordination across the entire fleet.

Earth's military could not make any move at all without being spotted and eradicated from above by the Jerrollite ships. The initial fighting had been over very quickly, as each Earth government capitulated in turn to the rule of the Jerrollite race. At first there had been many incidents of rebellion and insurrection on the part of individual humans, but they had been put down quickly and mercilessly by ruthless execution. It had been necessary on several occasions to exterminate as many as thirty thousand at a time, gathering them together in an open field and firing the ship's plasma weapons on the huddled crowd. Most of the time, the bodies were incinerated where they stood, but occasionally a victim would not burn completely, and a charred mass of flesh would be left where a human being had once been. The Jerrollites refused to remove these remains, so they stood in mute testimony as grim reminders of the disdain the Jerrollites had for human life..

In the command flagship, the supreme Jerrollite commander, T'chak, stood in the control center scanning readouts from the planet below. He shook his head in disgust as he looked over the heavy elements list that was just coming in from one of his ground commanders. This planet was very poor in resources that the Jerrollites could use. Every single element that they could have taken and used had been squandered by the human infestation on the planet. The commander again shook his head as he thought of all the time and energy that had been expended in conquering this planet. What had it gained them? Nothing! Not even a cargo of heavy elements to take back home. He had been against invading this puny planet from the beginning, seeing it for what it was—a waste of effort and resources. This conquest had been a politically motivated one, to be sure. There were members of the council who were attempting to puff themselves up by chalking up another conquest for the great Jerrollite empire. T'chak spat on the floor in disdain for the political maneuverings of others. Mulling over the situation in his mind, he grew angrier by the moment the more he thought of it. The commander came to a decision as he watched over his bridge crew. He spun on his heel and left the control center, headed for the communication core. He would put a stop to this waste before it could go any further.

He initiated contact with all the other command ships in orbit around Earth to inform them of his decision. As each commander appeared on the screen, he acknowledged his leader with a brief nod and waited for him to begin. When all five leaders were connected, T'chak began.

"After a long period of battle and glorious conquest, we have vanquished this planet and its inhabitants. There is nothing left for us to accomplish by staying here any longer. No heavy elements are available for us to take back home. Therefore, I make the following decree." He cleared his throat and began speaking in an imperious manner. "All ground squadrons will be immediately recalled to form up with the main battle group. A minor force will stay on the planet to enforce our rule over the population. Once the ground squadrons have rejoined the fleet, we will depart this system for the home planet within one rotation of the conquered planet."

T'chak could see in the eyes of his subcommanders that they felt the same way. They had quickly grown weary of this waste of their talents. He made a mental note of the discontent and continued. Leaning forward, he activated a private channel to Subcommander T'lal, the most senior member of his staff.

"T'lal, the honor of maintaining rule on this planet shall be yours. Move your squadron to the area on the planet the humans call Washington. Establish your command center in the Earth building called Pentagon. Our communications facilities are currently being run from there. Location coordinates are twelve-seven-oh-oh-two."

"Yes, Lord," T'lal said, clenching his fist over his chest in a gesture of honor and respect.

The commander nodded his approval and once again addressed his entire staff. "Implement now."

Communications were beamed out to every Jerrollite installation on the planet conveying the orders of the supreme commander. Ground commanders, caught unaware by the supreme commander's decision, scrambled to get their troops recalled and loaded onto transport ships in preparation for departure. After each ship was loaded, it left the surface for an orbital rendezvous with its own commander's ships.

The orbiting command ships executed a positioning maneuver and left the geosynchronous orbits they had been holding, coming alongside T'chak's flagship. As the ground squadrons began to rise in their transports from the surface, they headed for their respective commander's ships, taking position to the rear of each vessel. As the ground ships joined the assembling fleet, the formation began to look like a massive arrowhead, pointing straight at Earth's heart. Within a matter of hours, the entire Jerrollite armada was assembled and ready for departure.

The flagship lumbered into position as the point in a massive triangle. When the positioning maneuvers were complete, the supreme commander called for a communications connection to every ship in the armada. His voice and image would be seen by every soldier in the fleet simultaneously.

"You have fought well. This battle is done. We return now to our home world to bask in the glorious honor that is ours. T'lal, take your position."

T'lal's squadron broke formation and came to the head of the armada. T'lal ordered his ships to form two broad lines, between which the fleet would pass, a traditional honor guard in the way of the ancestors. Once the honor guard was in place, T'chak gave the order to proceed. The flagship was the first to enter the gauntlet of ships on its way home. Each ship passed T'lal's squadron, slowly and majestically, re-forming into a pyramid on the far side. The supreme commander felt a great pride in his men. They had served him well many times in the past and once again proven their ability as an elite fighting force—the home world's finest. It was infuriating that their efforts had been wasted on such a weak and unworthy opponent. Well, he considered, at least it was a good exercise.

As the flagship passed out of the gauntlet, T'chak ordered the hyperdrive engines engaged. As the engines came online, a brilliant green flash erupted from the rear, and the flagship streaked into the cosmos.

T'lal watched as the flagship left the system, followed closely by the other ships in the armada. When the last ship was gone, he ordered his men to descend back into Earth's atmosphere. He wondered at the "honor" of being selected as the commander to stay behind and monitor the humans' planet. To a warrior, the task could almost be considered humiliating. However, he was getting much older and slower than his younger counterparts, so he supposed he could have pulled worse duty. After all, the humans had already been beaten. Their military had been completely wiped out, and over 50 percent of the population had been disposed of. They had nothing left to fight with, their spirit was broken. His only problem was going to be one of boredom, and he was quite sure that he could still overcome that. T'lal gave a snort as his ship began its descent back into the atmosphere, headed for the Pentagon.

As the last remaining Jerrollite ship left orbit and reentered Earth's atmosphere, a small one-man TAC-WING fighter came out from behind the moon where it had been hiding. Thrusters set to maximum, the small spacecraft burst forward on a giant plume of burning exhaust for the safe confines of the *Hercules*.

CHAPTER 18

The fighter hurtled toward its destination. The pilot could barely contain his excitement over the developments he had just witnessed. Approaching the *Hercules* in its hiding place on the outer edge of the solar system, he entered the landing bay quickly and landed his craft. Without even waiting for the normal landing checks to be completed, he removed his helmet and leapt from the cockpit, his feet barely touching the floor as he raced from the landing bay. He could hear over his shoulder the cursing of the flight deck ops officer as the ground crew began swarming over his fighter. The news he carried was much too urgent to wait even the few minutes it would have taken to do his post-flight checks.

He rounded a corner as he headed for the bridge and ran smack into Mark Hunter. Both men went tumbling to the floor, the pilot sprawled in a heap against the far wall, Mark flat on his face. Mark shook his head, regaining his composure as he rose to his feet. He picked up his cap and smoothed his fingers through his hair. The pilot's face was burning red as he realized who he had just collided with. He collected himself and once again began running toward the bridge. Mark stood in the middle of the hallway, watching the young officer run in the opposite direction. Remembering what he had just done, the pilot called back over his shoulder.

"Sorry, sir. I've got some urgent news for General Matheson."

Mark shrugged and took off after the pilot, following him onto the bridge. They burst through the door together and came to a skidding halt in front of General Matheson. The young pilot was breathless and found himself unable to speak. Matheson stared at them while chewing on his cigar.

"Don't hyperventilate, boy! Speak up!" he said.

"Perhaps we should retire to a briefing room, sir," Mark said. General Matheson nodded his head, and they made their way into the nearest room. The general shut the door and took his seat.

"Now, gentlemen. You want to tell me what all the ruckus is about?"

The pilot began. "Captain Edwards, sir. I was on a surveillance mission on the far side of Earth's moon, and I saw the Jerrollite fleet assembling in orbit."

General Matheson leaned forward in his chair, expressing interest in this new development. Mark also focused on what the young captain was saying.

"After they were all in orbit, one group formed some kind of honor guard or something, and all the other ships passed through it and left!"

Matheson's eyebrows shot up. "What the hell do you mean, *they left*?" the general asked.

"Just what I said, sir—they're gone. They passed through this line of ships, engaged their engines, and were gone within seconds." Matheson sat back heavily in his chair, lost in thought. If the Jerrollite fleet had really left Earth, then perhaps a unique opportunity had presented itself.

"Did any stay?" Mark asked.

"I saw one contingent of thirty ships head back down to North America. I waited till they were out of sight and came back here as fast as I could," Edwards said, still breathing heavily.

Matheson and Hunter looked at each other and smiled as they realized that perhaps God had seen fit to give them a break after all. While thirty to one still weren't very good odds, it was much better than ten thousand to one. With the element of surprise on their side, they might just stand a chance of coming out on top. General Matheson scratched the stubble on his face and addressed the captain.

"Very well done, Captain, very well done, indeed. Dismissed." The captain stood, saluted both men, and left the briefing room. General Matheson banged his fist down on the table with a gleam in his eye.

"All right. We don't know why they left or how long they're going to be gone, but we are not going to waste this chance. Operation Phoenix commences in one hour. Make preparations to get under way."

"Yes, sir!" Mark said enthusiastically. He switched on the intercom and began issuing the orders that would set their plan in motion. Preparations, for the most part, were already complete, with only minor details left to attend to. The ship exploded with activity—personnel were elated to at last be going into battle. Flight crews began manning the more than one hundred TAC-WING fighters on the *Hercules*. The spacecraft were fueled, and engines were started. As Mark entered the launch area, he was amazed. Technicians were swarming over every fighter, checking and rechecking every detail. Every ship was critical to the success of the mission.

Mark walked over to the far side of the bay where the troop transports were loading the ground assault force. Johann Switzer was still in charge, barking orders to the men as they climbed on board.

"Coom ohn, you pahntie waists! Geht your butts in gear!"

Mark chuckled as several young recruits looked back over their shoulders, not really sure how to handle Johann when he was in one of his moods. Mark placed his hand on Johann's shoulder. His face lit up when he saw him.

"Mark, boy, will you be joinin' us today?"

"I wouldn't dream of interfering, Johann. I'll be above you, giving you air support!"

"Great, just what I need, my own guardian angel!" Johann said.

Mark clapped him on the back and wished him luck. "Your guys will go in about thirty minutes ahead of the fleet. You need to land as close as possible to the Pentagon and set up diversionary ground fire. If possible, get inside and destroy their communications facility. We sure don't want them to be able to send for help."

"Dahm streeight, mon!" said Johann. Mark laughed as he turned and headed for his fighter.

He settled himself into the cockpit of his TAC-WING, removing the BWI helmet from its alcove behind his seat. Placing the helmet on his head, he quickly ran through a complete check on every subsystem in the fighter in preparation for launch. The adrenaline pumping through his system wiped out any vestige of nervousness or fear. One at a time, each of his weapons systems came up green on his console. Satisfied that everything was ready, Mark leaned out and gave a thumbs-up sign to the loadmaster. A large grappling hook latched onto Mark's ship, lifting it onto the waiting launch rails. The TAC-WING fighter slid into the launch tube as the access hatch sealed shut. Mark could feel the vibration of the ship coming up through the launch rails. He gripped the joystick tightly, waiting for the launch order to come.

Up on the bridge, General Matheson was busy coordinating the thousands of details that had gone into their battle plan. The bridge was a beehive of activity: each element of the plan was being fed into the computer, checked, and rechecked for errors. Glancing at one of the status boards, he noted that one hundred TAC-WING fighters were online and ready to launch. All troop transports were in the launch tubes ahead of the fighters.

One by one each station signaled its readiness to implement the battle plan. Status lights on the main console went green as each unit reported in. When everything on the board was green, Matheson activated the intercom and addressed the entire crew.

"We are about to commence Operation Phoenix. The odds are against us, but right is on our side. We will prevail, or we will die. There is no other choice. Each and every one of you will play a vital role in the success of this mission. We are humanity's last hope. Godspeed."

He released the intercom with an air of finality. Moving to stand in the center of the bridge, he looked at the communications officer and gave the order that would begin the operation.

"Launch defense probes, now!"

The defensive probe ships were used as a confusion tactic, as each one gave off the exact same radar signature as the *Hercules*. On enemy sensors it would appear as if the entire fleet were attacking at once.

The only indication on the bridge that anything had occurred was a minor vibration felt through the deck plating as ten large probes left the main launch tubes. Riding pillars of flame, each one swung around in front of the *Hercules* and leapt into hyperdrive, leaving only a small wash of color behind. Even that faded quickly.

"Probes away, sir," a young ensign said.

"Very well. Launch three squadrons of fighters to act as an escort for us." The same tremble could be heard and felt beneath their feet as dozens of TAC-WING fighters were launched. Each fighter appeared on the main view screen taking up position around the ship, forming a protective umbrella. Matheson observed all of this in silence, satisfied at the progress of the plan.

"Engage main engines."

In the aft section of the ship, the giant engines roared to life, making the entire ship shudder violently. The general experienced a surge of adrenaline as he felt the vibration through the soles of his feet. The huge ship lumbered forward, slowly at first but gaining speed rapidly as the engines settled into a violent rhythm, propelling the *Hercules* toward its destiny. As the ship began racing toward Earth, Matheson ordered a course plotted to bring them in behind the moon and remain out of range of any enemy surveillance. Once the giant warship had attained cruising speed, Matheson opened a private channel to Mark's ship, which was still standing by for launch. Mark was going through systems checks in an attempt to make the waiting time pass more quickly. His heart skipped a beat as Matheson's voice interrupted his busywork.

"Is everything ready?" Matheson asked.

"All systems are green, sir. Just give the word," Mark said.

"Very good. Stand by for launch on my command."

Closing the channel, Matheson sat back in his command chair, content for the moment that all was going well. He looked over his bridge crew with admiration. They were all business, no wasted words or motions. The time for battle had come. They all knew it and were prepared to pay any price. The young ensign at the navigation console interrupted his thoughts.

"Coming up on lunar meridian, sir."

"Very well. Lay in an orbit that will keep the moon between us and Earth at all times."

"Course corrections laid in," came the crisp reply.

"Commence new course when appropriate, Ensign."

"Aye, sir."

The massive warship swung in low on the dark side of the moon, out of any sensor range from the planet. Using brief bursts of power, the battleship synchronized its speed with the rotation of the moon, appearing to hover over a single spot. A graphic display on the navigation console showed the desired orbit in relation to the current position of the *Hercules*. The image of the ship gently came into sync with the orbital path display. The ensign's fingers flew over the panel, locking in the ship's position and instructing the computers to maintain it. When everything showed green, the ensign turned to the general.

"Orbit achieved, sir. We are at station, keeping three hundred kilometers above the lunar surface."

"Well done." Turning to the command console, he keyed in the sequence to authorize the launch of the troop transports. The ship's computer system acknowledged his code and signaled the ships in the launch tubes. General Matheson switched on the intercom.

"Johann, you may launch your ships. Godspeed."

"We're off to see the wizard…and we're going to kick his butt…sir!" Johann said. Everyone on the bridge smiled briefly, sharing Johann's enthusiasm.

"Just make sure you do. Report in when you have taken your objective. Matheson out."

Each transport erupted simultaneously from different launch tubes around the ship. As each one cleared the outer shields, it headed toward the front of the *Hercules*, where it joined the lead ship in a massive flying V. Johann's face lit up the front view screen on the bridge.

"Well, General, looks like this is it. I will contact you as soon as our job is done," he said, all traces of his Jamaican accent gone.

"Good luck, Johann. We'll see you in a few minutes."

The main view screen flickered back to a view of the lunar surface. The formation of transports could be seen moving off the screen. The general switched on the ship-wide intercom.

"Silent running rules are in effect. No electromagnetic emissions of any kind are allowed. Use passive sensing devices and optical communications only." Silent running meant the *Hercules* would be out of contact with Johann and his troops until it was time to launch the aerial portion of the attack.

The general drummed his fingers on the armrest of his chair impatiently. He watched intently as Johann's ships dropped below the cloud deck after entering the atmosphere. Matheson was pleased to see that no response was forthcoming from the enemy. They had not detected the incoming ships. Now there was nothing left to do but wait for Johann and his men to execute their elements of the plan.

CHAPTER 19

Fountains of flame spat from the side of the *Hercules* as the troop transports left their launch tubes. Inside the lead transport, Johann Switzer made final preparations for planetfall. According to their plan, he had just two hours to achieve his objective of either taking over the Jerrollite communication facility or destroying it. It didn't really matter to him which course of action he followed as long as he got the job done. Johann was one of the lucky few who had not lost any family during the initial Jerrollite attacks, but he had seen his friends' lives destroyed by the invasion, and that was more than enough motivation to spur him on, hardening the resolve for victory in his heart.

Checking the status of the other transports on his board, he busied himself with checking and rechecking every detail of the attack plan. Everything depended on the element of surprise; even though the majority of the Jerrollite fleet had left Earth to head home, they still outnumbered the human ships by thirty to one. Each Jerrollite ship was more than a match for the *Hercules*, as great as it was, much less one of the transports. The humans' only hope lay with the weapon they had spent so much of their time and resources developing. Johann hoped it would work. If it didn't, there would be no second chances.

As the transports fell into formation, Johann brought his optical communications system online, establishing a link with the other ships. A brilliant red beam lanced out from Johann's ship and touched the hulls of the other transports, looking like the web of a giant spider with his ship at the center. Once valid communication connections had been achieved, he addressed his men.

"Oolright, gents, it's time to payh the piper. We'll be going in using maneuver Bomburst Seven." That maneuver was one of the most difficult but had the greatest chance of success. It involved pairing his ships, which would attack the target from four different directions at once, converging on the planned location simultaneously and laying down a tremendous barrage of lead rain and explosives. If all went well, the enemy would be taken completely by surprise, and the battle would be over before anyone on the ground could react. The transports were equipped with enough weapons and ammunition to make them a formidable force in the air. Johann planned on using their capabilities to the extreme.

"Transports One and Two take south, Three and Four take north, Five and Six east, Seven and Eight take west," he said.

"Roger, Leader. Flight control systems are locked in and fully functional," said Transport Seven. The message was repeated by every other pilot in the group.

"All ships converge on me, single file, for descent into the atmosphere," he said.

On cue each transport executed a pirouette and fell in behind Johann's ship, forming a line of ships over a mile long. Getting all the transports to the surface without being detected was crucial to the plan, so General Matheson had worked out a special maneuver to use to get down to the surface. Control of each ship in the line would be linked via optical relay to the lead ship, which would bring the entire assemblage to a point over the North Pole and dive straight into the atmosphere. Once down, the ships would break the link and head off in their assigned directions to eventually rendezvous with the other ships at the assigned coordinates.

"Engage optical link," Johann said. He watched his board as each transport complied. The onboard system acknowledged each ship as it came online and relinquished control to the lead ship. As the last ship docked, the ship-to-ship communication link buzzed to life.

"We're all yours, Johann. Take good care of us," said one of the other pilots.

Johann chuckled to himself and said, "Doon't worry, boy, it weel be like rockin' in your momma's cradle. Now hang on!" Johann thrust his accelerator forward. The other ships leapt after him, precisely duplicating his every move. He swept the line of ships completely around the dark side of the moon, bursting into the bright sunlight of dayside. Diving straight toward Earth, he brought the ships close to the orbiting Russian space station, keeping it between them and the surface. They could hide behind it until it passed directly over the North Pole. According to Johann's calculations, they were not going to have long to wait. Opening his front viewport, Johann could see the blazing white ice cap of the pole dead ahead. Gearing up the engines to make a run for it, he prepared to dive straight down to the frigid expanse. As the space station passed directly over the pole, Johann slammed his throttle to maximum and pushed his stick as far forward as it would go. The ships responded by rifling straight down like an express locomotive to hell. The surface rushed toward them, looming larger and larger in the viewport. Johann could hear the gasps of his men over the intercom but could not spare any effort in calming them. His attention was riveted on his control panel, carefully monitoring the hull temperature to make sure it did not exceed safety limits, as well as monitoring his airspeed to make sure he could pull up in time. The transports were designed to make atmospheric landings, but Johann was relatively sure the designers had never envisioned their ships being used in quite this way.

The outer hull groaned as it strained against the forces of reentry into Earth's atmosphere. The thick air shrieked as it whipped around the transports, buffeting them severely. Johann could feel the temperature inside his cabin begin to rise in response to the bright red glow surrounding the ship. The front end of each transport had been fitted with a special heat shield for this maneuver, but they had not had time to test it before launch. Johann muttered a prayer as their hellish descent continued.

Checking his long-range scanner, he could detect no enemy activity. At least that part was going right, he thought. Johann continued the descent, his entire being focused on performing the difficult maneuver. Suddenly a loud warning klaxon began screaming for his attention, accompanied by a flashing red indicator on his panel warning him that his approach speed was too high for a safe landing, Johann silenced the alarm—there was nothing to be done at this point. It was what it was.

Pushing to the very edge of the performance envelope for the ships, Johann waited until the last possible instant before yanking the throttle back and engaging the air brake. Everyone in the transports was thrown forward against the safety harnesses, breath crushed out of lungs by the sudden deceleration. The transports shuddered violently against the drag induced by the extended air brakes, rapidly losing airspeed. Johann had a fleeting thought that the air brakes could easily be torn off by the extreme forces pounding on them. If that happened, he would deal with it.

The stick was like a bucking bronco in Johann's hand, threatening to leap free at any moment. Every muscle in his body was stretched taut like piano wire. He pulled back with all his might, applying as much pressure to the stick as he could. The ground was coming up fast. Too fast.

Painfully slow to respond, the transport's nose crept upward, creating a cushion of high-pressure air that did nothing to soften the sudden deceleration. Each ship came within one hundred feet of the surface, barely completing the maneuver just before slamming into the ground. As each ship began to level out and stabilize, Johann relaxed a little more. He wiped the sweat from his brow, breathing a heartfelt sigh of relief. He made a mental note to look up the designers of this ship and thank them for building in the excessive tolerances that had allowed him and his men to survive. The airframe of each ship had endured forces that far exceeded the design limits of the spacecraft.

He reached forward and activated the communications link with the other ships.

"See? No sweat, mon!" he said, trying to maintain his facade of calm. He could hear groans from the other ships as each pilot realized he had survived.

"You are one insane SOB, sir," came a tentative transmission from one of the transport ships.

"Somebody mus' be to survive," Johann said, his accent now firmly back in place. "Remember that in the comin' battle."

Johann placed his hand on the switch that would disengage the control link with the other ships. "Okay, boys, this is it. Maintain radio silence while approaching the target. You all have your assigned courses. Any questions?" Receiving no response, he continued, "Well, then. Here we go."

He brought his hand down on the switch to deactivate the link. There was a slight jar as each of the ships broke free of the link, breaking formation and speeding off in its assigned direction. Within seconds all that was left to mark their presence were a few drifts of swirling snow and a fading rumble in the distance.

T'lal sat in his favorite spot in the building that had become his headquarters. He contemplated the series of events that had led to his assignment here as governor of the human population. This observation room on the roof of the Pentagon building provided him with the peace and quiet he longed for. From here he could see for miles in any direction, his solitude disturbed only by the whisper of air coming through the ventilation system. He took a deep breath, exhaling slowly as he patted his ample belly.

Yes, indeed, he thought, I definitely could have pulled worse duty. He took a long drink from a container of an Earth beverage he had acquired a taste for. While ransacking the building, he had found a supply of it in one of the sleeping quarters on the lower floors. He suspected it had been illegally stockpiled by one of the human soldiers that had been here before. He was sure his own men did the same at times, but he really didn't care. They had nothing like it on their own world. He looked at the label, not understanding what it said, but knowing enough of the humans' language to sound it out. "E-e-v-e-r-c-l-e-a-r G-grain Alk-e-hol," he slurred. He shrugged his shoulders as he took another long pull from the bottle. Although it burned like fire going down, it made him feel pleasantly unconcerned, the worries of his command temporarily forgotten.

He turned his head at the sound of footsteps coming in his direction. His subcommander poked his head into the tiny chamber where T'lal was lounging. The disgust in his eyes was evident. He was very dissatisfied with having been left behind and blamed T'lal. Saluting as a show of respect, an action performed out of duty that made the subcommander cringe, he reported, "Sir, we have detected unauthorized aerial activity in the vicinity of the North Pole." T'lal's hazy mind failed to comprehend the situation, so he simply dismissed the subcommander's statements.

"Track the targets and let me know what happens," he said, dismissing the subcommander with a wave of his hand, again raising the bottle and drinking long and hard. The subcommander clenched his jaw, seething as he repressed a stinging reply that had brought itself unbidden to his lips. Turning quickly, he closed the door and left.

"Overeager whelp!" T'lal said as a raucous belch escaped his lips. He satisfied himself with another long pull from the bottle of grain alcohol. Sinking back into the oblivion that he cherished so much, the commander failed to notice, off in the far, far distance, a tiny black speck on the horizon that was streaking toward a rendezvous with destiny.

Johann monitored the progress of his ships closely on his own sensor displays. Each ship was precisely on course and would converge over the Pentagon in less than three minutes. He brought his weapons systems online, removing all safeties, going hot and preparing to fire. As he made his preparations, identical actions were being taken on all the other transports. Men were readying themselves, making sure they had everything they needed, gripping their weapon controls tightly in anticipation of the upcoming battle. For many it would be the first taste of combat. Unlike other soldiers in the past who had been forced to fight for unclear goals and vague objectives, these men knew this fight was for the survival of the human race. There would be no losing this battle today. Each and every man knew that one of two things would happen. They would either emerge victorious, or they would die. Either way it was going to be finished—today.

As T'lal continued to drink, he noticed a small black spot on his bottle. Pulling the bottle down to examine it more closely, he was surprised that the speck had disappeared. Confused, he looked up at the sky and almost choked at what he saw.

Seen clearly now, unobscured by distance, were eight Earth military transports blazing toward his location, each leaving a clear vapor trail in the blue sky. They came from four directions at once, relentlessly homing in on the Pentagon. As realization finally made its way through the haze surrounding his brain, he made an attempt to shout for attention but could only manage a guttural scream. The bottle dropped to the floor, shattering into shards. T'lal fled the observation post and headed toward his command center, moving his huge body as fast as he could in his drunken state. He cursed himself for not listening to the subcommander when he'd tried to inform him of the incursion over the North Pole.

As he passed a window, a sick feeling came over him when he saw one of the ships under his command sitting unattended outside. He had allowed all thirty ships to come to the command center for a celebration of victory. That meant all thirty ships were parked outside in close proximity to one another. If one ship blew, it would take out several more. Staggering down the hallway, he burst into the command center, screaming, "Alert! Alert! There are human ships converging on our location! Recall all pilots to their craft for immediate launch!"

The subcommander displayed an open look of hatred and contempt for his commander. His incompetence would surely get them all killed. He resolved to do something about it. He placed his hand on his sidearm and prepared to take matters into his own hands.

The Jerrollite command center erupted into a flurry of activity as everyone realized what was happening and frantically began issuing orders to comply with T'lal's command. They halted in their tracks as they heard the low rumble—they were too late. Each member of the Jerrollite staff looked at the others, eyes wide with the realization that they were about to die. T'lal looked at the subcommander, who met his gaze and spat on the floor in disgust. The subcommander began to draw his weapon from its holster. T'lal recognized what was happening immediately. The alcohol in his system had long since been burned up by the adrenaline coursing through his veins; it in no way impaired his response to the subcommander's attack. T'lal was able to draw his own weapon and fire, striking the weapon and knocking it from his hand before the subcommander could pull his trigger. This elicited wide-eyed surprise in the subcommander's face as his weapon clattered to the floor. T'lal was nothing if not prepared for the uncontrolled desire of a subordinate officer to ascend the command hierarchy.

"Count this as your lucky day, Subcommander. If I did not need you right now, you would be dead. Control your ambitions and focus on the task at hand." The subcommander's face flushed a deep blue. He had been humiliated, and he knew his career was ruined. Even though assassination was accepted in Jerrollite society as a means to advance, if the attempt failed, there was no recovering. He had been bested by an old drunk at the end of his career.

"Yes, Commander," he said between clenched teeth. He would wait for a more opportune time to exact his revenge. He spun on his heel and retreated to the back of the command center. Turning his attention back to the matter at hand, he realized that his reprieve from death might have only been temporary.

The human attack had begun.

From the viewport Johann could see the other ships' vapor trails standing out in stark contrast to the brilliant blue sky. They were all converging on the Pentagon like fingers of God come down to smite unbelievers. Johann's fingers flew over his control board, preparing to attack. He reopened ship-to-ship communications.

"Transports Two through Five, land on the South Concourse and disembark your troops. Six, Seven, and

Eight, converge on me to begin an attack run." Johann looked up through his front view screen to see the transports veering off to implement the instructions he had just given. As the other three ships converged on his position, he scanned the area surrounding the Pentagon. His eyes almost bugged out when he saw all thirty Jerrollite battleships parked neatly in a row outside. It was an impressive sight but a severe tactical error on the part of the Jerrollites. He couldn't believe they were naïve enough to leave themselves so vulnerable to attack. It spoke to the level of contempt in which they held the human forces. They believed themselves to be untouchable. It was an underestimation they would sorely regret very shortly.

As the transports approached, they could see Jerrollite flight crews scrambling toward their ships in a frantic attempt to get airborne before the attack could begin. Johann smiled grimly to himself as he brought his finger down on the stud that would fire his missiles. His ship lurched violently as three incandescent arrows of flame shot out from underneath his ship, to be joined a split second later by several others from the other transports. The other pilots had seen the same opportunity and added their missiles to his own. Johann heard shouts of exultation over his communication link.

"What a bunch of dumbasses!" shouted one of the other pilots. Johann could not agree more, but right now he needed to maintain his pilots' focus.

"Okay, guys, cut the chatter. This ain't over yet! Stay focused on the objective. No mercy!" Johann said. He watched as each missile found its target, penetrated the outer hull, and disappeared inside the alien ship, followed immediately by a massive explosion, as each hull was consumed by a bright orange fireball. As the fire reached combustible materials in the ships, a final series of explosions rocked the surrounding area, throwing debris and Jerrollite bodies all over the compound. As each ship exploded, the ships parked next to it also caught fire and exploded in short order. Huge fireballs rose into the air from the missile hits and secondary explosions, scorching and destroying everything in their path.

"Watch out, boys!" Johann said as he pulled a hard right to avoid flying into the fire. The other ships in the attack followed him. They regrouped and began a flyover of the attack site.

As the smoke and flames began to clear, Johann and his team could see that most of the Jerrollite ships had been replaced by a smoldering black crater. Other ships that had not been destroyed directly by missile fire looked like sad, melted hunks of useless metal. Only four enemy craft were left intact. Johann swung his transport around as he sent orders to the other airborne ships.

"Seven and Eight, stay and finish off the rest of the alien spacecraft and mop up this mess! Six, follow me!" said Johann.

"Yes, sir!" came the quick response.

As the transports began a relentless pounding of the remaining ships on the ground, Johann and the other transport swung around and began an attack run directly on the Pentagon building itself, firing at and destroying any defenses that were visible.

"Bring your guns online. Take out any weapons you see on that building!" Johann said.

"Roger that."

Three large openings appeared in the front of each ship, a very large Gatling gun in each one. Johann flipped his safety off and depressed the trigger. All three guns fired simultaneously, spewing out long lances of fire. Out of his left eye, Johann could see tracer rounds coming from the other ship, striking their target alongside his own. The airframes of the ships bucked and vibrated violently as the guns chattered away, pouring thousands of rounds into the building. Portions of it began to collapse under the relentless assault, sending up billowing clouds of choking dust and smoke.

In short order Jerrollite soldiers began pouring out of the building, firing their weapons at anything moving in the air or on the ground. It was obvious to Johann that there was mass confusion and blind panic in the Jerrollite ranks. They had no idea what was going on other than that they were in real trouble. Human soldiers began pouring onto the scene from the opposite side of the building where their transports had landed. Johann could see them clearly as they attacked and killed everything with blue skin in sight. Their anger and frustration fueled the fight as they avenged their friends and families who had been devastated by the Jerrollite invasion.

The air around the Pentagon was blanketed with thick, black smoke, making it almost impossible to see. Johann fired his cannon at the fortifications on the roof. His thirty-caliber, depleted-uranium slugs ripped giant holes in the roof, destroying large sections of the building with every shot. Jerrollites were scampering frantically from one cover to the next, desperately seeking shelter wherever they could find it. Checking his scanners, Johann saw that two of the Jerrollite ships had survived the initial attack, gotten airborne, and were streaking away up into the atmosphere. Confused at first as to why they had failed to counterattack, he quickly realized what was happening. Abandoning the silent running rules, he opened a communications channel to the *Hercules*.

"General Matheson, there are two Jerrollite battleships headed your way. Be ready," he said.

General Matheson's voice came over his comm link. "We have them on our sensors, Johann. Tracking now." Johann closed the channel and returned his attention to the battle at hand. Sweeping high overhead, he brought his ship around the south side of the building, where he could see five of his troop transports continuing to disgorge their cargo of men onto the lawn. As the soldiers disembarked from the transports, they scurried away, crouching low to avoid enemy fire coming from the rooftop. As Johann watched, one of his men went down, grasping what remained of his leg after it had been burned off by an energy beam. He shifted his gaze to the Pentagon's roof in time to see a group of Jerrollites open fire with energy weapons. From their vantage point, the men from the transport were easy targets, and they were quickly racking up a large number of kills.

Anger filled Johann as he spun his ship on its axis and came in low and fast, heading for the enemy soldiers on the roof. Unaware that their lives were in danger, the Jerrollites continued to fire randomly into the men on the ground below. Hearing a low rumble, they turned their heads as one in time to see Johann's ship erupt from the swirling black smoke, spitting lead death in their direction.

Johann watched impassively as the Jerrollites were cut to ribbons. As the hail of bullets subsided, nothing was left that was even vaguely recognizable. After circling around once more to make sure there were none left alive and his men were out of danger, Johann brought his ship down next to the others. Opening a communication link with the other airborne transports, he gave them their orders.

"Six, Seven, and Eight, stay airborne until you hear from me. Continue patrolling the area from the air. Watch for those two ships that got away!" He turned off his link and leapt out of the ship. Glancing around, he saw that his men had already unloaded. Raising his weapon over his head, he motioned to them.

"Ohhkay, men. Let's kick some Jerrollite butt!" A roar erupted from the soldiers standing around the ship as they followed Johann into the building.

T'lal was frantically trying to contact his home world to inform them of the situation on Earth. Growing more frustrated by the minute, he slammed his fist into the communications console, sending sparks and smoke flying in all directions. He howled in pain as his fist made contact with the hard metal, sending white-hot jolts of pain shooting up his arm. T'lal jumped in surprise as the entire building shuddered with the impact of another large projectile. Spinning around from the console, he covered the area of the command center in two large strides and brought himself face to face with his subcommander.

"How did this happen?" he asked, standing toe-to-toe with the younger officer. "You reported no military capability was left on this planet! Does this look like no capability to you?" he said, gesturing wildly as he looked around the wrecked command center. The subcommander drew himself up to his full height and swallowed convulsively before answering. Seething anger evident on his face, there was no way he was going to take this treatment from this pig of an officer.

"Perhaps if you had not been so involved in exploring Earth's beverages, you would have detected this situation before it occurred!" said the subcommander. As the words left his lips, he immediately regretted uttering them. T'lal turned slowly, his frenzy of a moment before now replaced by a cold, emotionless stare.

"Commander—" the subcommander began but was cut short by the sizzle of an energy weapon being discharged. He looked down at his chest to see a gaping, bloodless wound where his heart should have been. His eyes returned to the commander as his body fell lifeless to the floor.

T'lal returned his weapon to its holster, grunting in satisfaction as he did so. He spun on his heel, walking away from the subcommander's body.

"Any other accusations?" he asked, addressing the personnel in the command center who were standing around with their mouths hanging open. In response to his question, everyone quickly averted their gazes from the body on the floor and back to their consoles.

"I didn't think so," said T'lal, harrumphing as he took his seat in the center chair. He was glad to finally be rid of that insolent pest anyway. Now to deal with these upstart humans in a way they would never forget. Spinning in his chair, T'lal addressed the entire center. "What do we have left?" he asked in a low, deadly voice.

A young soldier stood up. "Sir, when the ships on the ground were attacked, they were loaded with soldiers. Twenty-eight ships were destroyed, with all hands lost. Two of our ships got away and are currently keeping station in orbit above us. They are standing by, awaiting your orders."

T'lal let his head come to rest in his hands. Twenty-eight ships lost, each with a crew of 150 faithful Jerrollites. With a grim look of determination on his face, he realized that his career was over and that he would probably face a firing squad when and if he got home. With his communications facilities smashed, he had no way of contacting the home world and informing them of the situation. With only two ships left, he could most likely defeat the human force outside, but there was no way he could maintain control of the entire planet. His thoughts were interrupted by a squawk coming from one of the ground-to-ship channels. He turned toward the console and raised an eyebrow to the soldier manning the console.

"Contact has been made with our ships that got away, sir. They inform us that a large, *Mariner*-class battleship is just on the other side of the moon, sir." After a pause he added, "It appears to be the USS *Hercules*, sir."

T'lal felt the heavy weight of certain doom descend on his shoulders. "A battleship?" he asked incredulously. "All of the human space cruisers were reported as destroyed!" T'lal wondered how much more of their intelligence was in error. If the human military still had an operational battleship, he was in grave danger. Coming to a decision, he ordered his soldiers into action.

"Prepare a message buoy detailing all the events of the last couple of hours. Set its destination for the home world. Launch on my command. Get me in contact with those ships," he said.

The young soldier scrambled to obey his commander. "Contact established, sir; go ahead."

"This is Commander T'lal. You are ordered to send both of your ships to attack and destroy the human battleship. Do not fail me." The hidden threat in T'lal's words was not lost on the ship's commanders.

Their response came quickly. "Acknowledged."

The soldier severed the link with the ships and prepared the message buoy T'lal had requested. "Buoy ready, sir."

"Launch," said T'lal. A distant rumble could be heard as the buoy launched itself from the hangar and streaked out of sight.

"Everyone gather your weapons and follow me!" T'lal said as he drew his own and started for the exit. As he reached for the door, it erupted in a spray of flame and debris. T'lal was thrown back against his own men, all of them sprawling onto the floor. Johann and his men streamed into the room, sporadically firing their weapons as Jerrollites attempted to bring their own weapons to bear. The thick smoke made it difficult to see. Only muzzle flashes and occasional discharges from energy weapons illuminated the room. Pandemonium reigned as Jerrollite after Jerrollite fell, screaming in agony, their lifeblood spilling onto the floor.

Johann waded through the smoke in an attempt to find the Jerrollite commander. He scanned the room, his eyes coming to rest on a large pile of Jerrolite bodies.

T'lal was lying face down. . He could feel the human commander's breath on his neck. T'lal was hurt but not fatally. He decided that if he must die today, it would be on his terms and not lying on the floor like a coward.

Johann walked around the room, checking fallen bodies, trying to determine which one was the commander. Eyeing a uniform that looked more decorated than the others, he went over to investigate. Bending over to look at the corpse more closely, Johann was surprised when it rolled over and grabbed for his neck. Jumping back out of range, he brought his boot up and smashed it into the face of the Jerrollite commander. T'lal's consciousness faded into nothing.

Realizing that he had just kicked the Jerrollite commander in the teeth, Johann smiled. The thought gave him a kind of sadistic pleasure as he bound the commander and ordered one of his men to take him out to the ship and keep him under guard. Every other Jerrollite in the room had been killed, so Johann wanted to make sure this one got back to General Matheson for interrogation. Occasional shots rang out in the building as his troops moved through and ferreted out the remaining Jerrollite soldiers. Johann opened a portable communication link.

"General Matheson, do you copy?" he said. The response was almost instantaneous.

"I'm here, Johann. How goes it?" the general asked.

"Mission is accomplished, sir. We've met the wizard and kicked his butt, just as promised! Performing mop-up operations now."

"Glad to hear it. The *Hercules* is currently under attack. We could use your help as soon as you can make it." Johann could hear the sounds of battle in the background.

"Yes, sir. The cavalry is on the way! Over and out." Johann keyed in the recall code on his communicator and began to make his way back to the ship.

From outside, the Pentagon looked like it had just been through World War III. Pockmarks and streaks of black stood in mute testimony to the battle that had been raging only moments before. His men were assembling just outside the transports in response to his summons. He ordered one of his sergeants to radio the two circling craft and signal them to land. After both ships were down, he quickly explained the situation to the assembled crew.

"Okay, men, the *Hercules* is under attack. I want each pilot to get in your transport and follow me. We are going up to join the fight. The rest of you will stay here to maintain control of the Pentagon.

"Sergeant, deploy these men across the city in strategic locations. Kill any enemy soldiers you may find. No prisoners." Waving his arm to his pilots, he yelled, "All right, let's go!" and sprinted for his ship.

Eight transports lifted smoothly from the ground, nosed skyward, and roared off into the radiant blue sky.

CHAPTER 20

Two blazing red trails of fire erupted from the brilliant azure background of Earth. As they cleared the upper reaches of the atmosphere, one vessel veered off and headed for deep space, making a run for the Jerrollite home world. The other plunged forward, bearing toward a final confrontation with the *Hercules*. The commander could only hope that his counterpart would make it back to the home world in time.

The humans had surprised them with the suddenness and ferocity of their attack and had completely destroyed their communication facilities before anyone could respond. The commanders had agreed to split up even though T'lal had ordered them to stay together. They both felt that a message buoy would not get back to the home world fast enough and a ship must make the journey. One had been selected to stay behind and engage the human ship. He wondered if he would survive the coming fight. Never before had he seen a race react so violently to being invaded. He had been on countless expeditions like this one and never had a problem. As a general rule, most races simply acknowledged the superior force of the Jerrollite armada and capitulated with little or no resistance. This time, however, the situation had been completely different. The entire Jerrollite occupation force had been decimated in a single staggering blow.

The commander glanced around the bridge, keenly aware that for the first time in his life he was heading into a battle that he stood a good chance of losing. His crew remained in a state of high alert, ready for the upcoming fight. The commander was startled by an alarm.

"Sir! I have a pursuit from the surface! Range is seven hundred clicks and closing fast!" said the engineer.

Glancing down at his screens, the commander confirmed that this was one of the human ships that had attacked them on the surface. He pounded his fist on the console next to the screen. He wanted to attack the *Hercules* with no other distractions, but that was going to be impossible now. He was hemmed in, trapped between the *Hercules* and the pursuing ships from below. A dark resolve came across the commander's face as he made a final decision. There was no way his ship could withstand a combined attack from the *Hercules* and the ship from the surface, so he would channel all available power into the weapons systems in an all-out attempt to inflict a mortal wound on the *Hercules*. It was their only chance. He spun to face his engineering officer.

"Channel all available energy into the forward weapons battery."

The look on the engineer's face betrayed exactly how he felt about that course of action. "Commander, if we do that, we will be vulnerable to attack! One strike and our ship will be destroyed!"

"Don't you think I know that?" said the commander, menace dripping from each word. The engineer swallowed convulsively and turned to obey. The commander watched as power was rerouted from every nonessential system on the ship into the weapons. Finally the engineer turned to face the commander.

"All systems power has been rerouted. We no longer have any shield capacity."

"Understood. We're not going to need them." The commander turned his back on his openmouthed engineer and walked to the middle of the command center. "Give me maximum speed. Collision course with the *Hercules*." The commander noted the startled looks on the faces of his crew. "We have no choice but to ram the Earth ship. There is no way we can win against their entire fleet, but we can make sure that the battleship is destroyed." To their credit, his crew took the news of their certain death with dignity. They returned to the task at hand, changing the course of their ship to match that of the *Hercules* exactly. The helmsman brought the ship up to its maximum velocity, speeding forward on a course that would bring them head-to-head with the *Hercules* within minutes.

"Charge forward cannons. Track the *Hercules* and lock its coordinates into the system. Open fire as soon as we are in range," said the commander. He watched grimly as his crew carried out his orders without further question. Although he would never show it, he was proud of them as they prepared to face their last battle. His only solace lay in the fact that his crew would not be the only ones to die today. A sneer curled his lip as he watched the *Hercules* approaching rapidly, a lone warrior in the wilderness.

Johann's ship ripped free of Earth's atmosphere and began to pursue the Jerrollite spaceship in earnest. Through his cockpit window, he could see several other transports that had taken up formation on his ship. The pilots were intently studying their tracking systems to find the fleeing Jerrollite craft. Johann checked his own display and was surprised to discover that the two ships they were pursuing had split up and headed in opposite directions.

The other pilots made the same discovery simultaneously, and the radio erupted in chatter.

"Sir! I have one of the Jerrollite ships dead ahead and one retreating to the rear!"

"Oooch, I see him," said Johann. They could not spare any ships for pursuit. Protecting the *Hercules* was their first priority, and their chances of success were much greater if they had everything at their disposal.

"Lock his course eento tha computer, boy. Don't lose him, now. We'll chase him later, but right now we gotta protect the home front!" The other pilots radioed their agreement, and they all rocketed toward the *Hercules*.

General Matheson was gazing intently at the forward view screen when a warning siren sounded. Spinning around to his ops officer, he barked out his orders. "Red alert! Prepare to engage the alien vessel."

Immediately the ship's computer shifted the lighting to combat red and began an urgent announcement through-out the ship: "RED ALERT! ALL HANDS TO BATTLE STATIONS! THIS IS NOT A DRILL!"

Matheson nodded in approval as his order was carried out with maximum efficiency. The ops officer spoke quietly into his headset microphone, acknowledging a message coming over the ship's intercom. He turned to report to Matheson. "Sir, all stations are standing by."

Nodding in approval, the general stood. "Wings One and Two, you are cleared to launch. Deploy in front of the ship and form a wall between the *Hercules* and the approaching enemy craft."

Mark, who had been anxiously waiting in his fighter for this moment, replied first. "Yes, sir! Wings One and Two, launch on my mark. Three…Two…One…MARK!" The launch bay erupted in flame as twenty-four fighters launched simultaneously. Emerging from the launch tubes, each wing took up a defensive position in front of the ship.

"All fighters, this is Wing Commander. Bring your weapons systems online and prepare to fire," said Mark.

The weapons pod on the front of each fighter began to glow in response to the energy being channeled through it. As both wings fell into place, Mark was satisfied that they would be able to stop the approaching ship. He located the Jerrollite craft and relayed the information to the other pilots.

"Target at two hundred twenty mark four."

"Roger, targets locked. Ready to fire."

Mark gripped the arm on his seat tightly in anticipation of the coming battle, nerves manifesting as a bead of sweat rolling down the side of his head. As he watched, the Jerrollite ship loomed larger and larger in his display until he could see it unaided through his cockpit window.

"All hands, stand ready!" he said. The enemy ship was approaching faster, never reducing speed to engage the fighters. Almost too late Mark realized the Jerrollite commander's strategy. "Peel off! Peel off! Break formation!" he said into his microphone. The Jerrollite ship was on a collision course with the *Hercules*, and they were directly in its way. Both wings immediately broke formation and began buzzing around like angry hornets.

"Fire at will!" he shouted into his headset. The space around him exploded with the sizzling and crackling of particle beam weapons and laser fire. The Jerrollite ship seemed to momentarily wither under the barrage but with an iron resolve continued bearing down on them. As the TAC-WING weapons impacted the hull of the enemy ship, several large internal explosions were seen; large plumes of flame leapt from the gaping holes left by the particle weapons. Still the Jerrollite ship continued to bear down on them and the *Hercules*. Peeling off from the main fighting group, Mark radioed the *Hercules*.

"*Hercules*, this is Wing Commander. The Jerrollite ship is making a kamikaze run, sir. They are not defending themselves at all. They intend to ram the ship!"

"Acknowledged, Wing Commander. Are you having any effect at all?" General Matheson asked.

"Yes, sir, we are inflicting heavy damage but are unable to stop the mass of the ship. There will still be enough of it left that if it hits, the *Hercules* will be destroyed."

"Very well. Continue pursuit to within five hundred kilometers of us and then back off. I repeat, do not approach closer than five hundred kilometers."

"Yes, sir!" Mark said. He relayed Matheson's orders to the rest of the wing and then rejoined the battle. While the TAC-WINGs continued to batter the Jerrollite ship, a swarm of single-man fighters erupted from its belly. This action took the men by surprise, and Mark witnessed seven of his fighters disappear in puffs of flame, replaced by floating debris.

"My God! Watch it, everybody! Several enemy fighters are spaceborne. Watch your backs! Wing One, continue your attack on the main ship; Wing Two, engage the fighters!"

The Jerrollite ship roared past them, leaving only a swarm of fighters battling it out one-on-one. Mark saw several explosions but couldn't tell if Earth ships or Jerrollites were being destroyed. A proximity warning klaxon sounded in his cockpit. Mark slammed his stick forward, nosing his ship into a dive. Looking behind him he could just make out an enemy fighter on his tail. Weapons fire erupted from the nose of the Jerrollite craft, inching its way toward Mark's fighter. Mark jerked his control stick back as hard as he could, kicking in his auxiliary thrusters at the same time. The TAC-WING shot straight up, pulling a tight reverse arc. His ship groaned under the stress the maneuver caused but held together long enough for him to end up directly behind the Jerrollite fighter. Activating the targeting computer, he was rewarded with the steady tone of a target lock.

"Die, you son of a bitch!" Mark said as he activated the fire control with a single thought. His weapons pod blazed as a single burst of energy leapt from his ship to the hull of the Jerrollite craft. A blaze of bright green fire enveloped it completely, causing it to disintegrate in midflight. As the energy reached the fuel source, a brief explosion filled Mark's view screen. Diving through the middle of the fire, Mark came up behind another Jerrollite that was locked in on a TAC-WING. The human pilot was glancing frantically over his shoulder as he sensed that death was imminent. Mark could hear his pleas for help over the radio.

"Get him off me! Get him off me!"

"Stand by!" Mark frantically worked his controls. "I have a lock. Break left!" The TAC-WING pilot broke left as Mark fired. His laser swept up the back of the enemy fighter and made the outer skin bubble and blister. As the beams reached the cockpit area, the craft erupted into a brilliant flash. Mark peeled off to the right to avoid colliding with the debris.

"Thanks, sir."

"No problem—let's get back in it!"

Both craft turned to rejoin the fight. As Mark picked a target, his ship shook violently. An out-of-control Jerrollite fighter struck it, causing him to lose control. Mark struggled to regain proper orientation of his ship, firing his thrusters to counteract the spin his ship was in. He checked his display for a new target and saw that he was the target of three Jerrollite fighters bearing down on him from three different directions at once. Mark increased his thrust to maximum and dove into a spinning loop, whipping violently from side to side in an attempt to shake the Jerrollites off his tail. Completing the violent maneuver, he looked over his shoulder to see the Jerrollites were even closer than they were before. A fourth fighter had broken off from the main group, sensing the kill. All four of them moved in on Mark like a pack of hungry dogs. The newest fighter to join the hunt moved into a flanking position to the right of Mark's ship.

If I have to go, I'm not going alone! Mark thought. He slammed his stick violently to the right, causing his ship to spin ninety degrees on its axis. He opened fire on the nearest Jerrollite, completely destroying it. The other three ships opened fire on him at the same time, a lucky first shot impacting Mark's ship and damaging the control circuitry for his weapons pod.

Dammit! There was nothing left to do. Resigning himself to his fate, he applied full throttle in an attempt to ram the nearest Jerrollite ship.

"AAAIEEEEEEE!" he screamed, preparing to meet his maker. The Jerrollite ship loomed in front of him as he squeezed his eyes shut. His whole body braced for the impact and flaming death that he knew would come within seconds.

Mark heard the sizzling crackle of laser fire, followed by a brilliant flash of white light. Great, he thought, I'm dead. His comm link crackled with a cheerful voice.

"What's the matter, boy? Trying to kill yourself or sumpthin'?"

Mark gingerly opened his eyes to discover that he was, as hard as it was to believe, still alive. He thumbed his comm link control and responded. "Thanks, Johann. I think I owe you a big one." His voice was quivering with the adrenaline rush he had experienced only moments before.

"That you do, mah boy. That you do. Maybe you can buy me a cold one when we get through here. What you say?"

Mark laughed in amazement at Johann's attitude. "You got it! Now let's clean up the rest of this mess and go home!"

Both men kicked in their boosters and swung around to rejoin the battle. Even though Mark's ship was damaged, there was no way he was leaving Johann to fight alone. Jerrollite ships were rapidly being destroyed, one after another, with the additional firepower of the transports. Within minutes nothing was left but floating debris to indicate that the Jerrollites had ever been there.

The Jerrollite commander surveyed his situation as he cast his gaze over his bridge crew. His ship was rushing head-long toward the *Hercules*. They had suffered extremely heavy damage at the hands of the humans but had retained more than enough mass to utterly destroy the *Hercules*. The bridge crew cast nervous glances at him as they approached the point where collision was unavoidable. What they saw in their commander's face made them realize they had better make peace with their maker and very soon.

"No return point in three seconds," said a crewman from across the room.

"Acknowledged," came the terse reply from the commander. He stood stiffly, gazing out at the stars, preparing to meet his fate. If only that idiot T'lal had not been left in charge, none of this would have happened, he thought. Now we all have to die to correct his mistake. The commander could only hope that T'lal had suffered an excruciating death at the hands of the humans. The thought gave him a dark sense of pleasure.

"Point of no return has been passed, Commander."

"Acknowledged," he said, steeling himself for impending death.

The Jerrollite ship hurtled forward into the void like a silver bullet aimed straight at humanity's future.

"Evasive! NOW!" said Matheson.

The bridge of the *Hercules* was a flurry of activity as the helmsman brought the ship over, hard to port, in an attempt to avoid the onrushing Jerrollite vessel. The ship groaned under the stress of the sudden maneuver and rocked violently to one side as bodies, equipment, and anything else not bolted down skittered across the floor and crashed into the far wall.

"No use, sir! Every course correction we make is being matched exactly by the Jerrollite! Collision will occur in approximately two minutes!"

General Matheson pulled himself up from the floor and stood in the center of the bridge. He could see the Jerrollite ship on his forward view screen coming straight toward him.

"Open fire! All weapons, fire at will!"

Brilliant beams of energy leapt from the weapons pods all over the *Hercules*. Many scored direct hits on the hull of the Jerrollite vessel, but its armor was sufficient to withstand them. The enemy ship began to return fire; a massive energy beam danced down the hull of the *Hercules*, inflicting major damage along the port side. Explosions rocked the ship as the beam continued to burn through the outer hull.

"Strengthen the port shields!" said Matheson.

"Aye, sir. Shields are now stable and holding!" said an ensign.

"Sir, I'm not sure how long we can withstand that beam. It's taking everything we've got to keep it from ripping through the ship!" said the ops officer.

"Understood." Matheson realized his ship could not continue to take the pounding and most certainly would not survive being rammed by the Jerrollite ship. Feeling frustrated by an apparently hopeless situation, he was startled by a quiet voice from behind him.

"Use the weapon, General."

He spun around to see Bill Johnson standing at the entrance to the bridge. "Use it," Bill said again.

"We're too close to Earth, aren't we?"

"Yes, sir, but I would say that it's time to take a calculated risk. If we set the pulse duration to an absolute minimum, we should be able to control the reaction." Matheson raised his eyebrows as Bill continued. "Besides, if that ship destroys us, humanity won't survive, so either way we'll be screwed. If we use the weapon, we'll at least have a chance."

Matheson didn't hesitate. "Bring the generator online and prepare to fire on my command."

His crew leapt into action. They all sensed a sliver of hope if they could get the weapon online in time. The doors to the cargo hold lumbered open to reveal the generator still suspended in its latticework. The equipment surrounding the generator hummed to life. Coolant started to flow, causing a small stream of fog to cascade off the housing. Seconds later a bright green light came on.

"I have a green light on the generator, sir," said the weapons officer.

"General, one thing you need to realize. When you activate the generator and destroy the Jerrollite ship, it will still be coming toward us at the same rate of speed, with the same mass as before. Even though it may be microscopic in size, if it hits the ship, it will destroy us as surely as it would have before," said Bill.

Matheson digested this new information and then nodded his head in acknowledgment. "Helmsman, tie in fire control to your board and lock in a course change to implement at the same time the generator is activated. Bring us hard to starboard."

The young man's hands flew over his console, responding to Matheson's orders. "Yes, sir. Changes locked in, ready on your command."

Matheson cast a sideways glance at Bill, who simply nodded.

"Do it," said Bill.

The air was filled with tension, heightened by Matheson as he stood in the center of the bridge coiled like a spring, waiting for the opportune moment to fire the generator. The Jerrollite ship was closing faster and faster, crushing any hopes that the crew may have had about this being a bluff on the part of the Jerrollite commander. The massive alien ship filled the forward view screen, blocking the stars from view.

"Reduce magnification," said Matheson. The image on the screen reduced in size, allowing them to see more of the alien ship. The crew could see the damage that had been done and were amazed that the alien ship could still function. The general raised his hand as the helmsman poised his finger over the fire control button.

"Wait…wait…" Matheson said, causing everyone on the bridge to cringe, waiting for the inevitable impact. Several crossed themselves, praying for a miracle.

"FIRE!" he roared, dropping his hand and grabbing the rail surrounding the bridge. The helmsman's fist slammed down onto the fire control.

A screeching hum resounded throughout the ship as a brilliant blue bolt of energy shot out of the cargo bay, danced across the intervening space, and touched the Jerrollite ship. The generator had been set on minimum duration and intensity, creating a black hole that lasted only microseconds, but it was enough. The huge Jerrollite ship's hull buckled as they watched, collapsing in on itself. Huge plumes of air escaped into the vacuum of space, crystallizing in the deadly cold. As the hull continued to fold up, jets of flame erupted and dissipated, sending bodies and debris spinning off into the void. In a final, brilliant flash, the ship disappeared.

The bridge crew were mute, stunned by what they had just seen. An automatic proximity warning klaxon jolted everyone into action.

"SIR! The course change failed! Collision is imminent!" said the helmsman.

"MANUAL OVERRIDE! PULL UP! PULL UP!" bellowed the general. The helmsman slammed his hand down onto the manual override and jerked the flight control back. The engines screamed in protest as the ship bucked upward. The superstructure began to buckle, causing several panels to explode on the bridge. Showers of sparks and flame shot across the command center. The tiny ball that was once the Jerrollite ship closed on the *Hercules* with frightening speed. Passing within inches of its hull, the ball hit the left rear engine housing, ripping it free from its mounts and sending it spinning off into the depths of space. Fire erupted from the gaping wound left in the ship.

The ship was jerked violently backward, sending personnel careening into walls and consoles on the bridge.

"What was that?" yelled General Matheson.

"We were struck by the remains of the Jerrollite ship directly on one of our main engine housings, sir." The crewman gulped as he looked again at his console to verify his readings. "It's gone, sir. Completely ripped off the ship."

"Raise containment shields and close all access hatches. Seal off the area completely. Reroute all power to the remaining engines."

"Yes, sir!" The bridge again burst into a flurry of action as the crew responded to Matheson's orders.

The flame was snuffed out as the last hatch was sealed, leaving only the scarred and blackened remains of an engine mount. The bridge was dark, the power lost when the engine was destroyed.

"Get me emergency lighting, NOW!" barked the general. A dim blue glow emanated from the lighting panels built into the walls and ceiling. "What's left?" he asked. Reports came from each crew member on the bridge.

"Communications are okay, sir."

"Life support is nominal."

"Hull integrity is ninety percent."

"Weapons systems are out; engine power is down to sixty percent."

The general turned around, looking for Bill Johnson amid all the wreckage on the bridge. He found him in a crumpled heap underneath several panels.

"You all right?" he asked.

Bill replied by nodding, which he immediately regretted as it caused a severe jolt of pain through his head. "Ooowwwwww," he moaned.

The general chuckled and helped him stand. "If you have a headache, at least you're alive. Get down to sick bay and tend to your wounds." Bill complied, acknowledging the general with a wave of his hand as he exited the bridge.

Matheson walked to the front of the bridge, standing directly in the center of the view screen. He pulled his familiar cigar from his pocket and placed it in his mouth. Leaning over a console that still had some small flames burning inside, he lit his cigar and patted out the flame. Taking a long drag, he expelled the smoke slowly, savoring the taste of it.

Turning to face his bridge crew, he said, "Well, overall I would have to say we've had a pretty lively day!" A grin split his face from side to side. Laughter erupted from the crew—they were still alive to fight another day.

CHAPTER 21

Mark and Johann approached the *Hercules* cautiously, bringing their ships in slowly. It was floating, power-less, listing to one side with the nose of the ship pointed down at a severe angle. There was a gaping hole to the rear of the ship where one of the engines had been ripped from its mountings. Mark was stunned.

"Johann, we haven't lost the *Hercules*, have we?"

"I don' know, boy. It looks pretty bad from here." Much to their surprise, their comm links crackled to life.

"Looks can be deceiving, gentlemen. Didn't your moth-ers ever teach you not to trust your own eyes?"

"General Matheson! We thought you were dead, sir!" said Mark.

"Give us a moment to get the ship back on its axis, and then you can bring your ships into the main landing bay. See me as soon as you get on board. Matheson out."

As the comm link went dead, Mark looked out through the cockpit window, giving Johann a thumbs-up. They watched the *Hercules* began to right itself, turning slowly, leveling off, and stabilizing its attitude by using its maneuvering thrusters. Once the ship was on an even keel, the fires began to go out, extinguished by automatic systems. After a couple of minutes, their comm units once again sprang to life.

"Colonel Hunter, your wing is cleared to land in Bay One."

"Roger, Control. All ships, descend on my pattern," Mark said.

The TAC-WING fighters expertly and gracefully entered the landing bay, each ship doing a clean pirouette and coming to rest on the floor. Once they had landed successfully and were secured, the transports followed, landing in the center of the bay. When the last ship had touched down, the crew and pilots erupted in a joyous celebration of hard-won victory. Mark climbed down out of his fighter and made his way through the throng to Johann's ship. He was just coming down from the cockpit. The grin on his face gave away his feelings.

"How 'bout that cold one now?" said Mark.

"You got it, man," Johann said, as he shrugged off his flight suit and tossed it back up into the cockpit.

"I really thought my butt was cooked back there. I'm glad you came along when you did, old buddy!"

"No beeg deal, mon. Soombody's gotta look out for you, right? May as well be me!"

Mark laughed heartily as he clapped Johann on the back, and they left the landing bay together, heading for the bridge.

When Mark and Johann entered the bridge, they were startled by the sheer amount of destruction inside the command center.

"Man, looks worse on the inside than it did on the outside!" said Mark. Johann chuckled.

"If you boys had done any less, or any later, it wouldn't look this good!" said General Matheson.

"One o' dem nasty Jerrollite boys got away from us, General. We had to let him go so we could come help out here," said Johann.

"Where did he go?" asked Matheson.

"He was headed right for the Jerrol-1 star system. My guess would be that he was hightailin' it for home."

"Hmm. I guess we'd better be prepared for some more opposition, and soon," said Matheson, a dark expression crossing his face.

"That's probably a safe thing to do, sir. We have some time before we have to worry about a counterattack from their home world. I suggest we make use of it by preparing Earth's defenses and getting this ship repaired," said Mark.

"I agree, Mark. Comm Officer, tie me into the fleet broadcast channel," said Matheson.

"Tied in, sir. Ready to transmit."

Matheson cleared his throat before beginning the address that would be heard over most of the planet. "Earth Command, this is the USS *Hercules*, General Roy Matheson commanding. The Jerrollite forces have been defeated and are even now being routed from our system. Our foe is vanquished; the enemy's back is broken." He paused for dramatic effect before continuing. "However, we must not rest now, as a possibility exists that we will have to face a counterattack in the very near future. We must prepare ourselves for this final confrontation so that we may be ready when called upon once again to defend our freedom. We will be home soon. General Matheson out." He nodded at the comm officer to sever the link.

Holding out his hands in a palms-up gesture, he turned to Mark and Johann. "How was I?"

"Very inspirational, sir," Mark and Johann both said at once. They looked at each other and began to laugh.

"Helm, take us home!" said the general.

"Yes, sir!" was the enthusiastic response. The crew on the bridge settled back into their seats as the remaining engines came to life. The ship pulsated with power. Even with the extensive damage to their ship and exhaustion evident on their faces, everyone on the bridge beamed with unconcealed warmth and pride—they were going home as free men and women.

The *Hercules* entered Earth's atmosphere in a gentle arc, heading for a landing at the Washington spaceport. As the massive ship approached the surface, Matheson ordered the helmsman to make a low-level pass over the city.

"Bring us in low, Helm. Let the people see us. God knows they haven't had much to be happy about lately."

"Yes, sir."

The front of the ship dipped slightly toward the ground, coming to within five hundred feet of the crowds gathered on the streets below. As the *Hercules* made its pass, the crew gathered at the viewports to watch the crowds below.

Instead of the joyous celebration one would expect, a somber mood settled over the ship. As the ship slowly passed over the city, they could see the actual extent of the damage. Realization began to sink in as people at last began to grieve for lost loved ones. Their lives had been changed forever. No longer could Earth afford the luxury of arrogance, of believing it was the center of the universe. The Jerrollites had changed that attitude quickly enough. It was a lesson learned at an extremely high price and not to be forgotten, ever.

The ship descended toward the charred remains of the spaceport. The normal landing docks had been obliterated in the initial attack; nothing remained except a melted clump of black material.

"Engage standard planetary landing procedures," said the general.

"Aye, sir. Landing pods extending."

The *Hercules* came to a stationary hover above one of the few clear areas left in the spaceport. Massive landing gear extended from the belly of the ship as it began to make its final descent. The pods touched the tarmac as the landing jets flared briefly, kicking up clouds of dust and debris, and the huge ship came to rest for the first time since the attack.

"Secure all stations," said the general. He turned toward Mark and Johann, who had been standing behind him during the landing.

"Well, men, I guess we're home."

"Yes, sir, it would appear so. I just hope there's someplace left to go home to," said Mark. The grim look on the general's face showed that he shared Mark's feelings. Johann simply shook his head, his heart heavy in his chest. They felt as if they had been raped, violated to the cores of their souls.

Burying his feelings with a wave of his hand, Matheson broke the silence. "Well, we can't stand around feeling sorry for ourselves. We have to get ready for the future. Begin disembarking procedures now."

As the ramp lowered, Bill stood at the rear of the crowd, waiting to touch solid ground for the first time in months. His loss during the attack came rushing back to him, rending his soul. He began to sob uncontrollably as he thought of his child and wife. He leaned against the wall, tears staining his shirt, as he allowed the flood of emotion he had been holding back to all come out at once.

The ramp touched the ground, and people began to rush out into the cool evening air, anxiously looking for friends and relatives. Bill could hear the cries of triumph as the crew disembarked, whooping and yelling to let off the stress they had been under for the last several weeks. Soon there were only a few stragglers left. Bill looked up to see others around him going through similar throes of emotion. He sniffed loudly, removing his glasses and wiping the tears from his face. Mark appeared at the top of the ramp, breathless from sprinting up from the ground. He burst into the bay, shouting at the top of his lungs.

"BILL! BILL!" His shouts reverberated in the bay.

Bill waved at him halfheartedly. Mark ran over and grabbed him by the arm, practically dragging him toward the ramp. Bill's confusion was evident in the startled look on his face. Mark had a Boy Scout grin splitting his face from ear to ear.

"Come with me, you idiot! You're needed outside!" Mark laughed as they both stumbled and fell. "Come on, come on!" he said.

Bill's mind raced in confusion. He had no idea what could possibly be so important. He put his glasses back on and followed Mark outside. When he reached the top of the ramp and looked down, what he saw made his heart stop.

There, standing next to General Matheson at the base of the ramp, was his beloved wife, tears streaming down her cheeks as she began to sob. Bill stood still, dumbfounded. He turned to Mark, who was beaming with joy, and asked, "How…"

"The Jerrollites took her prisoner after your house was destroyed. They've had her in a cell since you left! She survived the attack on your house because she was working in the cellar doing laundry. Once the emergency crews arrived, they found her crouched in the corner of the cellar, a bit worse for wear but still alive!" said Mark, as he pushed Bill down the ramp toward his wife. Bill stumbled down the ramp, stopping when he reached his wife.

He looked at her, drinking in the vision of her standing there with outstretched arms. Emotions overwhelmed him as they locked in a passionate embrace. Tears began streaming down his face as he buried himself in her presence. The scent of her hair, the softness of her skin, everything he felt he would never again be able to enjoy threatened to overtake him as he continued to drink her in. His lips sought hers, delivering the most passionate kiss he had ever given in his entire life. They wept on each other's shoulders, unwilling to let go even for a fraction of a second, afraid they would be again swept away from each other. Bill thought his heart would burst with joy.

"I thought you were dead," he said. She reached up to his face and wiped a tear from his eye.

"I thought I was too…" she said. "The only thing I remember was the world exploding, and then nothing until those awful aliens dug us out of the wreckage." She broke down again into sobs. Bill clung to her, wanting desperately to take her pain.

"Don't worry, baby; we can start over now. We're together again."

"Daddy…Daddy…DADDY!" an insistent voice cried. Bill's mind didn't register the owner of that voice until he felt an unrelenting tug on his pant leg. He looked down to see his beautiful daughter, looking up at him with big brown eyes, tears welling up as she spoke.

"Don't forget me, Daddy!" she said. Bill yelped in delight, and both he and his wife laughed. He stooped and picked up the child he thought he would never see again.

"Never, sweetheart. Never."

They hugged as a family, heads and hearts pressed together in a joyous embrace that seemed to last forever. Unable to contain himself any longer, General Matheson joined in the young family's joy.

"Go home, Bill. You've done your job," he said, grasping Bill's shoulder firmly. "Take your family home."

"Thank you," Bill said, barely managing to choke out the words.

Mark stood with the general as together they watched Bill Johnson and his family walk off with the rest of the crew.

"I'm glad I was here to see that," Mark said, working hard to keep the emotion out of his voice.

"Yeah...me too," said the general, brushing his eye with the back of his hand and clearing his throat. Mark chose not to notice the tear. Matheson pulled his stogie out of his pocket, put it in his mouth, and began fishing in his pockets for a light. He was interrupted by Mark, who had pulled a match out of his pocket.

"I thought you never lit those things," said Mark.

"Well, generally I don't, but I figure what the hell?" They shared a solid laugh together.

"Allow me, sir." Mark struck the match and held it to the tip of the general's cigar. He took several long drags on it before allowing Mark to pull the flame away. Matheson got a quizzical look on his face, coughing violently. "Wow, these things taste like crap! No wonder I never light them!" Both men began to laugh. Matheson tapped out the cigar before putting the unlit stogie back in his mouth.

"Well, my boy...by the look of things around here, I would say we have a lot of work to do. Let's get to it, shall we?"

"You got it, sir!" Mark said enthusiastically.

"Very well, then. Let's go!" They made their way back up the ramp into the ship.

CHAPTER 22

General Matheson reclined in his favorite chair in his cabin aboard the *Hercules*. His mind was tired and his body fatigued from the incredible stress he had been under these last few weeks. Since the final battle with the last Jerrollite ship, he had been placed in charge of overseeing the rebuilding of Earth's fleet, which had been devastated during the war. Although everything was progressing at a reasonable pace, it was still very difficult for Matheson to bring himself down to a level to handle the day-to-day management of such a large project. The repair and retrofit of the *Hercules* were on schedule to be completed within days. The engine that had been damaged during the fighting had to be completely replaced. The new engine had been mounted successfully and was undergoing final testing. Matheson could hear the dissonant thrumming in the hull as his technicians worked to harmonically balance the new engine with the others.

The *Hercules* was relaunched into orbit as soon as the new engine was installed; the balancing procedure had to be performed in a weightless environment. He was glad to be in space again; sitting in spacedock was not his idea of a good time. He sighed to himself as he rubbed his temple with the palm of his hand in a vain attempt to alleviate his building headache. Shrugging it off, he stood and began to undress for bed. He mentally relaxed, allowing the worries of the day to slip from his mind. He yawned vigorously, allowing a wave of drowsiness to overtake him. Lowering the lights in his cabin, he made his way to bed.

As he was climbing into his bunk, the intercom chimed, signaling a message from the bridge. Cursing at the interruption, he reached out and swatted the respond button. "Please tell me you have a really good reason for bothering me!" he growled. Matheson chuckled to himself as he heard the ensign on the other end of the line nervously clear his throat.

"Uhh…sir, we just received a message from Earth Command. It's marked 'Captain's Eyes Only.' Would you like me to send it to your terminal?"

Matheson sat up in his bed, instantly alert, his mind racing. He had no idea why anyone at Earth Command would want to speak to him at this time of night.

"Send it down," he said, all traces of sleepiness gone completely. He got out of bed and moved to the corner of his cabin. His terminal screen glowed a soft blue, with a bright red *Message Waiting* flag flashing insistently in the center of the screen. He sat down, keyed in his personal security code, and waited for a response. As the message painted itself on the screen, he felt his heart sink into the pit of his stomach.

Message Dispatch	*Origin*: Ben Vorshauski, President
Urgent	Earth Command

Time: 2130

URGENT—At 2100 a communication was intercepted from the Jerrollite star system that seems to indicate that a new invasion force is on its way. Long-range scans have confirmed this. Initial estimates are that three thousand Jerrollite battleships have departed their system and are now heading this way. You are to assemble any and all forces you have at your command and proceed on an intercept course. You are authorized to use any weapon you have at your disposal. We will contact you en route with any data we can obtain. All personnel have been recalled and should arrive within the hour. You must depart as soon as they are on board.

Our prayers are with you.

End Transmission

Matheson was stunned as he read the message again, allowing it to penetrate his outer layer of shock and disbelief. He had known all along that the possibility of a counterattack existed but never believed it could happen so soon. He looked at the message again, hardly believing what his own eyes told him was true. It was practically a death warrant for his entire command. There was no way he could match the firepower of three thousand battleships, even on a good day, which this most certainly was not. His fleet was still in shambles, with only a handful of his main battleships ready for service. Hell, he thought, the *Hercules* just came back to one hundred percent operational status last week.

Matheson pressed a key on the terminal to print the message. He picked up the piece of paper, holding it gingerly in his hands. Matheson entered a number into the intercom system and asked Mark to join him in his cabin. Switching channels on the intercom, he addressed the bridge.

"All hands, this is General Matheson. The Jerrollite fleet is on its way back." He paused for a moment to let that news sink in. "We have been ordered to intercept and attempt to destroy it before it reaches our space. Prepare for departure in one hour."

He lifted his hand from the intercom. A gentle chime sounded at his door.

"Come," he said.

The door slid open to reveal Mark Hunter with an incredulous look in his eyes.

"Are you serious?" he asked.

"Deadly, Mark, deadly. You know as well as I do that we don't stand a snowball's chance in hell of winning. The last intelligence we have puts the number of Jerrollite ships at three thousand. The most we can do is attempt to stall them and hope for a miracle. What's our current status?"

Mark swallowed hard before answering. "Well, the *Hercules* is basically one hundred percent. We've got a bit of fine-tuning left to do on the new engine, but it is operational. We lost several TAC-WING fighters in the last battle that have not been replaced, but the three wings still onboard have been completely refurbished and are ready to go."

"What about Earthside?"

"Nothing, sir. We were able to muster three additional cargo freighters and equip them with laser cannon, but that's it. The Jerrollites did a pretty efficient job of wiping out our military capability completely," said Mark, a grim expression on his face.

"That's just about what I thought. Not even a snowball's chance in hell," said Matheson.

Both men stood in a somber silence, mulling over their current predicament. It was hard to believe that their victory would be so short-lived. Both men jumped as a buzzer sounded over the intercom. Matheson slammed his fist down on the respond button, making no attempt to hide his irritation this time.

"WHAT?" he said.

"Sir, we are receiving a communication from outside the solar system."

Mark and General Matheson looked at each other in surprise.

"Where is it coming from?" asked Mark.

"I don't really know, sir. It would appear to be coming from the approaching fleet, but I can't really be sure. All I can tell is that it is definitely not originating from Earth."

"All right, we'll be right up. Matheson out." He quickly put on his uniform and headed for the bridge. Mark was right behind him.

As the two men burst onto the bridge, all the frenzied activity ceased. Matheson made his way to the center.

"Comm Officer, what's the status of the message?"

"They are still sending, sir. It would appear to be a loop of some kind. It appears they ar—" the ensign's eyes were as large as saucers as he turned toward the general.

"Sir! The message is in English! And they are talking about you!"

"On speakers," Matheson said.

Everyone on the bridge listened intently, not really knowing what to expect.

"Attention, Earth Command. This is the *Razer*, flagship of the Jerrollite empire. You are accused of the criminal act of rebellion against the empire. This rebellion was masterminded by one called Matheson. Because of his insurrection and your willingness to follow him, your world has been scheduled for termination. Sentence will be carried out immediately upon our arrival. *Razer* out."

The message began to repeat, droning out the death sentence of billions of people.

"Cut that thing off!" said Matheson. The ensign on the comm board scrambled to obey. Mark had never seen Matheson so upset. He was pacing the bridge, muttering to himself. Mark saw a dark resolve on his face as he came to a decision. Matheson stopped pacing and turned to the communications officer.

"Comm, open a channel to the *Razer*."

"Open, sir."

"Attention commander of *Razer*."

The general caught Mark's eye, and a twinkle shone in his own. A gravelly voice emanated from the speaker. Matheson addressed the alien commander.

"This is General Matheson of the *Hercules*. In response to your previous message," Matheson paused for dramatic effect, "go screw yourself!" After a moment of shock, nervous laughter filled the bridge. Motioning to the comm officer to cut the channel before the alien commander could reply, he pulled out his cigar, placed it in his mouth, and began chomping on it in a smug fashion. Mark grinned, amazed at the testosterone levels in the general's bloodstream.

"Mark, come with me," said Matheson. Turning to address the ship he said, "Continue preparations. We depart in forty-five minutes." He spun on his heel and headed for the planning room.

Matheson locked the door and sat down at the table. Mark eyed him carefully, not knowing exactly what the general was up to. Matheson signaled the comm officer.

"Patch in a channel to the president of Earth Command."

"Yes, sir."

The general continued to eye Mark while they were waiting for the call to go through. Neither man said anything. A soft chime signaled that the connection had been made.

"I heard your usual eloquence in your response, General."

"Thank you, Mr. President. I tried to present just the right amount of fear."

"An admirable job, Roy," said President Vorshauski.

"Thanks. Sir, I want to send Mark here on a little side trip in preparation for the upcoming battle. As you know, we can't stop the approaching Jerrollite forces with the ships at our disposal, so I want to send Mark to the Jerrollite home world and use the black hole generator on their planet."

"WHAT! We don't know what would happen if you set that thing loose on a body the size of a planet! You could destroy this whole sector of the galaxy!" said the president.

"I don't see that we really have any choice, Mr. President. The Jerrollites have told us they intend to destroy our planet. We have no way to stop this from occurring. What I propose is that we use the generator to hold their world hostage, sort of. We wouldn't have to use it unless they refused to call off their attack. At least then we would have a bargaining chip."

Mark spoke up. "General, this is really a moot point anyway. We don't have any type of ship that could possibly get there in time to prevent the attack."

The twinkle came back into the general's eye. "Oh, but that is where you're wrong, my boy. Not only do we have the technology to build such a ship, but it already exists in prototype form. Hyperspace drives were under development a long time before the Jerrollites got here. Just before the attack, I received a report informing me that the engine was complete and lacked only trial runs, and a pilot crazy enough to fly it!" Matheson said, a wry grin on his face. "A TAC-WING fighter has already been fitted with the new engine and is ready to go."

Mark's mind began to play out various scenarios, each one giving him a renewed hope that they just might be able to pull this off. "Just how fast is this ship, anyway?"

"It could reach the Jerrollite home world in less than three hours," said Matheson.

"WHAT! How come we haven't used this before now?" asked Mark.

The president responded. "The ship was completed just before the attack. There was no time to outfit our ships with the new engine, and only the single prototype exists. If it's destroyed, the technology will be lost. All the plans, as well as the original designer, were destroyed during the attack."

"I see. Is the prototype operational?" asked Mark.

"Yes, it is. We can have it on board and ready to go in as little as thirty minutes. Are you willing to fly it?" said Matheson.

With no hesitation whatsoever, Mark replied. "Yes."

"Very well. General Matheson, you may proceed with my full authorization to do whatever you must in order to defend this planet. Keep me informed. Good luck, Mark. Out."

"Well, I guess we had better get busy," said Matheson. As the general outlined his plan, the kamikaze nature of this mission hit home.

"I don't have a very good chance of getting back, do I?" Mark asked.

"In all honesty, I can't say. It depends on how close you have to get to their planet. All I can say for sure is that this is our only shot. If it fails, Earth will fall."

Mark considered the alternative. He would rather go down fighting than just sit passively by, waiting to be destroyed. Stiffening his back, he responded. "I'm ready, General."

"Excellent. I knew I could count on you, Mark." The general placed his hand on Mark's shoulder. "We still have a lot of preparations to make before you can depart, so the sooner we get started, the better." The ship's intercom sounded as they were preparing to leave the room.

"Sir, the new ship has just arrived in Bay Twelve."

"Thank you," said the general. Turning to Mark, he made an after you motion with his hand as they both left the planning room, heading for Bay Twelve.

CHAPTER 23

As the two men entered Bay Twelve, crews were swarming all over the new TAC-WING that had just arrived. Its basic shape was much the same as before, with the curious inclusion of a small, bubble-shaped extension on the underside of the nose.

"That's an odd-looking modification," said Mark.

"That, my boy, is the hyperspace field generator. When that baby kicks in, you'll be goin' faster than a teenager with a new hot rod! It generates a field around the ship that in effect creates a tunnel that you go through to get from Point A to Point B. Pretty weird effect, from what I hear."

"Yeah, that's what I'm worried about," Mark said, running his hands over the curves of the ship, admiring its simplicity and deadly nature. The fate of the human race rested on this little ship performing well.

"This thing has been through the simulator thousands of times, Mark. Everything checks out. Anyway, if anything goes wrong, you won't ever know it," said Matheson.

"What do you mean by that?" Mark asked, nervous.

"Well, the containment field for the hyperspace field is not one hundred percent effective, so we had to build an auxiliary shield into the armor surrounding the cockpit. Because of the extra shielding, you'll be flying blind."

"What!? Oh my god. You mean I gotta fly this thing without being able to see where I'm going?"

"Yeah, pretty much. Along with the new shielding, we installed a tracking computer, so you will have a fairly realistic representation of your surroundings on your screen. Just like flying in the simulator back home!" Matheson clapped Mark on the back. Attempting to calm Mark's nerves, he said, "Maybe you could just use the Force…" Mark scowled at him through slit eyes.

"Why don't you hop in, and I'll show you the new controls." They walked over to the crew chief servicing the craft.

"Chief, let Mark get into the cockpit and see what's going on up there."

"Yes, sir," he said, stepping aside as Mark climbed into the cockpit of the fighter. Sliding down into the pilot's seat, Mark was at once familiar with the controls.

"Put your helmet on," Matheson said.

Mark reached behind him and slipped the helmet onto his head. Engaging the safety before activating it, he powered up the system and was startled by the display that came up. What he saw in front of him was a grid, with his current location mapped out and marked by a flashing dot.

"What is this?" he asked.

"That's the hyperspace grid display. Everything is tied in to the helmet. Basically, if you think of where you want to go, the computer will plot the proper course through hyperspace for you. Try it!" he said.

Mark thought of the Jerrollite home world, and after a brief delay, a set of coordinates came up on the screen next to a new dot with a connecting line drawn between them.

"There you are! All laid out and ready to go," the chief said proudly.

"I must admit I'm impressed with the navigational capabilities, but I'm still more than a little nervous about taking this thing out on its virgin run," Mark said.

"Well, I figured you might feel that way, so I took the liberty of asking Johann to join you. Here he comes now," Matheson said.

Johann entered the bay. "Hey, boys! We ready to rock or what?"

"I'm glad you're going, Johann." Turning to Matheson, Mark said, "When do we leave?"

"As soon as you both get suited up and ready to go—say, fifteen minutes or so."

"Mon, you don' give a body much time, do ya?" said Johann.

"Time enough when you both get back. We don't have enough time to install the singularity generator as a weapon on the ship, so we're going to load it into the cargo module. You're going to have to find a spot on one of their moons to set it up. Once you get there and get set up, you contact me here on the *Hercules*, and I will give you instructions at that time. If for some reason you can't reach me, you have full authority to use the weapon as you see fit. Good luck to both of you. Launch is in fifteen minutes." Matheson turned and headed back toward the bridge.

Mark and Johann left to don their flight gear as the generator was being rolled into the bay. Technicians loaded it into the cargo module of the fighter along with all the support equipment required to operate it. Once all the equipment was secure and the ship was ready to go, the crew chief took a moment to draw an image of a thunderbolt cracking a planet into two pieces, along with the words Jerrollite Enema on the nose of the ship. The chief smiled grimly at his artwork.

"Hey, Chief," someone said from behind him. The chief turned to see every member of his crew standing there. The man who had spoken to him took the marker from his hand and placed his name beneath the image. Each member of the crew stepped forward and signed it with a flourish, declaring the ship ready for the fight.

Mark and Johann put on their pressure suits and prepared for the upcoming flight. "Not really sure what to expect," said Mark.

"I know. Do you fully comprehend what they are asking us to do?" said Johann.

"Yeah. Yeah, I do. They basically want us to commit genocide on the Jerrollites," said Mark. The gravity of that statement hit Johann hard. He had known all along, but hearing it said out loud really brought it home.

"I hope I can do it when the time comes," said Johann.

Mark paused for a moment, turning to face him directly. "Johann, it's a tough burden, I know, but it really is our only hope. They are coming to destroy this planet, and we have no way to stop them. We can only hope that the fear of losing their own home will prevent them from committing genocide on us."

Johann hung his head and considered Mark's words. Raising his head, he looked intently into Mark's eyes and said, "I'm good. Let's do this." Mark and Johann emerged from the locker room in full pressure suits and flight gear and headed toward the waiting fighter.

"Mon, this stuff is heavy!" said Johann.

"Tell me about it, buddy," said Mark as he hoisted himself up into the cockpit of the new fighter. Johann climbed into the secondary seat, located behind and above the pilot.

Both men slipped the signal cables into their suits to activate the systems on the spacecraft. Because they were in full pressure gear, it would be necessary to use the helmets built into the suits instead of the one aboard the fighter. These helmets were specially designed to monitor the electrical activity of the pilot's brain, using that to derive the requested actions and take them as appropriate. Flight crews leaned into the cockpit, checking each connection to their suits and making sure everything was secure and showing green.

Once everything checked out properly, the crew chief patted each of them on the helmet and made a thumbs-up sign. Mark and Johann both responded with a thumbs-up in turn. As the cockpit cover slid into place, all the lights and sounds of the busy landing bay were blocked out—both men sat in total darkness. Overcome with a sudden sense of claustrophobia, Mark was relieved when the control panels in the cockpit sprang to life, illuminating the interior of the fighter. Mark checked his communications with Johann.

"How you doin' back there, Johann?"

"It's like sittin' in your momma's womb back here. I hope you know how to fly this thing."

"I thought you had the instruction manual!" said Mark. Johann stared blankly at him, pausing for a moment before realizing he was being teased. They shared a laugh.

"Don't worry about me; just make sure you understand how to handle that generator in the back!"

"Got the instructions right here!" said Johann, waving a sheaf of papers where Mark could see them. Both men again shared a nervous laugh. The radio crackled.

"Mark, this is General Matheson. Are your communications okay?"

"Fine, sir. We're ready to go."

"All right, stand by for launch on my signal. Flight Control, clear the bay."

Mark could hear the muffled warning klaxon going off in the bay, signaling the imminent launch of a fighter. Crews scrambled to clear a path so the fighter could be lifted onto the launch rails. Both men felt a jolt as a crane lifted the ship and placed it gently onto the rails. After a few seconds, the radio resumed its prelaunch chatter.

"The bay is clear. Opening outer doors."

The adrenaline began to surge through Mark's veins in anticipation.

"Very well, Flight Control. Mark, ten seconds to launch on my mark. Ready…mark!" the flight control officer announced over the radio.

The countdown proceeded as Mark and Johann watched the seconds tick by on the cockpit clock.

"Ten…nine…eight…seven…six…five…four…three…two…one…LAUNCH!"

The engines ignited, slamming both men deep into their seats as the fighter roared down the launch rails, headed for open space. Mark fought through the pressure of nine g's. Just as he felt he would black out, the fighter broke free of the gravitational field. Weightlessness took over. He throttled back the main engines and looked over his shoulder at Johann, who had remained silent during the entire launch procedure.

"How you doin' back there?" Mark asked.

Johann looked at him as a huge grin spread across his face. "I ahm doin' quite whell. Can we do dat again?"

Mark laughed out loud. "Maybe later, my friend. If we survive." He contacted the bridge. "*Hercules*, this is TAC-WING One. See you as soon as we can. Wish us luck!" Mark visualized the Jerrollite star system, and instantly a plotted course popped up on his display.

"Here we go, Johann! Hang on!"

With Mark's single thought, the hyperspace field activated and enveloped the small fighter, blasting it through a void never before traveled by man or machine.

On the bridge of the *Hercules*, the crew watched as the tiny ship disappeared in a brilliant burst of light, carrying with it the hopes of the human race.

CHAPTER 24

The ships of Earth's decimated fleet were assembling in orbit—three battleships and a handful of troop transport ships outfitted with as many weapons as possible during the short period of time they had to prepare. The *Hercules* was by far the largest and most battle-ready ship in the entire armada.

On the bridge Matheson stood in front of his view screen and surveyed his resources for battle. The grim expression on his face revealed his inner thoughts regarding their chances of surviving the coming battle, much less stopping the onslaught. It would be up to the *Hercules* to take on all offensive actions; the other ships would act in supporting roles. A report from his logistics officer interrupted his thoughts.

"All ships have reported in, sir."

"Understood," Matheson said. You've got to be kidding me. This is impossible, he thought.

Shaking his head in disbelief, he gave the order to move out. One by one, with the *Hercules* in the lead, the ships began to lumber out of Earth's orbit, heading toward a rendezvous with certain death.

"Helm, plot an intercept course for the Jerrollite fleet and relay it to all the other ships."

"Aye, sir," the helmsman said.

"Incoming message from Earth Command, sir," said the comm officer.

"Put it on screen."

The image of the stars was immediately replaced with that of the president of Earth Command. "I have some supplementary data on the Jerrollite fleet for you, General. Long-range scans are detecting a massive amount of energy being beamed out of the Jerrollite star system toward their fleet."

"Some type of weapon?" Matheson asked.

"Our men don't think so, General. It appears to be a power link with their ships. We can't detect any self-contained power sources aboard the approaching ships. The labs here theorize that the Jerrollites are actually powering their ships from the home planet using their version of a Tesla coil."

"Are you telling me they can actually transmit power through space?"

"Yes, it would appear so. Our guys here also tell me that there is no way such a transmitter could actually be located on the planet's surface. The residual radiation would be enough to kill even Jerrollites. So we think it's probably located on either a moon or perhaps an orbiting platform of some kind."

The wheels of Matheson's mind began to turn. For the first time since he had received the message informing him of the imminent attack, he could detect a thin sliver of hope shining in the cloud of despair surrounding him.

"If we could knock out their power source, their ships would be dead in space, right?" Matheson asked.

"We concur with that theory, yes," said the president.

"Then instead of attacking their home world, we should use the singularity generator to destroy their power station! That will leave their ships powerless and just might provide us with a reasonable chance of getting home alive!"

The president picked up on Matheson's line of thought, growing more excited by the moment. "Excellent idea, General. Work out the details and implement the change in plans immediately. I will contact you if any more information becomes available."

"Thank you for the update, sir. I will contact Mark and inform him of the plan. *Hercules* out." As much as Matheson hated the Jerrollites, he was relieved at the possibility of not having to destroy the entire race.

The view screen blanked momentarily and then returned to a view of the stars.

"Comm, contact TAC-WING One immediately."

"We can't, sir; the hyperspace field blocks all transmissions. We can't talk to them until they come out."

Matheson clenched his jaw in frustration as his mind quickly ran over all the possibilities.

"Very well, monitor his progress, and the second his ship comes out of hyperspace, I want you to transmit this message as a top priority." He tapped out the message on a keyboard. "Understand?"

"Yes, sir!"

"I want you to handle it personally. Notify me as soon as the transmission is made."

"Aye, sir. Message is ready to transmit; standing by."

The monitor that showed TAC-WING One glowed red, indicating that the ship was still in hyperspace. When the fighter emerged from the field, the monitor would glow green, and communications would be possible. Matheson could only hope and pray that they could hold out long enough to survive.

"Flank speed, Helm. Now."

"Aye, sir."

The engines of the *Hercules* flared briefly as it moved out and began to gain speed. The other ships in the fleet took their cue and increased their speed to match it.

"Time to intercept?"

"Two hours, nine minutes, sir."

"Notify me when we are fifteen minutes from intercept. I'll be in my cabin." Matheson stood and left the bridge.

In his cabin he sat at his desk and poured himself a glass of his best rotgut whiskey, but he could not bring himself to drink it, even though there was a very real possibility that this would be the last time he would ever have the opportunity to do so. Instead he sat in his cabin and reflected on his life, the paths he had taken as well as the ones he had left behind. There had been a woman once, but that relationship had failed. His first love was the military, and nothing else could stand in the way of that. Sometimes it was a lonely life, but he was doing what he loved, and most people could never say that. He laid his head down on his desk, closing his eyes, allowing the sounds of the ship—no, *his* ship—to calm his senses. His brain gradually relaxed as the soft song of the stars lulled him into a gentle sleep.

His dreams were interrupted by a soft chime from the intercom. Groggily he reached over and tapped the respond button. "Yes?"

"We are fifteen minutes from the Jerrollite fleet, sir."

He was instantly alert. "Very well. All hands to battle stations!" he said. Alert sirens began sounding the call to battle all over the ship.

Running his hand through his hair, he stood and straightened his uniform, placed his stogie in his mouth, and looked at himself in the mirror. "You are one mean-lookin' muther, boy. Time to go kick some Jerrollite ass!" Adrenaline pumping, Matheson made his way to the bridge.

When the doors to the bridge slid open, the comm officer greeted him with a welcome message.

"I just finished transmitting the message to TAC-WING One, sir. Colonel Hunter acknowledged and said he understood. He informs that he is still about an hour away from his target."

Matheson acknowledged the comm officer's report with a nod. He made his way to the center of the bridge. "Comm, patch me in with all the other ships in our fleet on a secure channel."

After a brief moment, the young officer said, "You're on, sir."

"Okay, Commanders, this is it. The main objective today is one of delay. If we can delay this fleet long enough, we can buy Colonel Hunter the time he needs to complete his mission. Our attack will concentrate on their flagship, *Razer*. Do not attempt to engage any other ships on an individual basis. We will attack the flagship in unison, in close proximity. That should keep the other ships from firing at us for the time being for fear of hitting their own flagship. Any questions?" Several negative replies came back. "Excellent. All ships implement attack formation now and open fire only on my command. Matheson out." The general walked over and stood behind his helmsman.

"Scan the approaching fleet and find the largest ship. That should be the *Razer*."

"Scanning…Found it, sir. Course locked in."

"Relay the coordinates to the other ships and implement course change now."

The *Hercules* made a minor course correction that would bring it into a direct collision course with the approaching Jerrollite flagship. The other captains made the same corrections until each ship was oriented directly toward the *Razer*. The group of ships together formed an arrowhead, aimed straight for the heart of the approaching Jerrollite fleet.

Matheson chomped his cigar in nervous anticipation of the impending attack. Everyone was startled by a shrill beeping sound coming from the comm board.

"Sir, incoming message from the Jerrollites."

"On screen, Comm."

Once again the view of the star field was replaced, not by a human face, but instead by a blue-skinned alien. Matheson growled under his breath as the Jerrollite began to speak, surprisingly, in English.

"Math-eee-soon, do you come to surrender yourself? It is too late for that. You have broken our laws and must pay the price. After we destroy your pitiful ship and laughable fleet, we will destroy your planet as well."

"We're not here to surrender. You will cease and desist your militant behavior, or we will be forced to destroy you," Matheson said aggressively.

Gales of sneering laughter erupted from the screen. The contempt in the Jerrollite's face was evident. Glaring down, he spat on the floor of his ship.

"I'll take that as your answer, then. See you in hell," Matheson said.

The Jerrollite commander turned a deeper shade of blue as his eyes began to bulge out in rage. Matheson made a cutting motion to signal the end of the conversation. The comm officer severed the link. The Jerrollite's image was replaced by the alien fleet once again, looming large on the screen.

"Well, here goes nothin'," Matheson said, motioning the helm to proceed. He sat down heavily in his chair as once again the engines flared, pushing the *Hercules* headlong into the jaws of death.

CHAPTER 25

The tiny TAC-WING fighter shuddered violently as Mark ordered the hyperspace field to shut down. With a loud moan, the ship once again emerged into normal space. Checking the chronometer, he noticed that a little over three hours had passed in real time, but to him and Johann it seemed like only a few minutes. He switched on his intercom.

"Jo, are you okay?" Mark asked, turning around. Johann was holding his head in his hands, moaning softly. Mark asked again, more insistently. "Jo! Are you okay?" Johann looked up at Mark with a slightly glazed look in his eyes.

"Mon, I don' tink I ever felt anythin' like dat before!" he replied, shaking his head, attempting to regain his composure.

"Well, shake it out, man. We're coming up on the Jerrollite system in just a couple of minutes, and I want you at one hundred percent." Johann continued to shake his head, slowly reorienting himself to his surroundings.

"I'll be all right in a minute. Just turn around and drive!"

Mark chuckled and turned back around in his seat. As he scanned his boards, a flashing light alerted him to an incoming message from the *Hercules*. Wondering if anything had gone wrong, he reached over and activated his communications system. Voice transmission was not possible because of the great distances involved, but it was possible to send and receive data packets between systems. Mark fine-tuned his receiver, making sure that it was locked on to the carrier frequency being transmitted by the *Hercules*. The message was decoded and displayed on the screen. Mark scanned it and felt a sense of relief wash over him. He had been thinking about having to destroy an entire planet and did not relish the thought of killing billions of life-forms, even if they were Jerrollites.

While the fighter was still well out of range of any planetary sensing systems, Mark engaged the electronic countermeasures this TAC-WING was equipped with, effectively hiding his presence from anyone below. Running down a quick equipment checklist, Mark and Johann ran checks on all their weapons and support systems.

"Everything looks like it came through the hyperspace field okay," said Mark.

"My boards check out green," said Johann.

Mark chose not to notice that his friend had dropped his Jamaican accent, a sure sign that he was scared.

"Relax, Jo, we're gonna be fine."

"Yeah, yeah. I'll just feel a lot better when we can get the hell out of here," Johann said.

Mark and Johann engaged their scanners and began looking for the source of the power transmissions. The Jerrollite system had four moons, each approximately the same size as Earth's. They were spaced at equidistant positions around the equator of the planet. The planet itself was roughly twice the size of Earth, with about the same proportion of land to sea. The only noticeable difference was the brilliant blue haze that seemed to pervade the entire planet, making it look like a giant sapphire hanging in space. After a brief scan, the computer locked in on a massive power source on one of the moons. The display in Mark's visor lit up like a Christmas tree, pinpointing the position of the generators.

"My God! Look at the power coming from that moon, Johann! That has to be at least…what…over five million terawatts!"

Johann swallowed hard. He had never seen anything of that magnitude in his life. Even under the best of circumstances, nothing human could come close to producing that much power.

"Whatever you do, boy, make sure you don't cross that power beam!" Johann said nervously. "Let's set down on the moon straight across from the one with the generators...there!" He pointed to the moon nearest to them currently, which would give them a direct line of fire for the singularity generator. Mark keyed the landing sequence into his flight computer and began to descend to the surface, disregarding all the landing procedures that dictated a slow approach speed. He wanted to get his ship down before they were spotted by any passing patrols in the area. He nosed the TAC-WING into a dive straight toward the moon's cratered surface, causing Johann to gasp. Swinging in less than five hundred feet above the gray surface, they flew around the area, surveying the terrain for a suitably level spot on which to set the fighter down.

"I got a plain coming up at two seven mark four," said Johann from the back seat.

Mark could see the plain coming up over the horizon. It was level and relatively free of obstructions. "I see it. That looks like as good a place as any to set this thing up. Here we go."

Mark brought the ship down in a perfect spiral, ending up in the shadow of a large mountain next to the plain to avoid any possible visual detection. As the ship came to rest, a brief cloud of dust and debris spewed up but quickly settled as Mark and Johann shut down the ship's systems.

Both men sealed their pressure helmets and started the flow of oxygen into their suits. Mark turned to look at Johann and tapped the side of his helmet as an indication to turn his radio on. Johann responded by hitting the comm button on the sleeve of his suit.

"You there, Johann?"

"Ready, boy. I got green on my suit. Pressure is okay; I'm ready to pump down."

"Okay, here we go."

Mark activated the sequence that would pump the atmospheric pressure in the cabin down to zero so that they could open the hatch without losing any air from the ship. A soft hissing sound was all Mark and Johann could hear as a gauge on the panel indicated that the pressure was falling rapidly. As the needle on the gauge touched the bottom peg, a small light flashed red when the atmospheric pressure finally reached zero. Mark looked at Johann to make sure everything was okay. Johann looked back at him and gave a thumbs-up. Mark reached up and jerked the handle that would release the cockpit cover. At first the handle would not budge, but it finally gave way. The cover slid backward, exposing Mark and Johann to the hard vacuum of open space.

Even for a seasoned veteran, it was difficult not to be taken aback by the sight. Stars seemed to leap out of a coal-black night sky as the surface of the moon stood out in brilliant contrast to the blackness, reflecting back the light from the local sun.

"Man, I don't think I'll ever get used to this," Mark said breathlessly.

"I sure hope I never do. I think I'll retire if it ever happens," said Johann.

They climbed out of the ship and down to the surface. Using a handheld scanner, Mark took several preliminary readings from the surface.

"Surface temperature is approximately minus two hundred twenty-five degrees Fahrenheit. No oxygen or any other gases. Surface gravity is approximately point seven five Earth normal. Radiation levels are nominal." Folding the scanner back into its pouch, Mark replaced it in his pack. "We should be okay for a couple of hours. Let's get to work." The men went around to the rear of the ship to unload the generator.

Carefully lowering the equipment to the ground, they began the arduous task of setting it up. Mark constantly checked the surrounding area for any signs of detection, aware that if they were caught out in the open like they were now, they would be defenseless. The thought did not make Mark happy.

After working nonstop for over an hour, both men stood back and surveyed their handiwork. The generator was ready to fire as far as they could tell. They had no way of testing the weapon without attracting attention to themselves, so they hoped for the best. Johann punched the coordinates of the Jerrollite moon into the targeting computer and stepped back. The tracking system on the generator brought the nose up and aligned it precisely with the Jerrollite moon.

"Good job, Johann! Let's contact the general and see if he's ready for us to fire," said Mark.

"You go ahead; I have a couple more adjustments to make before we can actually fire this thing." Johann turned back to his work and began to go over all the connections on the generator, making sure they were tight and everything was hooked up correctly. Mark climbed back into the cockpit of the TAC-WING and attempted to establish communication with the *Hercules*. Powering up the system, he keyed in a recognition code and transmitted it. Almost immediately he received a response from the system aboard the *Hercules*. Typing in his message, he informed the general that everything was ready and once again hit the transmit button. The reply came back quickly.

"ENGAGING ENEMY FLEET AS WE SPEAK. PREPARE TO FIRE ON MY COMMAND!"

Mark sent back a quick acknowledgment and tied the shipboard communication system into their suit comms. He had to get outside again and inform Johann of the situation. Mark noticed a small vibration in the hull of the TAC-WING and assumed that Johann was coming up the access ladder. He grabbed the edge of the cockpit to hoist himself out. A blue face appeared over the edge of the cockpit, glaring at him.

The space-suited alien was brandishing a weapon in Mark's face, motioning him to get out of the cockpit. The alien backed down the ladder so Mark could follow, never failing to point its weapon in his direction. Weighing his options carefully, he decided that it would probably be best to go along with the alien for right now. They didn't have much time; the *Hercules* was engaged in a losing battle while they dealt with this situation. He climbed out of the cockpit slowly, under the constant prodding of the armed Jerrollite. Mark glanced over and saw that Johann had already been taken captive and was being held well away from the generator. Hoping that his captor could not monitor their frequency, Mark tried to talk to Johann, speaking softly and barely moving his lips.

"Jo! Can you hear me?" he said.

"Yeah, but every time this guard sees me say anything, it threatens me with its gun! Man, this really bites, don't it!"

"We don't have time for this. If we don't fire that generator soon, the *Hercules* is going to be destroyed! I tied the ship communications into our suits. Right now we are waiting on the order to fire. When the order comes, we will simply have to get to the generator and fire it."

The two men watched as the Jerrollite soldiers, afraid to touch the generator, attempted to ascertain its function. Several of them were standing around it, pointing and then gesticulating wildly. Mark surveyed the situation, looking for an avenue of escape or at least enough of a distraction to give him time to fire the generator.

He glanced at the chronometer on his wrist and grew more anxious. It had been over five minutes since the general had told him to prepare to fire. He could only hope and pray that the *Hercules* and the others could hold out long enough. He watched the Jerrollite soldiers closely, waiting for the opportune moment to strike. The clock continued to tick.

CHAPTER 26

The Jerrollite fleet rapidly grew closer as the *Hercules* bore down on it. General Matheson was busy barking orders to his bridge crew, getting them ready for the fight of their lives.

"Bring all weapons online, shields up to full strength."

"Weapons charged, sir; shields up and at one hundred percent."

"Comm, put me in contact with the other ships."

"Contact established, sir."

"Attention, commanders, this is General Matheson. Bring your ships in close to mine in a triangle formation. Once we engage the enemy, the *Hercules* will stay in front of the flagship while the rest of you break up and attack her from all sides at once. Any questions?" Only the soft hiss of a radio carrier wave answered. "Good. You may open fire as soon as we are in range. Good luck, Matheson out."

The comm officer cut the connection to the other ships. Matheson clenched his fist in frustration, knowing their situation was almost completely hopeless. They didn't stand a chance against the combined strength of the Jerrollite armada. Their only hope for survival lay with Mark and Johann.

"In range, sir," said the weapons officer.

"Open fire!" said Matheson, a deadly, sinister tone in his voice.

The nose of the *Hercules* erupted in a blaze of fire, energy beams lancing out toward the approaching Jerrollite ships. As the first beam struck the flagship, its energy was rapidly dissipated by its shields, casting a dull green glow over the combat scene. The *Hercules* slowed to a stop not more than five hundred meters in front of the ship, continually blasting away, delivering a pounding to the shields of the enemy ship. The other ships in the Earth fleet broke off from the main formation, taking up positions all around the Jerrollite flagship to form a gauntlet with the alien ship trapped inside. As each gun swiveled into position and began firing, the Jerrollite ship was almost obscured as her shields flared and began to buckle under the onslaught. The other ships in the Jerrollite fleet couldn't fire on the Earth ships without the risk of hitting their own flagship, so they simply sat by, waiting for the opportunity to strike. From the bridge of the *Hercules*, Matheson could sense an impending kill.

"Keep firing! They can't withstand that kind of barrage for very long!" he said.

Almost as if in response to Matheson's statement, the forward shield of the alien ship buckled, as a full-power weapons blast from the *Hercules* impacted its hull. At the alien ship's he hull began to disintegrate, Matheson was startled to see the intensity of the beam begin to waver.

"What's happening?"

"Sir! Weapons are beginning to overheat! We must stop firing, or they're going to melt down!" shouted the weapons officer.

"Cease fire! All wings, launch your fighters NOW! Provide cover for us while the weapons systems are cooling down!" ordered Matheson.

Abruptly the fire from the *Hercules* ceased, providing the Jerrollite ship with a brief respite. Before the Jerrollite commander could respond, giant columns of flame began spewing out of the *Hercules*'s port side as the TAC-WING fighters were launched into space. They began swarming all over the Jerrollite ship like angry hornets.

Recovering from the initial onslaught, the Jerrollite ship began firing back at the *Hercules*, each hit delivering a staggering blow. The very core of the *Hercules* resounded like a gong. Several of the TAC-WING fighters were unfortunate enough to intersect the beam path and disappeared in small puffs of flame.

Matheson could feel his victory beginning to slip away faster and faster with each hit they took. Fires began to break out all over the ship, and warning sirens wailed in the background.

"Get those weapons back online, NOW!" Matheson bellowed.

"Trying, sir. We should be back up in—"

A cry from the comm officer interrupted the report. Matheson turned in irritation.

"What is it?"

"A message just came in, sir. From Colonel Hunter. He is ready to fire and awaits your order."

"Tell him to stand by for my order," said Matheson.

"Sending the message, sir." A worried look crossed the comm officer's face. "No acknowledgment, General. And it appears that his transmitter has gone offline!"

The frustration showed in Matheson's face as he attempted to keep his anger in check. "Very well. Let's see how well our Jerrollite friends can play poker! Open a channel to the Jerrollite flagship, now!" said Matheson.

The communications officer scrambled to comply.

"Weapons systems have returned to nominal operation, sir!" said the weapons officer.

"Hold your fire! I guess we're going to have to do this ourselves." Turning to the comm officer, he said, "Keep trying to raise Colonel Hunter. Inform me immediately if you have any success. Order all ships to cease fire and hold their positions."

Every officer on the bridge turned and looked at Matheson, wondering if he had gone insane.

"Uh, y-yes, sir," the young officer said as he relayed the orders to the rest of the fleet. On the main view screen, Matheson could see the fire die out as each ship obeyed his order, still hovering close to the flagship's hull. An eerie silence fell over the bridge as the scene played itself out like an Old West gunfight with the two greatest fighters facing each other to the death.

"I have a channel open to the Jerrollite commander, sir," said the comm officer. Matheson inhaled deeply and prepared to play out his hand. He nodded curtly at the comm officer and began speaking.

"This is General Matheson from Central Earth Military Command, commander of the USS *Hercules*. With whom am I speaking?"

The view screen wavered momentarily, finally resolving into a distinct image of the blue-skinned enemy they had all been fighting for so long. His gaze was fierce as he scowled out of the view screen at Matheson. His speech was thick and slurred.

"This is Commander T'chlo. Why do you bother me? Do you wish perhaps to beg for your life?" The Jerrollite's face split open in a wicked grin as a rasping, harsh sound emerged from his thin lips that could only be the Jerrollite equivalent of a cruel laugh. Matheson steeled himself as he answered, suppressing the burning desire to smash his fist square into T'chlo's mouth.

"On the contrary, Commander. I am offering you a chance for life." The Jerrollite's grin faded abruptly, replaced by an incredulous stare. "Cease your attack now and return to your world, or we will destroy your planet. The choice is yours."

Every person on the bridge again looked toward Matheson, now sure that he had gone insane. Gales of rasping laughter again erupted from the view screen, although not as confidently as before. The commander was simply saving face now. Matheson stood there until the laughter subsided.

"You sniveling, weak coward! You have committed high crimes against our empire, and you would dare to threaten us!" said T'chlo. The Jerrollite's eyes were bulging out of his head as the veins on his forehead stood out and his face flushed to an even deeper shade of blue.

"I don't dare, T'chlo. I merely state facts. If you don't back off now, we will destroy your planet. I will give you one minute to decide." Removing a cigar from his pocket and lighting it, Matheson took a long pull and exhaled the smoke slowly,

At a signal from Matheson, the communications officer severed the link to the Jerrollite ship.

"Comm, have you raised Mark yet?"

"No, sir. His transmitter is still offline."

"Damn. Keep trying. Without his help, I don't think we're gonna make it out of this one."

As the clock ticked toward the deadline the general had set, the comm officer frantically tried to establish communication with Mark.

"Sir, incoming communication from the Jerrollite ship," the comm officer said.

Matheson recovered quickly from his surprise as he turned to face the view screen. The comm officer completed the connection, and once again the Jerrollite face appeared on the screen.

"Matheson, this is Commander T'chlo. I thought you just might be interested in seeing this," said the Jerrollite as he turned and gestured toward a crew member in the background. The image of the Jerrollite was replaced with a stark, barren view of some dead planet.

"This was just received from the home system, taken on one of the moons orbiting our planet," the commander said, providing a somber narration to the scene before them. Matheson could feel his heart sinking into the pit of his stomach as the view panned to the left—there, in all its glory, was the singularity generator, with several figures clad in pressure suits standing off to one side. Two of the figures were being held apart from the rest of the group with weapons trained on them.

"One of our regular patrols spotted your ship and apprehended the crew. Although I must admit that I am somewhat surprised by your ability to get as far as you did, as you can see, you are no longer a threat to contend with." Once again the Jerrollite commander erupted into a fit of laughter. When his rasping laugh subsided, he continued. "Because I am a generous being, I will grant you one hour in which to make your peace with whatever gods you worship. In one hour your ship will be destroyed. If you attempt to move your ship in any way, it will be destroyed immediately. You have one hour. T'chlo out."

The view screen snapped back to a dismal view of the Jerrollite flagship looming in front of them like the grim reaper waiting for a victim to die before claiming the soul. Matheson sat down heavily in his chair and placed his head in his hands.

"Damn it all to HELL! I can't believe this is happening," he said, finally allowing despair to set in. As he was indulging in a well-earned fit of self-pity, he felt a hand on his back. He raised his head to see the young comm officer nervously standing beside him.

"We don't want to go down without a final fight, sir," he said, while the other officers on the bridge nodded their agreement. "We want to go out like warriors, not like a bunch of whipped dogs waiting to be executed. If we have to die, we want it to be on our terms, not theirs."

Matheson looked around the bridge into the eyes of his crew. He saw a firm resolve just below the surface, with no fear present in any crew member. In each face he saw the millions of people who had perished in the Jerrollite attacks and knew without a doubt that every man and woman on his crew wanted the same thing—to go down fighting.

Matheson stood up and walked around the bridge, looking each crew member in the eye to see if he could detect any regrets, any dissenting opinions. He could find none. Turning from the last member, he walked back to the center of the bridge and clasped his hands behind his back, facing the view screen. His heart swelled with pride.

"All right, people. Let's show these bastards what we're made of!" Matheson said. With a cheer the bridge crew returned to their stations with renewed vigor. "Shields on full," said Matheson.

"Shields up, sir. Weapons systems are online and functioning at full capacity."

"Very good. Comm, open a channel to the Jerrollite ship."

"Channel open, sir."

Matheson waited until the Jerrollite commander came into view before beginning. When the commander was seated, he queried Matheson.

"It has only been twenty minutes since we last spoke. Are you that anxious to die?" T'chlo asked, the same evil grin splitting his face.

"We just received our orders from headquarters, T'chlo," said Matheson.

The Jerrollite commander cocked an inquisitive eyebrow and unconsciously leaned forward in his chair, waiting for Matheson's next comment.

"We are hereby ordered to...kick your blue ass all the way to the Orion Nebula! FIRE!" Matheson bellowed.

Cannon and weapons fire erupted in a massive blaze from all defense pods on the *Hercules* as they hurled brilliant bolts of energy at the Jerrollite ship, again almost totally obscuring it from view. The TAC-WING fighters, momentarily idle, leapt back into action, again buzzing all over the flagship. The Jerrollite ships surrounding the area launched several groups of their own single-man fighters in an attempt to combat the Earth forces.

The image of the Jerrollite commander once again appeared on the main view screen.

"Why do you do this? You cannot win!" he said.

"Learn a lesson about humanity, pig. We might not be able to win, but we sure as hell can take you out before we go!" said Matheson. The Jerrollite commander's eyes grew wide in fear as he realized that the Earth commander was not bluffing. His comments were lost as the alien ship's bridge erupted in flames before their eyes. The bridge crew on the *Hercules* cheered their momentary victory. The view screen faded to static and then snapped back to an external view.

The TAC-WING fighters were inflicting much more damage than Matheson would have thought possible. Fires were erupting into the vacuum of space as atmosphere spewed out from gaping holes in the hull of the ship. The alien ship seemed almost to wither under the onslaught of combined fire from every human ship in the area. As Matheson was almost beginning to believe they might really be able to take out the Jerrollite ship, one of his officers screamed out a report.

"sir! The rest of the Jerrollite fleet is moving in to attack! Opening fire now!"

Wham! Before Matheson could even brace himself, the first beam struck from the attacking ships. The bridge exploded around him as debris went flying in all directions. Matheson himself was sent flying across the bridge to land in a pile of rubble directly underneath the view screen. The hammering that the *Hercules* was receiving at the hands of the Jerrollites was relentless.

"Concentrate all fire on the flagship! Ignore all other ships!" said Matheson to the young comm officer. Matheson looked up as he said it, only to realize that the officer was dead. He made his way over to him through what was left of the bridge. A large piece of metal had embedded itself in the man's skull, leaving his brain exposed. Suppressing a gag, Matheson gently lifted the body away from the communications console so he could relay his instructions to the rest of his ships.

As he watched, shields all over the Jerrollite flagship began to buckle under the continuous onslaught, finally failing completely. The deck beneath his feet bucked as the *Hercules* continued to take a pounding from the other Jerrollite ships as they increased the intensity of their attack, sensing that their flagship was in trouble. Matheson's teeth were rattling in his head as he fought to maintain his balance, keeping his eyes glued to the view screen. He glanced over at his weapons officer in time to see him launch several volleys of torpedoes toward the flagship in a final, desperate attempt to overwhelm the *Razer*'s defenses.

Looking again at the view screen, Matheson could see the torpedoes as bright pinpoints of light lancing through space toward the heart of the *Razer*. As the torpedoes reached their target, carrying with them the hopes of the *Hercules*'s crew, time seemed to stand still. Matheson and everyone on the bridge held their breath, waiting to see what would happen.

A blinding flash lit the view screen. Matheson winced at the brightness, forcing himself to keep looking at it so he could tell what was happening. As the flash faded, he was surprised and pleased to see the *Razer* listing to port, several gaping holes blown in its side. Several minor explosions continued to dance up and down the length of the hull, building in intensity. Suddenly a final, devastating fireball consumed the entire ship, ripping it apart and sending huge pieces of molten metal and Jerrollite bodies in all directions.

A debris cloud was all that remained of the *Razer*. Matheson blinked a couple of times, unable to believe what had just happened. Cheering broke out from the remaining crew on the bridge. His entire crew were rejoicing in the fact that they had exacted revenge for their loved ones who had been lost. Matheson smiled grimly to himself, satisfied at least that T'chlo would no longer be gloating at their expense.

He was startled out of his reverie as the *Hercules* was rocked by a renewed barrage from the rest of the Jerrollite ships. He ordered a channel opened to the other ships in his fleet.

"Commanders, break formation and attack one-on-one. All we can do now is try to stay alive long enough for Mark and Johann to do their jobs. Good luck!" He severed the link with an air of finality. He held no illusions about their chances.

Matheson moved to the communications console and typed in the order for Mark and Johann to fire the weapon immediately. His finger came down hard on the transmit button. He could only hope that they had been able to extricate themselves from the Jerrollites holding them captive. All he could do now was wait and try to survive.

After issuing the order, Matheson noticed that the link to Mark's transmitter was still open. As he reached for the button that would repeat the message telling him to fire the generator, another explosion ripped through the bridge, spraying white-hot chunks of metal through the air. Matheson was struck in the back by a three-foot steel support rod. Penetrating his body like a spear, the rod shattered bone and ripped muscle, continuing until it protruded from the front of his uniform, dripping with blood. Stunned momentarily, he was in too much shock to realize what had happened.

"Damn," he said, wincing at the burning pain in his chest, coughing spasmodically. He reached again for the button to send his message to Mark, but it was just out of his reach. Frustrated, he lunged forward. His hand came down on the button firmly, transmitting the message once again. A green light flashed in acknowledgment. Matheson grimaced in pain as he took a last breath of the acrid, smoke-filled air, hoping against hope that Mark and Johann would find a way to fire the generator as his world faded into deep black.

CHAPTER 27

Mark was beginning to sweat inside his pressure suit, even though the internal temperature was maintained at sixty-five degrees Fahrenheit. Beads of sweat trickled down the side of his face as he stood at the end of a weapon held by an alien soldier who looked like he would rather vaporize both of them than be bothered guarding them. The only reason both men were still alive was that the Jerrollite had been unable to determine the exact nature of the generator. Mark realized that if they did not fire the singularity generator soon, the *Hercules*, along with the entire Earth fleet, would be destroyed. That was a possibility that Mark did not want to even consider. He resolved to fire the weapon, no matter what.

Their captors continually circled the elaborate piece of hardware, gingerly touching it every now and then using some sort of sensing equipment to try to figure out its composition and purpose. It was clear from the angry motions Mark could see the Jerrollite commander making that their attempts to understand the weapon had been frustrated so far. Technical analysis failing, one of them had even gone so far as to taunt Mark and Johann, pointing at the generator and laughing.

"Man, I wish I could fire that thing. He wouldn't be laughing for very long," said Johann.

"Stay cool, Jo. We've got to think of something to create a diversion so that we can fire it. Got any ideas?" he asked, turning his head toward his friend.

The look of desperation in Johann's eyes told Mark everything he needed to know. There were at least ten Jerrollites between them and the generator, each of them armed and looking mad. The situation was not very bright from Mark's point of view.

"Johann, one of us is going to have to create a diversion so the other can have at least a chance of getting to the generator. Are you with me?" Johann's eyes were round with apprehension but filled with resolve as he nodded his head in the affirmative. "Okay, get ready."

Mark fell to the ground and began to writhe spastically, tugging at his restraints, making gagging faces. Their guard refused to budge, instead holding his weapon on both men, ready to shoot if either of them tried anything. The Jerrollite commander came running over to see what was going on. As the aliens gathered around Mark, the guard became distracted by the commotion and turned his back on Johann, who seized the opportunity to begin quietly inching toward the fire control panel next to the generator. As he stretched out his hand toward the lever that would fire it, he could hear Mark over his intercom radio, still screaming and creating a diversion. With a suddenness that almost took him unaware, the screaming stopped and a very clear statement came over his earpiece.

"JOHANN! WATCH OUT!"

Johann whipped his head around just in time to see a Jerrollite level an energy weapon at him and open fire. He jerked back as the beam narrowly missed his outstretched hand, scorching the ground where it had been. Scrambling up from his crouched position, he lunged toward the fire control as the Jerrollite fired again. This time the beam did not miss its mark and burned a hole in the lower back of Johann's suit, passing through his body and out the front. Johann stared in horror as he watched his blood trickle out of the hole in large globs, floating slowly toward the moon's surface. He slapped his hand over the hole in his suit in an instinctive but futile effort to stop the escaping air. As the pressure in his suit fell toward zero, his consciousness faded, and his body doubled over in pain and fell toward the generator. As he hit the ground, his body jerked spasmodically and came to rest only inches from the firing control.

Mark stared wide-eyed in disbelief. A rage overcame him. He leapt from the ground and dove toward the Jerrollite that had just gunned down Johann, reaching him before he could react.

Mark caught the alien full in the midsection. The weapon flew to one side as both of them went down thrashing. Mark's hand closed on the air feed into the Jerrollite's suit. He grasped it firmly, pulling the alien's helmet around to where he could see the evil blue face as it died. Mark yanked the tube free from its socket, causing a plume of atmosphere to leak out. Even as the atmosphere crystallized and began to fall, the Jerrollite writhed in agony as the pressure inside his body began to press outward. His face turned a shade of blue that Mark had never seen before, just before it burst inside the helmet, smearing a blue liquid all over the inside of the visor.

Mark staggered back in surprise and was immediately kicked in the midsection by one of the other Jerrollite guards. He rolled with the kick, absorbing the impact and using its momentum to carry him away from the rest of the guards. He landed on something hard—one of the energy weapons the Jerrollites were using. Unable to believe his good fortune, he snatched it up as he rolled, bringing himself up to one knee and firing a sustained burst into the crowd of onrushing attackers. Three of the Jerrollites fell dead instantly, the unfortunate recipients of the brunt of Mark's attack. All three had large holes burned into their torsos. The others began to flee as Mark continued to fire, picking them off one by one. They attempted to return fire but were immediately cut down by blasts from Mark's gun. As the last Jerrollite fell, the alien weapon sputtered, its energy supply exhausted.

Mark stumbled in exhaustion, falling to his knees and letting the spent alien weapon drop from his grasp. His body was shaking from the surge of adrenaline. His rage slowly subsided, and he surveyed the scene before him.

All around lay dead Jerrollites. The generator was still waiting patiently to be fired, oblivious to the battle that had just been fought. Mark's eyes fell on the crumpled form of Johann at the base of the generator. He staggered over to the TAC-WING to check his communication board. The screen was lit up with a single word: *Fire!* Mark slammed his hand down on the acknowledge button and slid back down the ladder. He moved as fast as he could toward the generator, stumbling on a small rock and landing in a heap next to Johann's body. The bloody form of his friend filled him with the resolve he needed to continue. Pulling himself up, he staggered over to the fire control panel and placed his hand on the firing lever. Looking up once again at the Jerrollite moon, Mark gritted his teeth and slammed the lever home.

He heard an ominous crackle over his headset as the generator built up a charge. He bent over and grabbed Johann's suit, dragging him to a sheltered spot behind a large rock. He ducked down, sheltering Johann's body with his own. As the charge in the generator reached its peak, a brilliant blue burst of energy erupted from the tip, bolting across the intervening space and striking the distant Jerrollite moon dead center.

A blinding flash of light occurred when the beam struck the moon, causing a microscopic black hole to form deep in its core. Mark watched as the surface seemed to shudder and then began to collapse in on itself. The brilliant blue beam disappeared, and the tiny black hole dissipated. The process that had begun was irreversible, and as Mark watched, the moon collapsed in on itself. A blinding flash of plasma energy was hurled from the center of the event and traveled outward rapidly, creating a stunning halo effect around the entire area. The mass of the moon was compressed more and more until it reached a critical stage. It exploded once again, sending huge chunks of rock and debris hurtling toward the planet below.

With a final thunderous roar, the moon collapsed completely, at the same time creating a massive electromagnetic pulse that discharged along the path of the power beam feeding the Jerrollite home world and all of their ships. The pulse was visible: a massive red and gold dart of fire, lancing its way across space.

Part of the pulse impacted the Jerrollite home world. The surface of the planet erupted into a hellish, fiery scene of death and destruction. The power packs on the suits of the dead Jerrollites around him exploded as the feedback from the pulse struck their ship and was in turn relayed to their suits. Across the plain Mark saw the Jerrollite patrol ship ripped into small fragments by the force of the explosion. The feedback into the alien systems was simply too much for them to handle, and each was overpowered by the pulse and promptly exploded or was made useless by the shock. The surface of the Jerrollite home world seemed to erupt into a massive blaze that quickly spread and consumed everything in its path. Mark felt a grim satisfaction that they had been able to avenge their loved ones at home. He hadn't wanted to become the instrument of destruction for the Jerrollite race, but he had had no choice. It had been do or die.

A stirring beneath him caused him to look down. Johann was looking up at him, grinning from ear to ear.

"I thought you were dead!" exclaimed Mark. "I saw your suit get punctured when that blue devil shot you!"

"Doon't ya know, boy, that ya can't keep a good mon down?"

"How did you survive decompression?"

"Our suits are equipped with emergency pressure bands that seal off different parts of the suit whenever pressure is lost. When I was hit, the bands constricted and probably saved my life. But man, am I gonna have sore ribs when we get home!" Johann laughed again but broke into a fit of coughing that made Mark doubt his ability to make it back to the *Hercules*.

"C'mon, Jo. Let me help you back to the ship."

"What about dem Jerrollites, boy?" Johann asked nervously.

Mark grinned as he answered. "I don't think you'll have to worry about them anymore." He looked up meaningfully at the Jerrollite planet. Johann followed his gaze and was startled by the scene. Blue fingers of fire continued to dance all over the surface of the planet, causing colossal firestorms that could be seen even from their vantage point.

As both men watched, the largest piece of what had been the Jerrollite moon struck the surface of the planet, sending ripples of tectonic energy through the crust and shaking it to its core. They could only wonder at the amount of destruction the resulting quakes were going to cause.

Johann continued to stare open-mouthed as he reached up and placed his arm around Mark's shoulders.

He let Mark support his weight as they hobbled to their TAC-WING fighter. Brilliant flashes and explosions continued on the surface of the planet as the feedback from the pulse wrought havoc on the Jerrollite home world. As both men watched the scene unfolding on the planet below, they came to the same realization at once.

"If that pulse hit the Jerrollite fleet while the *Hercules* was in close proximity…" Mark didn't have to finish his thought. He eased Johann to the ground and tore down the generator as quickly as he could. After storing the equipment in its compartment on the TAC-WING, Mark returned to Johann and helped him up.

"Let's go, buddy," said Mark, grunting as Johann shifted his weight onto Mark's shoulder. They scrambled into the TAC-WING and quickly strapped themselves in. A worried look crossed Johann's brow as he gripped Mark by the shoulder.

"Mark, there is no way we can make it back in time. You've got to use the radio. It's our only chance."

"You're right. I hope they're listening for us."

Mark keyed in an urgent message describing the situation with the pulse and the danger the *Hercules* was facing and pressed the transmit button. A green acknowledge light flashed on his panel.

"Well, that's that. I sure hope they get it, or we won't have anything to go home to," said Mark.

"Let's get the hell out of here," said Johann.

"You got it."

The engines of the TAC-WING roared to life, and the small fighter rose from the surface of the moon. Mark nudged the craft forward, arcing across the surface in a low-altitude pass. Kicking in his turbo thrusters, he executed a perfect barrel roll as the Jerrollite home world faded from view. He keyed his transmitter again and again, trying to get a response from the *Hercules* by the sheer force of his will.

"Relax, Mark, there's nothing else to do," said Johann.

"Yeah, I know," Mark said, not wanting to accept Johann's statement but knowing it was true.

As the TAC-WING climbed out of the Jerrollite system, Mark activated the hyperspace field generator, and the small fighter disappeared out of normal space, leaving behind a burning world with three moons and a glowing red cloud where a fourth moon had once been.

CHAPTER 28

Matheson raised his head, the dull pounding inside providing a constant reminder that he was still alive. Looking down, he noticed that his uniform was caked with blood. Confused as to why he was bleeding, he realized he was suffering the symptoms of shock. He couldn't remember why until he tried to move his arm. A searing pain shot through his body. He gasped as his arm touched the metal rod protruding from his chest.

Grasping the steel rod, Matheson realized that the shaft was sticky with his own blood. To hell with it, he decided and braced himself. Clenching his teeth, Matheson mustered his courage and pulled. Waves of searing pain washed over him, bringing him to the brink of unconsciousness. The rod slid smoothly out of his body. He let it fall to the deck with a loud clang. Gasping from the intense pain, he placed a hand over the hole in his chest and called for a medic, as he expected to bleed out and die. His world was fading to black very quickly.

His ship was continuing to take a beating as the Jerrollite ships sensed that the end of the battle was near.

The *Hercules* shuddered under the continuous onslaught of enemy fire. Sirens were blaring all over the bridge as system after system either failed completely or was on the verge of doing so. Matheson fought back the waves of pain and nausea that threatened to overwhelm him and looked around the bridge. He assessed the damage and found it difficult to believe that the *Hercules* had not disintegrated or been blown to bits by now. The ship had been severely abused and would not last much longer.

Despair reared its ugly head as he realized they were not going to make it. It was a shame to have come this far, only to end up being defeated by the Jerrollites. Beating back his desperation, Matheson stood up and staggered back to his command chair. With each impact of an enemy weapon, he almost lost his footing, bracing himself against consoles until he was finally able to collapse into his chair. He felt weak and dizzy from the loss of blood. He looked down at his wound, and somewhere in the far reaches of his mind he realized he was bleeding to death. He turned over in his mind the events of the last few months, wondering if there was anything else that could have been done to win the fight.

"Medic…" he said weakly. A young corpsman burst onto the bridge and sprinted to the general.

"I got here as fast as I could, sir," he said, pulling Matheson's hands away from his wound. A worried expression traversed the young man's face as he opened his emergency medical bag and retrieved a bag of hemostatic blood-clotting agent. The medic poured this over Matheson's wound and applied pressure.

"Doesn't look too—" Matheson was interrupted by a racking cough that made his entire body convulse in pain, "good, does it?"

"No, sir, it sure does not. You're going to need a surgeon to fix you up good 'n' proper. Here, hold this," he said, placing a cotton bandage in Matheson's hand and gently pressing it into the wound. Matheson grimaced in pain as the bandage touched the exposed flesh.

"Sorry 'bout the pain, General. I put medicine on the pad to keep any infection from setting in."

Matheson squeezed his eyes shut as the corpsman raised his shirt and placed a large gauze bandage over the entry and exit wounds to prevent the lung from collapsing. He tightly wrapped gauze around the general's chest to hold both bandages in place and keep the wound sealed.

"Okay, sir. You seem to be breathing okay, and those bandages will hold until we get you down to medical." He motioned for one of the other crew members to help him lift the general out of the chair.

Matheson looked up at the corpsman and put his hand on the young man's shoulder. "Hold it, son. I'm not leaving the bridge." The corpsman hesitated only for a moment before waving off the other people he had summoned.

"It's against my better judgment, but I understand, sir. Just sit still and get down to medical as soon as possible." He placed his hand on Matheson's shoulder. "Okay?" he asked, looking Matheson squarely in the eyes.

"You got it."

With a curt nod, the corpsman moved off to attend to the other wounded on the bridge.

"Get that damn view screen working!" said Matheson. Other crew members on the bridge breathed a sigh of relief as Matheson once again assumed command of the bridge. Picking his stogie up off the deck, he placed it in his mouth and chewed vigorously. His normal grumpy demeanor gave confidence to the bridge crew.

"Resume fire! Keep up a continuous barrage. Let's give 'em everything we've got left," Matheson said to his weapons officer.

"Sir, the systems will overheat if we fire continuously," the weapons officer said.

"Let 'em melt, then!" Matheson said firmly, a hardness in his eye. The young officer took the comment with a grim resolution. He knew this was a last-ditch, all-out effort to survive. He entered the instructions into the ship's computer to keep the main gun batteries firing continuously, at the same time overriding all safety systems. The main view screen flickered once and sprang back to life just in time for the bridge crew to get a good view of their situation.

A gasp escaped the lips of almost everyone on the bridge. The scene was akin to something right out of hell. The fleet was in shambles, with every major battleship under heavy attack from the Jerrollites. Individual fighters were darting in between the big ships on kamikaze attacks, inflicting as much damage as possible.

Matheson gripped the arms of his chair tightly as crimson bolts of light and fire once again erupted from the main weapons battery of the *Hercules*. As it poured on the power, the other ships in Earth's fleet realized that this was all or nothing and joined in on the attack. Most of the commanders figured they didn't have anything to lose and wanted to go out fighting. The Jerrollite ships were momentarily taken aback by the ferocity of the renewed assault from the Earth fleet but quickly recovered and matched the increased firepower.

The replacement officer who had assumed the communications station was startled when the incoming message indicator on her board began to flash insistently. It took a moment for the meaning of the flashing alert to become clear; the officer had given up hope of ever seeing a message on that channel again. The message filled the screen, causing her heart to skip a beat as she read it and realized who it was from.

"General Matheson! Incoming message, sir!"

"What? From who!" he said, turning in his chair, afraid to let his hopes rise. "Let me see it, Ensign." She complied by displaying the message text on the main view screen.

Message Dispatch   *Origin*: Mark Hunter, Colonel
Urgent   Central Earth Military
                                  Command

Time: unknown

Enemy power base destroyed. Destruction caused feedback pulse that is causing destruction of all enemy power receivers. We are monitoring massive explosions and firestorms on the Jerrollite home world. Pulse appears to be travelling the same path as the original power beam, which means that it is headed directly toward the Jerrollite ships in your vicinity. Destruction of Jerrollite ships is a certainty.

You must not be anywhere near one of those ships when pulse arrives.

End Transmission

As Matheson read it, his heart leapt at the news, but he quickly realized the danger they were in. For the first time, a flicker of hope kindled in his soul. He immediately began shouting orders to his crew. He hoped the Jerrollite commanders would think they were running to save their lives.

"All weapons, cease fire! Navigation, get us the hell out of here! All engines FULL POWER!"

"Relay full emergency retreat orders to the rest of the fleet. No delay—cease fire and retreat, NOW!" he said to the ensign at the communications console.

The young ensign rushed to obey. Her fingers flew over her keyboard faster than they ever had before. She hit the transmit key and turned to the general. "Aye, sir. Message sent."

The *Hercules* used its maneuvering thrusters to reorient itself, its powerful engines causing its frame to groan as they came up to full thrust. Matheson knew their survival depended on rapidly putting distance between the *Hercules* and the Jerrollite fleet. The tremors could be felt throughout the whole ship as the entire hull and frame resonated to the harmonic frequencies caused by the straining engines. The crew could hear the muffled roar of the engines as they consumed massive amounts of fuel and converted it to energy, spewing flame and pushing the great battleship to the very limits of its structural integrity.

Matheson returned his gaze to the view screen to watch as his fleet put more and more distance between themselves and the Jerrollite fleet. Every ship that was still capable of motion began to pull back from the battle.

The Jerrollites were surprised at the human retreat. The crucial few seconds that it took for them to recover allowed the fleet to gain more and more distance. Recovering from their initial surprise, the Jerrollites brought their ships about and began an earnest pursuit of the fleeing Earth ships.

"Incoming message from the Jerrollite fleet, sir," the communications officer said.

"Put it on the main screen," Matheson said.

The leering blue face of a smug Jerrollite commander appeared on the screen, taunting Matheson. "Do you tire so soon of our little game, General?" Matheson refused to answer, so the alien continued. "Coward! You have no hope of escaping our fleet. As you did me a personal favor by getting rid of T'chlo, perhaps if you shut down your engines now, I will kill you quickly." Mocking laughter erupted from the screen.

Unable to contain himself any longer, Matheson said, "Are you prepared to die today, Commander? Very soon, I think, you will be greeting your god…personally." Menace seethed in his voice.

The Jerrollite bit his upper lip as he fought to maintain control. His face turned three deeper shades of blue as he bellowed, "I will kill you first and then smash your puny flee—"

Matheson cut him off in midsentence. "I refuse to speak to a dead man. Don't bother me again." He motioned for the ensign to sever the connection. The Jerrollite commander's anger was evident in the violence of the attack—the *Hercules* was jarred as a renewed assault began, the intensity and frequency of the bombardment more than doubled.

"Sir, uh…I think we pissed 'em off," the weapons officer said.

"Good guess, soldier," he chuckled, grimacing in pain as the movement reminded him of his wounds. "Maybe he'll have a heart attack or something." The bridge crew shared a nervous laugh together, the tension momentarily lessened.

"Increase speed! The Jerrollite fleet is gaining on us!" said Matheson.

"Already at top speed now, sir," said the crewman.

Matheson sighed heavily as he digested that report. If the alien fleet got too close, they might be destroyed as well. The *Hercules*'s deck bucked and lurched beneath him as the ship sustained another direct hit from behind.

"Sir, rear shields have failed! One more direct hit, and we're done for!" cried the weapons officer.

"Damn," muttered Matheson. "Damn."

The Jerrollite commander saw the rear shield on the *Hercules* flare and die out where their last energy bolt had struck. He knew that the Earth ship was heavily damaged from their attacks, barely managing to survive intact until now. Before striking the final blow to destroy Matheson and the *Hercules*, the commander wanted to savor this moment as long as possible. The destruction of the human battleship *Hercules* would provide him with the political clout he needed back home. How he had longed for this moment! Now that T'chlo had been exterminated and his flagship *Razer* destroyed, he and his ship would be given command of the entire fleet! Yes, this human had most definitely done him a favor, but now it was time to stop the game.

"Targeting, lock in on the main reactor pod of the human ship and prepare to fire on my order!"

"Yes, Commander."

The bridge of the Jerrollite ship was a prime example of military precision and efficiency of motion. Even though it had sustained some damage from the combined attack of the Earth ships, it was more than a match for any single ship, especially the once mighty and now pitiful *Hercules*. The damage the human ship had sustained was substantial, and the commander was truly surprised that it was still flying.

"Ready to fire, Commander."

The wicked gleam in the commander's eye revealed the blackness in his heart. He would glory in this kill, avenging the death of his brothers at the hands of Matheson and bringing an end to the human ability to fight once and for all.

"Prepare to fire!" he said.

Just as he was ready to give the order to unleash the barrage that would sound the death knell for Matheson and the *Hercules*, his tactical officer's console erupted into a shower of sparks and flame. At the same time, the systems in the entire bridge flickered as power began to fail. Reports of failures began coming in from all over the ship. The tactical officer turned to his commander with an undeniable look of fear in his eyes.

"Report! What is happening?" the commander cried.

"Commander! Power beam is not stable! Energy level is falling rapidly!"

He glanced around the bridge and saw the same result from each station. Warning indicators were flashing everywhere. The commander jumped as a siren began to sound, insistently warning of an imminent power failure.

"Commander! We must power down! If we fire again and the beam drops, we will not have enough power to get home!" the tactical officer said, his face reflecting the anxiety he felt.

The commander considered his options for only a moment. There was no way the *Hercules* could get away. As soon as power was restored, they would once again track it down and then destroy it once and for all.

"Power down, NOW! All weapons, cease fire. Begin emergency power conservation procedures. MOVE!"

In all his time as a commander, he could not remember ever seeing the power beam fail. It was the basis for their entire technology. Only a severe problem at the generator outpost on the second moon could cause the beam to fluctuate as it was currently doing. The commander had been briefed that the humans had been captured on the third moon. Could they have caused this? He dismissed the thought quickly as too ludicrous to consider. Humans were simply too stupid and weak to pose any threat to the Jerrollite race. Glancing at his view screen, he could see the Earth ships still retreating as his ship slowed down to conserve power.

"Contact the generation outpost and find out what is happening!" he said to the communications officer.

The officer's hands flew over the controls, attempting to establish a link with the power station. After several seconds the officer turned to face his commander.

"No response from the station, Commander."

Considering the significance of that statement, he decided to contact the team on the third moon to get first-hand information. The communications officer feverishly began attempting to establish contact with the team leader. Unable to raise the station on the moon, he began searching for alternative communications from the moon. Identifying a video feed coming over another channel, he switched to it and established a visual. What he saw caused the blue color to drain from his face. He reported to the commander.

"Sir…Commander, I cannot establish communications with the team, but I have a visual from an automatic camera running at the site," he said nervously.

The commander was disgusted with the shaken look on his officer's face but chose to ignore it for now. He would deal with that later. "Let me see it."

His mind would not accept as truth what he saw with his own eyes. The video showed Jerrollite bodies lying contorted into unnatural shapes by explosive forces. He could see frozen blood running from blast wounds on several of the bodies. He carefully counted the bodies of the team members that had been stationed at the moon facility. Conspicuously absent were the bodies of the two humans who had, only a few hours before, been held at blast rifle point.

As realization dawned in his mind, the commander slammed his fist into the side of the nearest console and began bellowing in rage. "Bring the engines back online! Plot an intercept course for the *Hercules*!"

"Commander, if we do that, we won't make it home."

"We're dead already, you fool. Obey my orders or die," screamed the commander, drawing his sidearm and leveling it at his second-in-command. Their eyes locked for the briefest of moments, the commander glaring down the barrel of his gun at his underling. The young officer seemed to melt under the fierce gaze of his superior.

"Y-y-yes, Commander," he said.

The commander holstered his weapon and turned to the view screen, eyeing the *Hercules* in the distance.

"Perhaps, General, we will both die today," he said, slumping in his seat.

Matheson watched as they began to pull away from the Jerrollite ships, leaving them far behind. He had been surprised when they stopped firing and was even more so now.

"What's going on? Tactical?" Matheson asked.

"I can't tell, sir. It would appear that they just shut down all their systems. I can't get anything but minimal power readings from them at all."

"Interesting. Hold our position here till we figure out what's going on."

"Aye, sir."

The constant groan of the engines died down to a dull throb as the *Hercules* drifted to a full stop.

"Are we out of the path of that power beam?" Matheson asked his navigator.

"Yes, sir. The beam is off the port bow, approximately one hundred kilometers away."

"Fine. Maintain that distance."

His shoulder and chest were beginning to throb, making it difficult to breathe.

"sir! The flagship just powered back up! It's heading this way!" the tactical officer said.

"Bring the ship around! Divert all power to the front shields. Let's keep our weak spot protected!" Removing his cigar from his pocket, he lit it and took a long drag from the smoldering weed, sending coughs racking through his body again.

"We'll just wait here and get this over with!"

An exclamation from the scanning station made them all turn and look in that direction.

"General, something is happening! I'm reading a massive energy surge coming along the power beam!"

Matheson smiled at the timing.

As the pulse approached the Jerrollite ships, it appeared as a curtain of white fire sweeping across everything in its path. Matheson and his crew watched, unable to comprehend what was happening. The pulse intercepted the lead Jerrollite ship, causing its hull to buckle as a massive amount of electromagnetic energy washed over it in wave after wave. The energy receptors on board overloaded quickly, unable to contain the pulse. Tongues of blue fire began dancing all over the ship's hull, scorching everything they touched. As more and more internal systems were assaulted by the extreme amounts of energy, they overloaded and exploded in brilliant flashes of light. The alien ship began to list to one side as system after system erupted in massive fireballs. It spun on its center axis, end over end. The bridge of the *Hercules* was silent as they watched the extermination of the Jerrollite fleet. The massive alien ship shuddered violently once and then was ripped apart as her main drives overloaded and exploded. As the lead ship was coming apart, a blinding flash revealed the detonation of her main reactor. Within seconds all that was left of the Jerrollite ship was a tumbling pile of debris.

"Oh my God! Look at that!" said one of the crew, pointing at the view screen.

Every ship in the Jerrollite armada began to explode, hurling large chunks of debris in every direction. Flash after flash, detonation after detonation, the scene replayed itself over and over as Matheson and his crew watched until all that was left of the enemy fleet was a large field of floating wreckage, spinning lazily in space, silent, all life extinguished.

Silence reigned as every person on the bridge sat, stunned by the scene they had just witnessed. No one said anything; only the whisper of the ship's ventilation systems reminded them that they were still alive. From the communications console, the intership channel crackled to life.

"*Hercules*! *Hercules*! Come in." The message repeated insistently. "*Hercules*! This is Mark and Johann—are you okay?"

Matheson limped to the communications station and keyed his transmitter. "Mark, Johann, you don't know how good it is to hear your voices. Come on in, boys. Let's go home." Tears were streaming down Matheson's face as he collapsed into the arms of a waiting medical team. The entire bridge discharged all their pent-up emotions at once, laughing and crying, clapping one another on the back, grateful to be alive. Matheson could hardly believe the magnificent stroke of luck that had allowed all of them to survive.

"Let's go home," he said again as the medical team loaded him onto a stretcher.

A young medic's face appeared over Matheson as he heard a voice say, "We're on our way, sir. You just relax and hold on so we can get you fixed up." The team wheeled him off the bridge to medical. The bridge crew watched him go.

The first officer assumed command as the doors whispered closed.

"All right, everybody, let's see if we can get this crate home, shall we?"

With renewed vigor, the crew began making preparations for the voyage home.

A young ensign slipped behind the communications console. The first officer smiled as he gave the order they had all been waiting for.

"Recall all fighters to their home ships. We will depart for home in ten minutes."

A cheer erupted from the bridge crew as they prepared to get the ship under way for the voyage home.

"Comm, dispatch a message to Earth Command informing them of the outcome of the battle." As the ensign complied, the first officer said, "And tell them to have a cold beer ready for all of us!"

"Yes, sir!" said the ensign enthusiastically.

The large battleship lumbered into position, orienting itself toward Earth. Even with battle damage evident on the blackened hull, its crew still maintained their sense of pride as the main engines powered up, accelerating the *Hercules* on its final journey home.

CHAPTER 29

The Jerrollite home world was on fire. The brilliant blue atmosphere was dotted with flecks of red over the entire surface of the planet as every power-receiving station that had been online when the moon was destroyed burned to the ground. Cities were in chaos as the government tried to maintain control over the population but was rapidly discovering that it was an impossible task with no power. Jerrollite technology had evolved over the eons to be based entirely on the transmission of power from a central facility. This technology had allowed the Jerrollite armada to travel to any star system without the need to carry fuel, as the power beam supplied everything they needed. When the technology had matured, it had been placed on the surface of the nearest moon to protect it from any planetside dangers and avoid impacting the planetary environment. As the Jerrollite race considered itself impervious to attack, the controlling powers had never even considered that the subject of one of their many conquests would be able to penetrate their system and actually pose a threat to the power transmitters. But it had happened, and now the Jerrollite civilization had been smashed because of their conceit.

In its arrogance the Jerrollite government had never given serious thought to building a backup system for the power station on the moon. The governors had always assumed that it, and they, were invulnerable to destruction, as they had indeed been for hundreds of years. Never in their wildest dreams would they have imagined that it could be destroyed. The shutdown of the power generators would have been bad enough, but because of the feedback pulse that had been generated when the station was destroyed, every aspect of Jerrollite civilization was affected. Their entire technology base had been tied into the power beam and as a result had been destroyed when the pulse had hit. It would take years just to repair the destruction caused by the explosions, much less bring their technology back to the level it had been before the attack.

The home world was not the only aspect of Jerrollite civilization to suffer. Every Jerrollite installation in the galaxy had been tapped into the same power source and suffered the same effects. In one fell swoop, Jerrollite rule of that sector of the galaxy was smashed completely.

The Jerrollites had conquered hundreds of other planets, and Earth had been scheduled to become another victim—to be raped of resources and then discarded like so much garbage. They realized too late the tenacity and sheer will of the human race. The Jerrollites had allowed themselves to become complacent and as a result had been caught completely by surprise. They had never seen a race so fiercely opposed to being ruled by another. They had severely underestimated Earth and its inhabitants.

It was a mistake they would not be able to rectify for a very long, long time.

Mark expertly piloted his TAC-WING onto the landing deck of the *Hercules*, flaring his flaps at the last minute to execute a perfect emergency landing. Mark climbed out of his fighter, frantically waving to a medical team for assistance.

"I've got a wounded man in there!" he said, jerking a thumb toward the cockpit of the TAC-WING fighter. Several men climbed up the access ladder and began to extricate Johann from the ship under Mark's watchful eye. They lowered him gently onto a stretcher, but Johann yelped as the movement of his body brought renewed pain. Grabbing the sleeve of the lead medical tech, Mark spun him around, face-to-face.

"Is he going to be all right?" he asked nervously.

"I think so, sir; he's lost a lot of blood, but I think we can pull him through."

"Please don't let him die. He saved all of us today," Mark said, releasing the sleeve. He walked over to where Johann was being attended to by the medical team.

"Take care of yourself, buddy. I'll see you in a little while," Mark said.

Johann's only reply was a weak thumbs-up from his stretcher. The medical team bustled him off to the emergency triage ward in sick bay. Mark followed the stretcher down the long corridor. Trying to avoid all the activity as doctors and nurses tended to the many hurt and wounded in the bay, Mark located General Matheson's bed. He was surprised at how bad Matheson looked. His face was ashen, and there was a bead of sweat on his brow. His breathing was shallow and irregular.

Mark hesitated, unsure of how to proceed. He had been through so much with this man that he felt a strong bond of kinship with him. There was no way Mark could stand to see his life end—not when the fight had been won. He placed his hand on Matheson's shoulder and was relieved when the general's eyes fluttered open. The old twinkle was still quite evident, not only in his eyes but also in his voice.

"It's good to see you, sir. We thought you weren't going to make it when we heard you had been injured on the bridge," said Mark.

"It'll take more than a piece of government steel to kill me!" Matheson said weakly.

"I don't doubt that at all, sir."

"Are you okay?" Matheson asked faintly.

"Yeah, but I can't say the same for the Jerrollites." Mark grinned, and both men laughed. Matheson was overcome by a wracking cough for several seconds. When he regained his composure, he continued.

"Johann?"

"Hurt, but the doc thinks he's gonna be okay. Without him, we would not be standing here right now. His actions today saved us all."

Matheson nodded in acknowledgment.

"You take it easy, sir. There will be a lot of rebuilding and work to do when we get home. Just let me take it from here."

The general closed his eyes in response and relaxed, allowing the weariness and exhaustion to finally overtake him. Mark lingered a moment longer and then turned and left, heading toward the bridge.

He stopped in the doorway and looked back at his friends. Johann was unconscious, being prepped for surgery, but a thumbs-up from the attending doctor made Mark feel better about his chances. Matheson had finally drifted off to sleep, confident in Mark's ability to get them home. He smiled to himself, tired but content that everything had worked out in the end.

Humans had lost much in their encounter with the Jerrollites, but perhaps they would also gain something that not very many people could lay claim to—a fresh start. Mark thought about what lay ahead of them and was almost overwhelmed as he thought of the monumental task of rebuilding their homes, cities, and governments back on Earth. It would be a difficult journey, but he knew the human race was more than up to the challenge. With the help of Matheson and the surviving members of government, the remnants of the human race would be able to not only survive but flourish once again. The human race had done it many times in the past when all hope had seemed lost. It had bounced back over and over again against impossible odds. The situation was now perhaps more severe, but the challenges were the same. The very best of humanity always seemed to rise to the top in times of crisis, and this time would be no different. All the petty politics and squabbles of the past between nations would finally be put to rest as all humans were now united in a common cause for their very survival. It would be tough for a while, but they would be back. Mark knew it in his gut.

Shrugging his shoulders, Mark spun on his heel and made his way to the bridge. There was a lot of work left to do, and now was as good a time as any to get started.

—THE END—

ABOUT THE AUTHOR

Jerry Reynolds is a computer software engineer with twenty-five years' experience in the field. He is the president of his own company.

Science fiction filled Reynold's world growing up and still influences everything he does. Reynolds is married, and his home is decorated with life-size replicas of movie robots.